The Wise Child

The Wise Child

Jeanne Whitmee

ROBERT HALE · LONDON

ISBN 978-0-7090-8486-0

Robert Hale Limited
Clerkenwell House
Clerkenwell Green
London EC1R 0HT

www.halebooks.com

2 4 6 8 10 9 7 5 3 1

Typeset in 11½/14½pt Palatino
by Derek Doyle & Associates, Shaw Heath
Printed and bound in Great Britain
by Biddles Limited, King's Lynn

CHAPTER ONE

'PLEASE close the door, Danielle.'

Mr Dains, the manager of Bestways supermarket glowered at Danni from the other side of his desk. His small colourless eyes glinted through his spectacles and his pallid jowls cascaded over his starched collar. Danni reflected, not for the first time, that he looked exactly like a bad-tempered hippopotamus.

The fact that he did not invite her to sit down confirmed for Danielle that she was in trouble. 'This is not the first time I have had occasion to reprimand you for insolence, Danielle,' he went on. He pronounced it Dan-yell which made Danni bite the inside of her lip with irritation.

'That woman was rude to me first,' she protested. 'She said I was more interested in my nails than her shopping and I wasn't. I'd cut my finger. Look.' She held out the injured finger, which she'd caught on a sharp piece of foil packaging.

Mr Dains waved a podgy hand at her. 'I do not wish to hear your feeble excuses,' he growled. 'As you well know, rudeness to customers will not be tolerated at Bestways and the customer said that you swore at her.'

Danni gasped. 'Oh, I *didn't*! What I said was, did she want her shopping all bloodied?'

Mr Dains waved a dismissive hand. 'You have had more than the statutory two warnings . . .' He cleared his throat.

'*Many* more. In fact I think I have been extremely tolerant in view of your belligerent attitude. But this time I'm afraid I have no alternative but dismiss you.' She opened her mouth to protest but he went on quickly, 'You may serve one week's notice or collect your cards and P45 from Personnel at the end of your shift. The choice is yours.'

Danielle felt the familiar pounding in her chest and felt the colour flood her face as her hot temper flared. Leaning forward, she planted her palms flat on the desk. '*You know what you can do with your flaming job!*' she shouted into Mr Dains's outraged face. 'Do you think sitting at that flamin' check-out all day, putting up with everyone's bad temper and nasty remarks, is fun? I'd like to see you try it!' She stood up, her hands on her hips. 'I'm not staying here another minute to be treated like dirt. Stuff the rest of the shift. I'm off – *now*.'

'You'll forgo your wages if you flout the rules.'

She threw him a look of contempt. '*More than the statutory two warnings*.' She mimicked his reedy voice. 'Flout the *rules*? Oh *dear*! Can't upset the gods of Bestways, can we? If you want to be a lackey to them you're welcome. I'll get my cards and P45 and as for your week's money, you know where you can stick it!' She flounced to the door, then turned. 'Tell you what, though, you'll hardy feel a thing, the pittance you pay!'

Outside in the corridor she leaned against the wall, her temper deflating like a pricked balloon. *Oh no, I've done it again*, she told herself, biting her lip. Letting her anger get the better of her had been her downfall more times than she cared to remember. Why on earth had she told him what to do with the week's money? She must have been mad. And what would Mum say when she went home and confessed that she'd lost yet another job? She sighed. Oh well, it was done now. Better get on with it.

On the way to the personnel office she suddenly remembered Maurice Dains's startled look at her outburst and a bubble of laughter rose in her throat. He'd jumped back in alarm, his glasses slipping crookedly down his nose. He must have thought she was about to attack him. The thought of her fist connecting with his pile of flabby chins made her chuckle again. It was almost worth a week's money – almost but not quite. As Mum had told her many a time: speaking her mind was a luxury she couldn't afford.

It was still only mid afternoon when she turned into Crane Row. The narrow street of 1920s council houses looked bleak in the February drizzle. Most of the curtains were as grey as the pebble-dashed walls. Many of the windows were boarded up due to the gangs of youths, whose main interest in life seemed to be roaming the streets after dark and chucking stones through windows. The front gardens were overgrown and neglected, the fences broken and the gates swinging drunkenly on their hinges. As she passed number 23 the Alsatian that was always tied up by the front door barked at her, straining on his length of rope.

'OK Rex. It's only me.' She fished in her pocket for a piece of chocolate and leaned over the rickety fence to deliver it into his slathering jaws. Poor thing, she was sure he didn't get enough to eat.

Danni found it all deeply depressing, even on a good day. Mum had a good job in the personnel office at Preston's, the engineering factory, and she often wondered why they couldn't find somewhere better to live. There were better council estates than this one; places where the residents took a pride in their surroundings. The rents were higher, of course, but she was sure they could afford it. But Mum would never discuss it, saying that Danni didn't know when she was lucky. *Lucky!* That was a laugh.

She'd worked really hard at school. Eight GCSEs and an A* in art. Mr Pellham, her art teacher, had wanted her to study art and take A levels at evening classes then try for a fine arts degree at university later, but Mum had said they couldn't afford it. She said it was time Danni earned some money and helped out. That had been just over a year ago and so far she'd had – and lost – four jobs.

'What do you mean, you told him where to stick his money?' Ruth Emerson stared at her daughter. 'My God, Danni, how many times have I told you to curb that temper? You'll be the death of me before you're finished.'

'It was so unfair, Mum,' Danni protested. 'I never swore at that woman but old four-eyes'd rather believe her than me. Look, I'll sign on tomorrow. And I'll go to the job centre afterwards and see what they've got.'

'It's too bad, Danni, really it is.' Ruth closed the oven door on the casserole she had just made and threw down the oven glove. 'Every job you've had so far, you've lost. And it's always caused by that temper of yours.'

'I do my best, honestly.'

'Do your best to muck things up, you mean! You never think before you speak. You're so rude to people.'

'Not unless they're rude to me first. Honestly, Mum, some people treat you like dirt at those check-outs. You wouldn't believe it how horrible they can be.'

'When will you learn to bite that tongue of yours? When you're serving the public you have to take the rough with the smooth.' To Danni's dismay tears welled up in her mother's eyes. 'You've got no idea how hard it's been for me since we've been on our own,' she said. 'Struggling to make ends meet, week in and week out; never any money to spend on little extras; no holidays or days out. I thought that when you left school and were able to bring another wage in we'd be better off. But you can't hold a job down because of that tongue of yours. The job centre, you say! Do you think anyone is going to give you a reference? Not on your life. Soon you'll be on the unemployable list. A permanent giro-junkie.'

'It would've been different if you'd only let me go to art college.'

Ruth groaned. 'Not that again. When will you *learn*, Danni? Art college is a luxury for those who can afford it.'

'Natalie went,' Danni said. 'She's already done her first year and she's really enjoying it – even talking of going on to uni to do fine arts.' She sighed. 'All through school we've been planning to go to art college together. It's not fair.'

'Natalie Frost has a mother and a father – both working,' Ruth pointed out wearily. 'You know that, Danni. Now, help me set the table. Jim is coming round at seven.'

'*Jim*?' Danni pulled a face. 'Jim Crawford is eating with us? Oh, Mum! He's such a drip. Why do you bother with him?'

Ruth shook her head. 'I'm warning you, Danni. Don't you dare be rude to Jim. He's good to me and he'd be good to you too if you'd let him.'

'You're not getting serious about him, are you?' Danni asked.

Ruth coloured. 'No! Well, yes, in a way. Jim and I – we're thinking of . . .'

'Not *moving in together*?' Danni turned an appalled face towards her mother.

'Would it really be that bad? You'd come too of course, that's understood. We'd be able to move away from here – go and live in Jim's house in Parkside. You'd like it there.'

'Living with all his dead wife's stuff? No way!' Danni stood with her feet apart and her hands on her hips in the stubborn way that Ruth knew so well. 'You can count me out, Mum. I'm not going to live with Jim Crawford. It's up to you if you want to, but . . .'

'Don't be silly,' Ruth interrupted. 'Where would you go?'

'I don't know but I'd find somewhere. Why can't we stay as we are, Mum? We've always been OK, the two of us. Why change things now?'

'Oh Danni, don't go on.' Ruth sank on to a chair. 'Have you

any idea what it's been like for me? I'm so sick and tired of struggling, making ends meet, counting the pennies. I'm not getting any younger and—'

'So why have you never asked my dad to help?'

The question stopped Ruth in her tracks. 'Your dad?'

'Yes. You remember; that man you used to be married to – the one who dumped us and took off before I was born; the reason why we've had to live like paupers all these years. Where is he, Mum? Why haven't you ever made him pay some maintenance?'

Ruth sighed. 'What brought this on?' she said. 'You haven't mentioned him for ages.'

'That's because he's a stranger to me,' Danni said. 'Someone we're not supposed to talk about. He's not a stranger to you though, is he, Mum? Why have you always let him get away with dodging his responsibilities?'

'He's in the past,' Ruth said. 'We're divorced. He's nothing to do with us. We don't even share his name any more and I don't want him back in my life. Anyway, you're grown up now. It's too late.'

'He's still my father though,' Danni insisted. 'He must owe us thousands in back money. If he'd been here for me I could have gone to art college. I don't even know the first thing about him. If I met him in the street I wouldn't even recognize him.'

'Just as well too if you ask me! I'll tell you about him, shall I?' Ruth said, her mouth twisting bitterly. 'The first *and last* thing about Tom Emerson is that he's a gambler. All his money goes on poker games and the horses and if he was here now there'd be even less money than there is now. So take it from me, he'd have been no help to you. Gambling always came first with him, before me, before everything – 'specially us!'

Danni stared helplessly at her mother's tear-filled eyes. 'I'm sorry, Mum.' She reached out a hand to touch Ruth's shoulder. 'But can you imagine how I felt last year when Natalie started college without me? Every time I see her I have to hear all about the fabulous time she's having. It makes me feel *sick*! I want a career in *art*, Mum. I know I can do it. It's the only thing I'm any good at; the only thing I want. I hate the thought of being stuck behind a counter in some dead-end job for the rest of my life – taking orders from people like old Fatty Dains.'

Ruth shook her head. She recognized only too well the passion in her daughter's voice. 'I know, love, and believe me, nothing frustrates me more than not being able to make your dream come true. But listen, if you behave yourself and play your cards right you might still be able to go – next year perhaps.'

For a moment Danni's face lit up, then her eyes clouded. 'Oh, I get it. You're saying that if you and Jim . . .' She turned away. She hated Jim Crawford. He was so stiff and formal. He had no sense of humour at all and, she was sure, nothing in common with Ruth. She had always wondered what her mother saw in him. Now suddenly she knew. 'You can't go and live with him just because of his money,' she said. 'So if you're doing it for me, forget it!'

Ruth turned away. 'It's not like that.'

'It can't be like anything else, not with Jim! I wouldn't want him to pay for anything for me. I'd rather go without for the rest of my life. I'd rather *starve*!'

Ruth sighed. 'It's all very well having high ideals, but they don't pay the bills. Nothing's decided yet, anyway. Go and tidy yourself up before he gets here.'

'No! I'm going out. You and Jim can have a lovely romantic meal without me.' She flung out of the kitchen and started up the stairs, Ruth following.

'Danni! Come back here. You can't—' But the rest of her sentence was cut off by the sound of Danni's bedroom door slamming.

Determined to get out of the house before Jim arrived, Danni decided to go round to Natalie's. They hadn't seen each other for several weeks. It had been Danni's decision to allow their friendship to cool. Since Natalie had started her course at the local art college Danni felt she had moved on to other friends. She felt hurt and left out, and, if she were truthful, heart-achingly envious.

The Frost family lived in a semi-detached house in Meadway Avenue. It was only a short walk from Crane Row but so great was the contrast that it might have been a hundred miles away. The avenue was tree-lined and all the houses had neat front gardens and smartly painted exteriors. As she opened the gate of number 7 and walked up the path between borders of geraniums Danni felt afresh the familiar stab of bitterness for the social gulf that existed between herself and her best friend. It was all her absent father's fault, she told herself. If only she knew where to find him she would go and give him a piece of her mind.

Natalie herself answered the door and her face lit up when she saw her friend.

'Danni! It's ages since you came round. Come in.' She held the door wide and Danni stepped into the hall with its soft rose-pink carpet. A delicious smell of cooking drifted out from the kitchen, reminding her that she hadn't eaten this evening.

'Hope I'm not interrupting your tea,' she said.

Natalie shook her head. 'No. We've just finished. Come and say hello to Mum and then we'll go up to my room.'

Natalie's mother was washing up in the trim kitchen. She looked round when the girls came in. 'Hello, Danielle. Long time no see.'

'I know. I – I've been doing late shifts at the supermarket,' Danni told her, half-truthfully.'

'We're just going upstairs for a natter, Mum,' Natalie put in. 'Leave the drying up. I'll do it later.'

Molly Frost smiled good-naturedly. 'Go on, I'll let you off this once. If you see your brother you can tell him it's his turn to help anyway.'

As Danni followed her friend upstairs she reflected wistfully that it must be great to be part of a family like the Frosts. Natalie had two brothers; Jack, who was nineteen and just finishing his A levels and Nicky who was ten. There was never a dull moment in the cosy, secure Frost household, and although they were often noisy and quarrelsome their closeness was always apparent.

Natalie had the smallest bedroom, her brothers sharing the second largest of the three. Her father had built her a corner desk space and she had her own computer and TV. Danni looked round with envy.

'You are lucky, having a room like this,' she said.

'Lucky? You can't swing a cat,' Natalie complained. 'When Jack goes to uni I'm going to make Mum move Nicky in here so that I can have the back bedroom.' She threw herself down on the bed and patted the space beside her. 'So – what have you been doing with yourself? And why haven't you kept in touch?'

'I walked out on my job today,' Danni said, sinking on to the bed beside her friend.

'What, at Bestway's?'

'Yes. I was accused of swearing at some frumpy old woman and I didn't. They had a real down on me there, Nat. I just saw red.'

'Oh dear. What did your mum say?'

'Need you ask?'

Natalie nodded. 'How is she?'

'She's thinking of moving in with that creep Jim Crawford. And she expects me to go too.'

'Oh. Don't you like him?'

Danni pulled a face that made her friend giggle. 'I'd rather go and live with a gorilla.' She reached out to touch Natalie's arm. 'Nat – I suppose I couldn't come and stay here for a bit, could I?'

Natalie caught her lower lip between her teeth. 'Oh, Danni! We've no more rooms. You know how crowded we are.'

'I'll get another job and pay proper rent, I promise. Just a mattress on the floor will do. You said that when Jack goes to uni . . .'

'I know, but that won't be till October.'

'Couldn't you just ask your mum? I'd keep out of the way and be ever so quiet. I can't go and live with Jim. I just *can't*!'

Natalie looked at her friend's desperate face. 'Well, I'll ask of course, but I don't know.'

Danni took a deep breath and shook her head. 'No. It's all right. Forget it. I shouldn't have asked.' She gritted her teeth. 'If only my dad had stuck around I wouldn't be in this mess now and neither would Mum. If only I knew where he lived!'

'Does he still live here in Meadbridge?' Natalie asked.

Danni shrugged. 'As far as I know he does, although I suppose he could be anywhere.'

'If you really wanted to find him you could always start by looking on the electoral roll,' Natalie said.

'What's that?'

'It's a list of all the streets in the town – all the people who live in the houses are listed; everyone who's old enough to vote, that is,' Natalie explained. 'They use it for elections.' She stood up. 'I think Dad's got a copy of it. I'll go and ask him if we can look at it, shall I?'

A few minutes later Natalie was back with the thick document and the girls sat on the bed to pore over it.

'This could take all night,' Danni said despondently. 'There's pages and *pages* of it. It's all very well if you know where a person lives. All I've got is a name: Tom Emerson.'

'Well let's keep looking anyway,' Natalie said. 'You never know.'

Half an hour later they were still looking. By now they had

reached H. Hadley Close; Hereford Street; Hickson Road. Then suddenly Danni spotted it. At number 7 Hobson Lane – Thomas Gareth Emerson. Could it be her father? She didn't know whether Gareth was his second name, but Emerson wasn't a very common surname so it was a distinct possibility. She took a scrap of paper from her handbag, scribbling down the address. It was certainly worth a try. She had nothing to lose after all.

It was late when she got home and Ruth had been worried. 'Where on earth have you been till now? I've been worried to death.'

'Natalie's. Can't I even go and see my friend these days without you getting your knickers in a twist?' Danni said truculently.

'You could have said,' Ruth complained. 'You didn't even stop for your supper.' Danni turned to leave but Ruth closed the kitchen door. 'No – sit down, Danni,' she said. 'We have to talk.'

Danni sat down opposite her mother with a feeling of trepidation. 'OK,' she said. 'Tell me the worst.'

'Don't be like that. Listen – Jim has invited us to move in with him. No . . .' She held up her hand as Danni opened her mouth to protest. 'Let me finish. It's just for a trial period – to see how we all get on.'

'*All*? I'm not going,' Danni said. 'You can if you like but I'm not.'

'Don't be silly, Danni. Where would you go? Just give it a try – for my sake. Jim knows we come as a package, you and me. And he's happy with that so don't let me down.' She reached out to touch her daughter's hand. 'Listen love. I'll be forty next birthday. I'm not getting any younger and I'm tired of being on my own and struggling to manage. It's no life.'

'You're not on your own. You've got me.'

'But you'll have your own life soon,' Ruth said. 'You'll be

spreading your wings before long and that's what I want for you. You deserve better than I can give you on my own. Can't you see, love? This is the chance of a better life for both of us.'

'I'm not taking anything from *him*.'

'Just let's give it a go. Look, if it doesn't work out what harm will have been done?' Ruth asked. 'At least it would give me the chance to save up a bit and we could look for somewhere better to live. Just give it a try – please – for me?'

'Not much choice, is there, the way things are?' Danni sighed. 'But if I can find somewhere else to live that I can afford, I'm going, Mum, so don't say I didn't warn you.'

Ruth seemed reassured. 'I'm sure I don't need to remind you that you don't have a job, Danni. Look, it'll work out. You'll see.'

'Yeah, yeah.'

'All I ask is that you keep that temper in check?'

Lying in bed that night Danni weighed up the pros and cons of moving in with Jim Crawford. There was always a slim chance that Mrs Frost would let her go there but if there was no alternative she would somehow have to make the best of it. She turned over and shut her eyes; the thought was too horrible to contemplate. She had to admit that it would be great to move out of Crane Row with its violent, marauding kids and nosy neighbours. And who knew – maybe there'd be a better chance of a decent job out in the suburbs? She turned over. One thing she'd do before she left – she'd take poor old Rex to a rescue centre and to hell with the consequences! He was entitled to a better life too, poor moth-eaten old thing. But at the back of her mind was the thought of that scrap of paper in her handbag, an address scribbled on it. Dare she go and find out if this man was her father? Would it make a difference to her life if she did find him? She couldn't go through the rest of her life not knowing what the man who had fathered her was like, and why he had deserted her. But how did you go about getting to know someone who hadn't been around for almost eighteen years? She was going to have to find the courage to do it.

It was almost a week before Danni found a chance to go to Hobson Lane. It turned out to be on another council estate, this one on the other side of town from Crane Row and she had to take two buses to get there. Her heart was beating fast as she knocked at number 7. After a short while the door was answered by a woman with long blonde hair tied back in a ponytail. She wore tattered jeans and a T-shirt and she looked Danni up and down suspiciously as she took a cigarette out of her mouth.

'Yeah?'

'Does Tom Emerson live here?'

The woman turned and shouted, 'Tom! Some girl here wants to see you.'

Ruth had kept no photographs so Danni's image of her father was all in her imagination. The man who appeared in the hallway did not match up to it in the slightest. He was short and bald with a stomach that hung over the belt of his trousers. He peered at her, frowning slightly.

'Yeah? Do I know you?' he asked.

'Not really, no,' Danni said smarting inwardly at the irony of the remark. She glanced at the woman who was still hanging around in the background. 'Er – can I have a word with you?' she ventured. 'In private?'

The man's eyebrows rose and he glanced round at the woman. 'Give us a minute, Trace, will you?'

She glared at him. 'OK, but if I find out you been up to your tricks again . . .' She left the rest of the sentence hanging in the air as she disappeared through a door and closed it behind her. The man beckoned Danni inside.

'Better come in the front room.'

She followed him into an uncarpeted room with little furniture and he closed the door.

'Right, so what can I do for you?' he asked. 'If you've come from Bill Langley about that money I owe him you can tell him he's got to give me a bit longer.'

'It's nothing like that. My name is the same as yours and I wondered . . .' She bit her lip. 'I'm Danielle.' When he still looked blank she added, 'Ruth Emerson's daughter.'

Light dawned on his face and he hit his forehead with the palm of his hand. 'Ruth! My God, after all these years. How is she?'

'She's OK.'

'So – you're her kid. How old are you now?'

'Nearly eighteen.' Something about his casual manner irritated her. 'I'm your *daughter*,' she pointed out. 'And I think it's about time you recognized the fact. Do you have any idea how Mum and I have struggled all these years?'

'Woah!' He held up his hand. 'Woah now! Hold your horses, love. Look, sit down. I think you've got the wrong end of the stick. First of all, how did you find me?'

'From the electoral roll.'

His eyebrows rose. 'Oh, I see. I'm impressed. Your mum put you up to it, did she?'

'*No*! She has no idea I'm here. If she knew she'd be furious.'

'Mmm, I bet,' he said drily. 'So why are you here then – if you don't mind me asking?'

'Because I think it's time you faced up to your responsibilities,' she told him. 'I want to study art at college and maybe even go on to university but when I left school Mum couldn't afford to let me stay on. It's all I've ever wanted to do and I don't see why—'

'Hang on.' He held up his hand. 'Look around you. Does it look as if I'm loaded? I'm sorry, but your education's got nothing to do with me.'

Danni felt her temper beginning to rise. 'Still gambling, are you?' she flung at him. 'Still chucking money away at cards and on the horses?'

His colour rose and he sprang to his feet. 'Don't you start

getting stroppy with me, my lady! What I do and how I live is none of your business.'

'No? That's what you think and I daresay that's how you like it, but there's such a thing as the CSA.'

His colour deepened. 'Don't you quote the Child Support Agency at me!' he said. 'Anyway, they'd have a job to stick anything on me!'

'You proud of yourself, are you?' Danni was into her stride now and gathering momentum. 'What kind of man walks out on his wife when she's expecting his child? Are you proud of yourself for dumping me before I was even born?'

He waved a finger at her. 'Now just you button it a minute, little Miss Gobby, and listen to me.' His face was as red as hers. 'I didn't want to say anything but I can see you're not going to let it go. Just pipe down. You're going to hear the truth your mother should've told you years ago. *I am not your father.*'

She stared at him, taken aback. 'Not my . . . What are you saying – that Mum was – that she had. . . ?'

He shook his head. 'I'm not saying *nuthin'*. Not another word. What I've just told you is the truth, like it or not. If you want to know any more you're going to have to ask your mother. It's her place to tell you and she should have done it long ago.' He opened the door. 'Now I think you'd better leave.'

CHAPTER TWO

'YOU'VE been to see Tom Emerson?' Ruth's face was pale as she looked into her daughter's blazing eyes.

'I went to find the man I've always thought was my father,' Danni told her. 'Only to hear that he isn't.'

'Oh, Danni.' Ruth sat down suddenly, looking defeated. 'Why do you always have to make life so difficult?'

'Why do *I* make life difficult?' Danni shook her head. 'I can't believe you've just said that! Look – Tom Emerson says he's not my father. Is he telling the truth or isn't he?'

'He had no business telling you anything!'

'But he did and now I want the truth, Mum. I think you owe me that at least.'

Ruth sighed and for a moment they stared at each other in silence, then Ruth capitulated. 'All right then – yes,' she said wearily. 'Yes, he's telling the truth.'

'OK. So now that's out of the way I need to know who my father is. I think I've got a right to know that, don't you?'

It was Sunday morning and Jim was expected for lunch. Ruth and Danni were in the kitchen where Ruth was making pastry for an apple pie. She put down the rolling pin and washed her hands at the sink.

'Sit down, Danni.' She sighed. 'I've been dreading this moment.'

'Dreading owning up to me that you're a cheat? I suppose

you thought I'd never find out. Is that it? You were going to keep me in the dark for the rest of my life!'

'I'm not a cheat,' Ruth said patiently. 'I never was. It was all a long time ago now. Your – Tom and I were young. We hadn't been married very long and he was up to his neck in debt through his gambling. There were people after him, making threats, getting nasty – really nasty, I mean.'

Danni frowned. 'What has all this got to do with it?'

'Everything. We were desperate. I had a cleaning job at the time. I had several actually – had to earn as much as I could to keep us going. One of these jobs was with a young doctor and his wife. They badly wanted a family but Claire, the doctor's wife, couldn't have children. They knew about Tom's debts because in desperation I'd asked them for a sub on my wages, and one day soon afterwards they asked me if I would be a surrogate for them.'

'What? You mean have a baby for them?'

'Yes. It wasn't heard of much back then and for reasons of their own they wanted it all done on the quiet. At first I wasn't sure, but the money they were offering was beyond my wildest dreams. It was like the answer to all my prayers. I thought it would be the end of all Tom's problems. It would more than pay off his gambling debts with some left over to set us up.'

'So – you agreed?' Danni's mind was spinning. She could hardly take in what she was hearing.

'Yes, out of sheer desperation. As I said, he – Mark – was a doctor so it was all done clinically. It worked first time and there I was – pregnant. The plan was to pay me half of he money as soon as the pregnancy was confirmed and the other half when the baby—'

'Hang on a minute. Is this me?' Danni interrupted. 'Are we talking about *me*?'

'Yes. I was to receive the other half of the money when you were born.'

Danni frowned. 'So – what went wrong?'

'To begin with Tom was all right about it. He was pleased and relieved to be able to pay off his debts and get the heavies off his back. He swore he'd give up gambling for good. But as time went on he started to get difficult.'

'Difficult – in what way?'

'Resentful – jealous, I suppose. He couldn't come to terms with the fact that I was carrying another man's child. We had a lot of rows about it and then I found out that he was still gambling. In the end, after one final blazing row, he just left.'

Danni shook her head. 'After you'd paid off his debts! What a rat! So what happened then? Did they – this doctor and his wife, let you down too?'

'No. They were wonderful. Claire and I went away to a cottage they had down in Devon and we stayed there. You see, they were going to let everyone think that the baby was hers – Claire's. The time came and I went into labour. Mark himself delivered the baby. They'd hoped for a boy but they were just as happy with a girl.'

'So . . .' Danni shook her head. 'I don't get it. What happened?'

Ruth looked up, her eyes full of tears. 'What happened was that I fell in love with my baby. The moment I saw you and held you in my arms I knew that there was no way I could ever let you go. As soon as you were born Claire started feeding, bathing and changing you, just as though you were hers. Bonding, she called it. She was like a little girl with a new doll. She was going to call you Imogene. I hated it. Right from the first you were my Danielle. They'd bought all this expensive stuff: cradles, prams and clothes galore. It tore me apart. I knew in my heart that they couldn't possible love you as I did and I just couldn't bring myself to give you up.'

'So – you told them?'

'I tried, but they refused to listen. Mark reminded me that it was a business arrangement and that I couldn't afford to go back on it. I'd paid Tom's debts and given up my home. I was alone. I needed the rest of the money to make a future for myself. I knew he was talking sense. I knew that they could give you the kind of life I never could. I knew they'd be devastated and that I was letting them down. I realized that bringing you up on my own would be hard.' She shook her head. 'I knew all of this, Danni, but it made no difference. You were my child and what I felt for you was so strong. I think secretly Claire sympathized. I think she understood how I felt even through her sadness and disappointment. But Mark was a different cup of tea. He was just plain angry. He said that if I took his child away I'd be homeless and penniless and that I needn't look to him for help. He made it clear that if I let them down I was on my own, and I knew he meant it.'

'He couldn't have cared much what happened to the baby if he was happy to let it – *me* – in for a life of poverty.' Danni said.

'I don't think he ever really believed I'd have the nerve to do it,' Ruth said. 'He was calling my bluff.'

'But you called his instead.'

Ruth nodded. 'Yes, even after he played his trump card.'

'What was that?'

'He told me that he'd let me go – take you and all of the clothes that they'd provided for you, as long as I promised to pay back the money I'd already had.'

Danni's mouth dropped open. 'But you had none of it left.'

'No.'

'He couldn't make you though, could he?' Danni argued. 'You said they wanted to keep the surrogacy secret. You could have spilled the beans.'

'He said he'd deny everything – that he'd go to the police and accuse me of theft; say that I stole the money while I was working for them. With an absent husband and a fatherless baby who do you think would have been believed?'

'Yet you still went. You still kept me.' Danni was silent for a moment. 'And paid back the money?'

'Every week, a few pounds at a time. The debt was paid in full just a month ago. But it kept us poor, Danni. I didn't mind for myself but it deprived you of so much and I'm sorry.'

Danni shook her head. It was so much to take in all at once. It was impossible not to admire Ruth for sticking to her guns and keeping her child. She couldn't imagine how hard it must have been when she, Danni, was little. So many things were coming back to her now; the birthdays and Christmases when there had been no parties or friends round to tea; no special presents or birthday cakes. She remembered being mercilessly teased at school for wearing the hand-me-down clothes Ruth had bought at jumble sales; the school trips there was never any money for. She'd resented it all so much at the time but now the reasons were all too clear. She went to Ruth and put her arms around her.

'Oh, Mum. I wish you'd told me all this a long time ago.'

'How can you tell a child a thing like that?' Ruth asked. 'It would have been too much for you to take in. But now you know. I just wish you hadn't been to see Tom. I hate the thought of him telling you he wasn't your father when it should have been me.'

'Don't worry about that,' Danni said. 'After what you've told me I'm *glad* he isn't my dad. Who wants a father like him?' She frowned. 'What's his name? My real father, I mean.'

Ruth looked at the clock and stood up. 'Heavens, look at the time. Jim will be here soon and I still have to make this pie. Will you set the table, Danni? Use the best cloth and see if you can find enough matching china. Oh, and there's a packet of paper serviettes in the sideboard drawer.'

'I asked you a question, Mum. What's my real father's name? Surely I have the right to know that.'

Ruth sighed. 'Doctor Mark Naylor.'

'And he was practising here in Meadbridge?'

'He was working at the local hospital at the time,' Ruth

admitted. 'But they moved away years ago. For all I know they could even have gone abroad by now.'

'Do I look like him?'

'No – well, maybe, a bit. I hardly remember what he looked like now.' Ruth shook her head. 'Danni – you wouldn't? Please love – it wouldn't do any good. If you've got any ideas about trying to find him, please forget them. It could only cause trouble and heartache now.'

Danni shrugged. 'Just curious, that's all.'

As she set the table for lunch Danni thought over what she had just heard. It was hard to take in all the implications. It was more than likely that Mum would marry Jim – just for security. And probably she'd eventually marry some deadbeat too, for similar reasons; for security and so as not to be alone. Ruth had struggled for almost eighteen years to bring her up; tried hard to do the best she could, but even now it wasn't really working. Instead of developing the one talent she had, she was destined to work all her life for the minimum wage in a series of dead-end jobs. It wasn't Ruth's fault but surely someone had to be answerable for it. Here they were, trying to impress Jim Crawford with paper serviettes and the best tablecloth. And if it worked, just where did it leave her?

After lunch Danni helped her mother with the washing-up while Jim settled down with the Sunday papers. *A taste of the future*, Danni told herself ruefully as she put away the last plate. She'd already decided that somehow or other she would not be a part of that future.

'I think I'll go round to Nat's,' she said, watching Ruth surreptitiously smooth her hair in front of the kitchen mirror. 'I expect you and Jim would like some time to yourselves.'

Danni pulled up the zip of her anorak as she stepped out of the house. It had started to snow and the wind was bitingly cold. As she was passing number 23 she noticed that Rex, the Alsatian, was crouching against the fence, his coat caked with snow. His water bowl had a layer of ice on it. On impulse she made up her mind. Slipping in through the gate she untied his rope.

'Come on, Rexie boy,' she said. 'Let's leg it.'

At the end of the street she took the belt off her jeans and slipped it through the dog's collar. 'Come on, boy,' she said. 'We're going to find you a better home.'

In the nearest telephone box Danni thumbed through the pages till she found what she was looking for. To her relief the local RSPCA animal rescue centre was only two streets away.

'You say he's a stray?' the officer on duty said, examining Rex.

'As far as I know,' Danni fibbed. She'd taken off his thread-bare collar, which now reposed in her pocket. 'You can see he's half-starved. He looked so miserable I couldn't just leave him.'

The man smiled at her. 'Well, you're right about him being half-starved and he's certainly in poor condition.' He patted Rex. 'Come on, lad, let's find you something to eat and a dry kennel.' He looked at Danni. 'If no one claims him do you want to give him a home?'

Danni shook her head. 'I wish I could. I'd like to give you a donation. I know that's what people do but I . . .'

The man patted her arm. 'Don't worry about it, love. We'll see that he's OK.'

Danni gave Rex a final pat and left. As she walked to Natalie's she reflected that she and Rex had a lot in common. Just where did she belong? Who was she really? *Doctor Mark Naylor.* She said the name aloud. It was odd to think that was her real father's name. 'I bet he's got loads of cash,' she told herself. 'I wonder if he ever thinks of me – if he wonders where I am or what I've grown up like. Maybe he just put the whole thing out of his mind when Mum took off with the baby he'd fathered. But surely a man who had no hope of having a child of his own must have regrets and at least some curiosity about what might have been, just as she had.

I could have had a good education, she mused. Gone to uni or art school – no problem. I'd have had a wardrobe full of designer clothes and a posh bedroom – even better than Nat's; with my own telly and computer – even a DVD player. Instead of all that she and Mum had spent the last eighteen years struggling on the breadline. Poor Mum, having to slave away to pay back money that Doctor Mark flippin' Naylor wouldn't even have missed. It was all so unfair. A thought suddenly occurred to her. Had Mum been telling the truth? Did she really not have an address? A tiny spiral of excitement stirred in the pit of her stomach. If she'd been paying the money back surely she had to have had an address. Mum had begged her not to look for him but she hadn't promised not to, had she? She shook her head. Contemplating trying to meet her real father was too big a deal – too important to attempt on impulse. She still wasn't even sure if it was what she wanted. But if she did decide to do anything about it she would have to plan it carefully. As yet she had no idea where or how to begin.

By the time Danni was on her way home it was dark and the afternoon's snowfall had turned to rain. Soon her trainers were wet through as she slithered her way through the slush on the pavements. Mrs Frost had invited her to stay to tea. She'd been kind and apologetic.

'Even when Jack has gone to university he'll still want to come home,' she explained. 'I couldn't let his room out. And Natalie's is far too small to share.' She smiled. 'I'm sure your mother will want you to move with her anyway, Danni, and you'll probably get along with her new partner just fine once you get to know him.'

What did she know about anything? Danni asked herself. Her with her nice neat home and a husband to support her. She sensed that Natalie hadn't been all that keen for her to stay either. She'd started going out with that nerdy Jason Williams – hadn't stopped talking about him all afternoon. Danni sighed, her heart heavy. Why should she care about them? First thing tomorrow she was going to have to find herself a new job. And soon she'd have to start thinking about finding herself somewhere to live. It was a bleak prospect.

At Crane Row she let herself in and sensed at once that the house was empty. Mum and Jim had probably gone out for a run in his car or maybe over to his house. She went upstairs and took off her wet things. On the landing the door to her mother's bedroom was open and on impulse she went in. Perhaps Mum would lend her the dark grey suit she sometimes wore for work. It might make a good impression at the job centre. She took the jacket from the wardrobe and slipped it on. She and Ruth were roughly the same size. For a long time she looked at herself in the dressing-table mirror. She'd always thought that she looked a bit like Mum; tawny brown hair, worn long and tied back; an oval face with clear hazel eyes and a straight nose. *Nothing to write home about*, Mum always said. She grinned ruefully at her reflection. It was wonderful what a bit of make-up could do though. She opened the top drawer and took out her mother's modest make-up bag. Mum didn't wear make-up very often but when she did she favoured blue eye shadow. Danni didn't really go in for make-up but when she did, she preferred grey or brown. But, as Mum said, she was young enough to be able to take them without looking washed out. Opening a pot of Ruth's blue shadow Danni dabbed experimentally, peering into the mirror. Quickly she rubbed it off.

'Yuk! I look like something off a Christmas tree,' she told herself She zipped up the bag and pushed it back, but the drawer wouldn't close. Something was catching at the back. She pulled it open and tried again but it still caught. Danni pulled the drawer right out and reached her hand in to the void. Her fingers closed round a thick envelope. She tugged it out. For a moment she stared down at the thick brown package then slowly she opened the loose flap and drew out the contents. There were two snapshots of herself as a baby, a wedding photograph, presumably of Ruth and Tom, though Tom was barely recognizable. A marriage certificate, Ruth's birth certificate – then another, which she realized with a small shock, was her own. *Blake – Danielle Ruth.* She traced a finger along the columns and her stomach gave a lurch as she saw that the column reserved for *father* was left blank. No man was officially named as having fathered her. She was a nobody – a *nothing.* There it was in black and white. Her chest contracted with hurt and her lip trembled. 'Well, we'll see about that,' she said aloud, her voice shaking.

As she gathered the items together and pushed them back into the envelope a scrap of paper fluttered to the floor. She bent to pick it up. On it was scribbled an address. Charlesworth Avenue Medical Centre, Haylesmere, Suffolk. There was no name, but to Danni there was only one person to whom it could belong. She sat thinking for a long moment. Suffolk wasn't a million miles away. An idea began to form in her mind. At first it seemed mad but the more she thought about it, the more reasonable it seemed. At last she pushed the scrap of paper into her pocket and stood up resolutely.

'Right! You might think the debt has been paid, Doctor Naylor, but you're going to find out that you've got some paying back to do too! I'll show you whether I'm a nobody or not!'

CHAPTER THREE

CLAIRE placed the bowl of snowdrops and cream chrysanthemum heads in the centre of the table and stood back to take in the effect.

She had tried really hard to make sure that everything was up to her mother-in-law's standard. White lace place-mats; gleaming silver cutlery; sparkling crystal and, last but not least, the Georgian silver candelabra that George and Mary had given them as a wedding present, complete with slender white candles (Mary would have considered coloured ones vulgar).

Downstairs in the kitchen everything was ready; melon slices laced with Cointreau chilling in the fridge, duck à l'orange keeping warm in the oven; delicate lemon cheesecake awaiting its sifting of icing sugar – cheese and biscuits attractively arranged on a board and covered with foil. Maddie, Claire's beloved Yorkshire terrier, was safely shut up in the utility room in her basket. Mary did not approve of pet dogs. All she had to do now was to change and get ready.

Halfway up the stairs Claire paused. Had she remembered the wine? Yes, white, chilling in the fridge; red, uncorked and 'breathing' on the sideboard. Mark had promised to deal with the brandy and liqueurs when he got home from the surgery.

The house in Grafton Place was Regency. Built as one of an elegant terrace it overlooked a small private park where the residents exercised their dogs and children. On the ground floor was a dining-room overlooking the park and a morning-room to the rear. A large drawing-room took up most of the first floor and boasted long windows that gave on to a wrought-iron balcony. There were four bedrooms on the two floors above, two of which had *en-suite* bathrooms. The massive basement kitchen had been renovated to accommodate a smaller, compact kitchen and a studio, reached separately by the area steps from which Claire, under her maiden name of Claire Cavendish, conducted her successful interior design business.

To Claire the house had never felt like home. It had been her father-in-law's choice for them when Mark first qualified and returned to his home town of Haylesmere to join the family practice. That had been in the days when he had cherished fond hopes that Claire and Mark would present him with a large brood of grandchildren. She often longed secretly for the semi-detached villa on the outskirts of Northampton where she had grown up with her parents.

In her bedroom Claire put on the dress she had chosen for the occasion: a midnight-blue silk creation with shoestring straps, and slipped her arms into the little matching jacket of chiffon spangled with tiny crystal beads. She applied a discreet make-up, adding a dash of pale lipstick and brushed her blonde hair into a shining halo. She was about to go downstairs again when the telephone beside the bed rang.

'Hello, Claire Naylor.'

It was Mark's partner, Doctor Adam Bennett. 'Hi, Claire, it's me. Mark asked me to ring and tell you that he's on his way.'

'Thanks, Adam. It's good of you to take his calls this evening.'

'Not at all. It sounds as though the old man has something important to say to you.'

Claire sighed. 'I hate to say so but that usually means problems. Ever since he retired from the practice last year he's been coming up with all these bright ideas.'

'Tell me about it.' He chuckled. 'The whale noises instead of piped music in the waiting-room were a bit of a disaster.'

Claire laughed. 'The patients thought there was something wrong with the plumbing!'

'This new extension means that at the moment we're up to our necks in building materials. Some people just don't know when to let go.'

'Well, I suppose George does still have an interest in the practice, in as much as he sees the odd private patient there.'

'So – what do you think he's got up his sleeve this time?' Adam asked.

'I dread to think, though I doubt if it's anything we're going to like.'

'You really should put your foot down,' Adam said. 'Or at least Mark should. George has retired. You'd think he'd have better things to do.'

Claire said nothing, knowing that Mark would be the last to rock the boat as far as his father was concerned. He considered that they had short-changed him enough. 'Thanks for ringing, Adam,' she said. 'I really should get on now.'

'Claire . . .' There was a note of urgency in his voice. 'When am I going to see you again?'

'Oh, Adam, I don't know. I think we should . . .' She stopped speaking as the distant sound of the front door was heard slamming. Mark called out:

'Claire! I'm home.'

'Mark's here,' she said quickly. 'I'll have to go. See you soon, Adam.'

'Lunch maybe? Monday, my day off'?' There was a pause, then he said softly, 'Please, darling.'

'I can't talk now, Adam. I'll be in touch – I promise.' Already she could hear Mark taking the stairs two at a time.

'I must say it smells good.' He stood in the doorway

regarding her. 'Bloody hell! Is that what you're wearing?'

She turned to look at him. 'Of course. Why?'

He frowned. 'Isn't it a bit – well, you know . . .'

'A bit *well, you know* what?'

'Well – *frumpy*, not to put too fine a point on it. For heaven's sake, Claire, you're forty-five, not eighty-five!'

'I bought it specially,' she told him. 'I thought your mother might actually approve for once.'

He laughed. 'Since when did you dress to please my mother?'

Claire swallowed her irritation. 'I thought you'd be pleased.'

'For God's sake put something else on,' he said. 'And take that thing back to wherever you got it. It makes you look like something out of the Addams Family. What are we having for dinner?'

'Melon, duck à l'orange and lemon cheesecake.'

He pulled a face. 'Is that the best you can do? Claire, why don't you get someone in to help you? We've talked about this time and again. You just can't manage your work and the house as well. At least, not efficiently. It's not so bad when it's just the two of us but you're totally not up to entertaining.'

She shook her head. 'I've been working hard all afternoon, Mark. I thought . . .'

He looked at his watch. 'Hell! Look at the time. I'd better shower and change.'

Claire sighed. Nothing she did was ever good enough for Mark. Or so it seemed. She was almost ready to give up trying. She took off the midnight-blue dress and selected a black silk Jacques Vert skirt and white lace top from the wardrobe. Hurriedly fastening the skirt she ran down to the kitchen. In ten minutes they'd be here. Her in-laws were always punctual.

*

'How is the new extension coming along?' Doctor George Naylor leaned back in his chair as Mark poured him another glass of wine.

'Slowly,' Mark said. 'You know what these builders are like.'

'Oh well, There's no great hurry, I suppose.' George had done full justice to Claire's dinner, which was more than could be said for his wife, Mary, who had left a considerable amount of her food untouched, pushing her plate away from her with an expression of barely concealed aversion.

'Is everything all right?' Claire had asked her.

Mary's lips forced themselves into a pained smile. 'Yes dear, it's very nice – really, though since you ask, perhaps you've overdone the fruit theme a little. I'm afraid my digestion just can't handle it.'

'Oh. Can I get you something else? Will you have some cheese and biscuits?'

Claire could see Mark out of the corner of his eye mouthing *leave it*.

'The extension, Dad.' He turned to his father. 'It was good of you to offer to foot the bill for a minor ops theatre but at the moment we don't really have anyone to man it.'

'Ah – *at the moment*.' George patted his ample stomach and looked at Claire. 'My dear – would you mind if I had another slice of that delicious cheesecake?'

As Claire cut him a slice she could feel Mary's eyes boring into her like resentful lasers. She passed the plate to her father-in-law with a smile.

'As I said, "at the moment" is the operative phrase.' He took a spoonful of cheesecake and chewed thoughtfully. 'As you know, your cousin Gerald is a general surgeon.'

Mark frowned. 'At St Mary's hospital in Edinburgh.'

'Exactly. He's had a bit of a health scare recently – a bit of angina. Nothing to worry about, but he's been advised to take things more easily. He's going to take early retirement but he doesn't want to give up working altogether.'

Light began to dawn. Mark forced a smile. 'So you're going to suggest he moves down here and takes on our minor ops?'

'That's the idea. I've already suggested it and he's delighted. He and Anita have been thinking of moving further south for some time.' George nodded with satisfaction. 'Our nearest hospital is in Ipswich so it will be a godsend to local patients. And of course it'll be a tremendous boost for the practice.' George clearly still felt connected to the practice even though he had retired. He cleared his throat. 'There's something else. As you know, Paul, Gerald and Anita's son is twenty-five and qualified now. He's just coming to the end of his pre-reg year but he wants to become a GP. I thought it would be ideal if he joined us.' Seeing Mark's doubtful expression he went on: 'You were saying only the other day that the practice could do with another partner since my retirement.'

'Well, I'm not sure that we can afford to take anyone else on board at the moment. Anyway, isn't it a bit soon to be talking of partnerships? He's only just qualified.'

George nodded. 'I meant eventually, of course. He'll have to make his mark first.' He chuckled. 'Though from what I hear that won't take long. Seems he's a bit of a prodigy, passed his finals with the highest marks St Mary's had ever seen.'

'And of course we have to think of the future, don't we?' Mary put in. 'Your father has always been keen to keep the practice in the family and as you have no sons to pass the practice on to, Paul would be the obvious choice.'

Silence fell over the table. Claire stole a look at Mark and saw that his colour had deepened. She rose from the table. 'Coffee, everyone?' She went to the sideboard where the filter machine was bubbling away, relieved to have something to occupy her.

'One thing I'm going to have to insist on.' George paused to light a cigar. 'When we've got this minor ops theatre up and running there are to be no terminations carried out in it.' Mark frowned. 'It has come to my notice that you recently referred a couple for IVF treatment,' George went on. 'I'm sure you know my views on that subject only too well.'

Mary coughed delicately. 'Really, George. Is this a subject for the dinner table?'

George ignored her. 'If there's one thing I draw the line at it's tampering with nature,' he said. 'Some of the ideas they're coming up with lately; stem-cell therapy, freezing sperm and embryos, not to mention the appalling prospect of human cloning! It's all getting hopelessly out of hand and no good can come of it. In years to come no one will know who they are or where they come from. As for surrogacy! Getting some strange woman to give birth for you! Nothing short of obscene if you ask me! What's wrong with adoption? Plenty of poor kids out there needing good parents.'

'Most couples want a child who is their own,' Claire put in.

'Of course. And if a woman can't give her husband a child herself she should give him his freedom in my opinion,' Mary said, taking a sip of her coffee. She stared pointedly at Claire. 'That might sound harsh but it's what I believe; unless of course they decide mutually not to have children. Messing around with other people's homes is no substitute for motherhood.' Claire bit the inside of her lip so hard that she tasted blood.

When George and Mary had departed Claire carried the dishes down to the kitchen and began to load the dishwasher. Mark looked round the door.

'Can't you leave that for the morning?'

'I need something to do,' Claire told him without looking round. 'I can't go to bed yet. I'm too angry. Your mother is quite impossible sometimes.'

Mark was silent for a moment. 'I know it's hard on you,' he said. 'But we always said, didn't we, that we'd keep everything that happened from them. If Dad had known what we did he'd never have spoken to me again, let alone allowed me into the family practice. You know how hidebound he is.'

'Now it seems we needn't have bothered!' Claire wiped her hands on a teacloth. 'It looks as though your cousin and his genius son will be taking control before long.'

'Not while I'm still the senior partner,' Mark said grimly.

'And just how long will that be?' Claire said under her breath. Aloud she said, 'What gets me is that we were just *told*. Your father didn't even feel it necessary to discuss it with you. And what about Adam?' she asked. 'Where does he fit into this new arrangement?'

Mark shrugged. 'I doubt if he'll consider it the end of the world. He'll find another practice without any trouble,' he said. 'He's young. The Charlesworth Avenue practice doesn't mean anything to him.'

'Whereas it means everything to you. So much in fact that we have to live a lie for the rest of our lives.' She shook her head at him. 'Why don't you make a break and look for work somewhere else, Mark?'

He frowned. 'You know why, Claire. This is my place, my birthright if you like. Why should I give it up just because of a quirk of nature?'

She gave a bitter little laugh. 'Is *that* what you call it? You know, sometimes I can't help wondering if there isn't something in your father's reservations. Messing around with nature certainly did us no favours, did it?'

An expression of slight irritation crossed Mark's brow. 'We were just unlucky. Nothing is ever infallible,' he said. 'We have to move with the times. If the medical profession had never accepted new procedures we'd still be doing operations without anaesthetics and seeing children die of measles!'

'That's easy for you to say,' Claire said. 'You didn't suffer the devastation of a botched abortion and have your dreams of becoming a doctor shattered. You didn't have the child you thought was going to be yours snatched from your arms.'

The colour left his face. 'That's not quite true.'

'As for your mother,' Claire went on, 'she's never stopped sniping at me. What about that crack she made tonight? *Messing around with other people's homes is no substitute for motherhood.* As if I didn't know!'

Mark shook his head impatiently. 'Oh, that's just her way. Take no notice of her.'

'How can I help it?' Claire demanded. 'I'm the innocent party here, Mark. But she'll never know that, will she? I can't defend myself. According to her I should stand aside and let you marry someone who can give you a child.' Her eyes challenged him. 'But then maybe you agree with her!'

He turned away. 'Oh, don't be so melodramatic.'

'But how would I *know*, Mark? We never talk. I haven't a clue what you want or how you think any more.'

'I've had enough of this. I'm going to bed.' He walked to the door. 'If I were you I'd advertise for some help around the house. It seems to me that you're overtired.'

Claire threw down her teacloth. 'And that's all down to my work, I suppose? Messing around as your mother calls it!'

He sighed with exaggerated patience. 'Calm down, Claire,' he said. 'There's nothing to be gained by raking up the past.'

She stared helplessly at the door he closed behind him. Walking out was always Mark's way of ending an argument. It never occurred to him to stay and talk things through. *There's nothing to be gained by raking up the past.* No, he was right there. Nothing they could do or say could ever put right the terrible things that happened all those years ago. Only she was the one who would have to live with the injustice of it all for the rest of her life.

'What is it? You've been miles away ever since we met.' Adam looked at Claire across the table. They were lunching at a tiny riverside pub out in the Suffolk countryside; a place that had become their favourite haunt since they'd started meeting the previous summer. 'There's something worrying you, isn't there?'

She looked up. 'I shouldn't really have come,' she said. 'I told you I wasn't fit company for anyone today.'

He reached across the table for her hand. 'But I flatter myself that I'm not just anyone.'

'No. That's the trouble.' Her eyes met his. 'Adam, this really can't go on, you know. We—'

'*Don't*,' he interrupted. 'We have so little time. Can't we just enjoy it?' As she shook her head he asked, 'Does this have anything to do with the dinner party last Friday evening?'

'It's what started it, I suppose.'

'Do you want to talk about it?'

Claire pushed her barely touched plate away. 'Let's go,' she said. 'Let's take Maddie for a walk along the river bank. There might even be some early primroses out.'

Adam hurriedly paid the bill and followed her outside. He was worried by her mood; afraid of what she might be about to say. Seeing his partner's wife behind his back was despicable. He was always telling himself so, but he couldn't help it. He was hopelessly in love with Claire. He felt her sadness and vulnerability whenever they were together and all he longed for was to make her happy, whatever the cost.

The late March sunshine was watery, with white clouds blown raggedly across the sky. The wind was still cold. Adam hunched his shoulders.

'Are you sure this is what you want?'

She nodded. 'I need to breathe some fresh air.' They walked in silence for a while, then she turned to him. 'George is planning to bring his nephew, Gerald into the practice. His son is newly qualified and George is planning for him to join the practice too; and take over eventually – Mark and me not having provided him with an heir apparent.'

'I see.'

'No you don't. Not really. Adam, look – there's a lot you don't know about us,' about Mark and me. It's only fair that you should know the truth. Our marriage is more complicated than most.'

He smiled wryly. 'I had already gathered that.'

'And I want you to know why. I feel I owe it to you.' Claire turned up the collar of her jacket and quickened her step. 'We met at university.'

'I knew that.'

'What you didn't know is that I was studying medicine too. We fell madly in love and planned to marry as soon as we both qualified.'

'So – what happened?'

Claire took a deep breath. 'I got pregnant; something we hadn't visualized.' He looked surprised and she laughed bitterly. 'Yes, naïve or what? After the initial shock I would have been happy to keep the baby, but Mark was horrified by the idea of parenthood before either of us had finished studying. As far as he was concerned there was only one course.'

'Termination?'

She nodded. 'I hated the idea but I went along with it against my better judgement.' She swallowed hard. 'I suppose I saw that it was either that or lose Mark. To cut a long story short, things went horribly wrong. I suffered a severe haemorrhage and almost died. I had to have emergency surgery and as a result I was told that I would never have another child.'

Adam took her hand, forcing her to stop walking. Turning her towards him he looked into her eyes, his own full of compassion. 'Claire. I'm so sorry, darling. And of course I can see that Mark would want to keep it from George, with his strong views about abortion.'

'But that's not the whole story. Mark and I were married some months later, as soon as he'd passed his finals. I think I already knew that he was marrying me out of misplaced shame and a certain amount of guilt. I'd had to drop out of university, you see. All my hopes of a career in medicine were smashed. Looking back I suppose I realized he'd stopped loving me but I chose not to notice. I suspected – rightly as it turned out, that he'd been seeing someone else but I just kept burying my head deeper and deeper in the sand – until I discovered, six months after we were married, that the girl he'd been seeing had given birth to a baby son.'

'Oh, my God! Poor Claire.' Adam took her arm. 'You're shivering. Let's go back to the car.'

On the way back it began to rain and they ran the last few yards. Claire scooped up Maddie and put her on her blanket on the back seat before climbing gratefully into the passenger seat. Adam drove to a quiet spot close to some woods where he pulled over and stopped. He turned to Claire who had been silent and drew her into his arms. He kissed her and for a while she sat with her head on his shoulder. 'Thanks for letting me tell you, Adam,' she whispered.

'Are you going to tell me the rest?' He cupped her chin with his hand and made her look at him. 'There *is* more, isn't there?'

'My tragedy was knowing I'd never have a child. Mark's was not being able to acknowledge his illegitimate son. I think he felt it was some kind of judgment on him, but instead of coming to terms with it together he put all the guilt on to me.' She sighed. 'We went through a very bad time. I almost made up my mind to ask him for a divorce so that he could marry the mother of his child.' She looked at him. 'But George would have been just as shocked by that as by my abortion.'

'Why is Mark so afraid of his father?' Adam asked. 'He's a brilliant doctor. He could work anywhere. Why does it matter so much to be here?'

'The Charlesworth Avenue practice has been in his family for four generations.' She shrugged. 'It's one of those pride things. Mark's been conditioned to it since childhood.'

41

'You could have left him; made a new life on your own.' He looked at her. 'Why didn't you? Did you love him so very much?'

'I did love him, it's true. But more than that I felt I'd invested so much of my life in him; sacrificed so much.' She shook her head. 'I think by that time we were bound together more by this awful guilty secret than by love.'

'So you stayed together.'

'We stayed together, with an ever deepening sense of regret and resentment.' She took a deep breath. 'Until a solution presented itself.'

'What kind of solution?'

'We found a woman who was willing to be a surrogate for us. She was in financial difficulties and was only too glad to accept our offer. It was like the answer to everything and for a while we were happy again. We planned it very carefully – managed to keep the whole thing under wraps. A baby girl was born, at a holiday cottage we used to have down in Devon. We were to have brought her home as our own.'

Adam raised an eyebrow. 'But?'

'But when the child was born the mother decided she couldn't be parted from her. Mark was furious. He told her she would have to pay back the money we'd paid her.'

'He could hardly make her, could he?' Adam looked shocked. 'After all, the arrangement wasn't exactly legal.'

'No. It was Mark who delivered the baby, too. He could have been in deep trouble – probably struck off. She could have been in trouble too. It was stalemate. Mark argued with the woman, made all kinds of threats, but it made no difference and in the end we had to let her take the child and go.' Her eyes filled with tears. 'I couldn't blame her. She loved the baby so much she'd have done anything. We were powerless to stop her.'

'Did Mark carry out his threat of making her pay back the money?'

'Oh yes. As far as I know she paid back every penny.' She shook her head. 'How she managed to bring the child up on her own I dread to think. I begged Mark a dozen times to let her off the payments for the child's sake but he was adamant. It's hard for him, you see. He's bitter. He now has two children he can't acknowledge.'

'That's hardly your fault.'

'It might as well be.' Claire looked at her watch and shivered. 'I think we should go now. It's getting late.'

As he drove back to Haylesmere Adam said, 'With two more doctors joining the practice it looks as though I'm going to be surplus to requirements soon.' He glanced at her. 'I'll start looking for another job. When I find one why don't you come with me, Claire? We could go abroad – anywhere.'

She sighed. 'You're younger than me, Adam. You don't want a woman with all my baggage round your neck. I'd just be a burden.'

'Of course you wouldn't. I'm only five years younger and anyway it doesn't matter. You deserve better than this, Claire. I love you. Come with me, please.'

'You're very sweet but I can't. It's too late. You should find someone of your own age. You'd regret it and I've had enough of regrets.'

'I wouldn't!' He drew up at the end of Grafton Place. 'Promise me you'll at least think about it.'

She gave him a wry little smile. 'Oh, I'll think about it all right.'

'Seriously, I mean.'

Glancing round she leaned over and kissed his cheek. 'Why do you think I told you all that about our past, Adam?' she said softly. 'I want you to know that our – I don't know what you'd call it – affair, for want of a better word, has to end. You need someone with a clean slate, or at least with fewer complications. This has to be the last time for us, Adam. No.' She laid a finger against his lips. 'I mean it.' Reaching for his hand she squeezed it gently. 'Find a lovely girl and be happy, Adam,' she said. 'You're a lovely man and you deserve it. You really do.' And before he could protest she reached into the back seat for Maddie, opened the door and slipped out of the car.

CHAPTER FOUR

D ANNI closed the door of her bed-sit and looked around her. What a dump. Not that she could summon up much enthusiasm for her surroundings after a shift at the supermarket, stacking shelves.

She'd been in Haylesmere for almost a month now. She'd found the job at the Savemore supermarket easily enough. It didn't pay very well and by the time she'd paid the rent of this grotty little bed-sit there wasn't a lot left, but at least she got a reasonable midday meal in the canteen.

She had seen the single bed-sit advertised in the local paper on the day she arrived and had gone right round to 28 Church Street to see it. She soon discovered that Church Street was not in the most salubrious part of town, but, as she told herself, beggars couldn't be choosers. Up two flights of stairs on the second floor of a Victorian semi the eight by ten room boasted a single bed, a rickety table and chair, a wardrobe and chest of drawers. There was a spluttering gas fire, paid for by a meter that sat beside it in a little cupboard. The one small dormer window had a view of the adjacent weed-infested cemetery, and the bathroom was on the floor below and shared by two other tenants. Mrs Bell, the landlady, was however a cheerful soul; an elderly lady with an ample figure and a throaty laugh. To Danni's relief she hadn't demanded a month's rent in advance and she had trustingly handed over a key to the front door.

'I've been around long enough to know a face I can trust,' she said. 'We don't stand on ceremony here, love. Come and go as you please as long as you remember that last in locks up. And any problems – just knock on my door.' Danni had very gratefully taken the room on the spot.

Ruth had been upset when she had announced her intention of leaving Meadbridge. It wasn't that she hadn't tried. She'd stuck it out for three weeks after they'd moved into Jim Crawford's house. But his pernickety ways really got on her nerves; that and lying in bed at night knowing that only a thin wall separated her from the two of them in bed together. The thought made her want to throw up.

She had refused to tell Ruth where she was going. For one thing, she didn't know that Danni had Mark Naylor's address and for another she was afraid that she might guess at the germ of a plan that she was still carrying around in her head. Danni had hedged, saying she would go wherever there was likely to be a job and Ruth had reluctantly accepted the plan. But on the day Danni left she had presented her daughter with a mobile phone.

'If you can't tell me where you're going to be at least promise me that you'll keep in touch,' she said. Danni had promised.

She wasn't even sure that she could call it a plan; as yet it was only a half-formed notion in her mind. She hadn't a clue where to start. Obviously, finding her biological father wasn't something she could rush into. It would take a lot of careful thought and preparation and she wasn't even sure she could do that. But of one thing she was sure – that one way or another – somehow – sometime she would meet him and get to know what kind of man he was.

She found Haylesmere pleasant with its quaint stone

houses and pretty riverside walks. It was a lot more attractive than Meadbridge. On Sundays, if the weather was fine, she would take her sketchbook down to the river and while away the time drawing the trees and the boats on the water. The early signs of spring were everywhere and she planned to go out sketching more in what spare time she had. The one thing she wasn't going to do was lose touch with her drawing. Maybe when she could afford it she'd attend some classes.

Although she got along well enough with her new workmates at Savemore she kept them at arm's length. She had decided from the start not to make any close friends. The fewer people who knew about her background the better. She recognized the flaw in her nature that made it hard for her to resist confiding in people. She never meant to but somehow the words just came tumbling out before she could stop them. She decided that it probably came from being an only child, brought up by a single parent.

For the first few weeks everything was fine, then, in mid April, Danni went down with the flu. At first she thought it was a cold and that she would shake it off. But overnight her temperature soared and the following morning when she tried to get out of bed her legs crumpled under her and a searing cough tore at her chest. She managed to call in sick to Savemore on her mobile, then sank into a restless, cough-racked sleep.

It was midday when there was a knock on her door. Raising her head she managed to croak: 'Who is it?'

'S'only me, lovie – Mrs B.' The landlady put an anxious face round the door. 'I never heard you go out this morning and I wondered . . . Oh, my dear Lord, look at the state of you!' She bustled into the room and tugged at the rumpled bedclothes. 'Feelin' bad, are you, duck?'

Danni nodded. 'I think it must be flu,' she said. 'Mind you don't catch it, Mrs Bell.'

The old woman laughed. 'Never you mind about that. I've had my flu jab so I'm all right. Now, what you need is some nice soup. I bet you ain't had no breakfast neither.'

Mrs B looked after Danni like a mother hen for the next two days and when she was well enough to get up again the older woman asked her if she'd registered with a doctor. Danni shook her head.

'Never thought I'd need one.'

Mrs B laughed. 'We all need the doc from time to time, duck. Maybe while you're still off work you should pop along and do it. Get him to give you a certificate and something for that nasty cough while you're there too.'

Danni thought about the suggestion. It was as though fate was taking a hand. If she was looking for a way of setting her plan in motion maybe this was it. Going downstairs to the payphone in the hall she leafed through the Yellow Pages till she came to the section marked 'General Practitioners'. Running her finger down the column she found what she was looking for: 'Naylor, Doctor M. Charlesworth Avenue Medical Centre.' For a long time she stared down at it. Well, why not? Mrs B had said she should get checked over after the flu – maybe get something to clear up her cough. And she might as well go to Charlesworth Avenue as anywhere else.

She found it easily enough. The surgery was on the edge of town, close to the park, in quite a smart residential area. She went in to reception and asked if she could register. The receptionist gave her a form to fill in.

'Can I see one of the doctors now?' Danni asked. 'I've had flu, and I can't shake off this cough.'

The woman consulted her computer screen. 'As it happens Doctor Naylor has had a cancellation,' she said. 'It's not for another half an hour though. Can you wait, or come back at three o'clock?'

'Thanks, I'll come back.' Danni felt her heart skip a beat.

The receptionist entered her name on the computer.

'That's fine then, Miss Blake. See you in half an hour.'

Danni went for a walk round the park. Signs of spring were everywhere. New leaves were bursting on the trees and there were daffodils blooming in the grass. The air was warmer. She sat on a bench near the lake and wished she had her sketch book with her. Today was a milestone, she told herself. Today she was actually going to get her first look at her father. She would take things slowly, though. Rushing would ruin everything. Anyway, maybe he'd be horrible and she wouldn't like him. In that case she'd go away and say nothing – put the whole idea out of her mind. But at least today she would know.

At five to three she walked back into reception again. The girl at the desk smiled and nodded. 'You can go through to the waiting area now,' she said. 'Doctor will be free in a moment. You're his last patient.'

In the waiting area she sat down and thumbed unseeingly through a magazine. Her heart was beating like a drum but she swallowed hard and tried to calm down. When the door opened and he stood there calling her name she stood up slowly on shaky legs. *This is it*, she told herself. *The moment of truth.*

Her first impression was that he looked like any other middle-aged man. Quite nice-looking; tallish with dark hair, going a bit grey. He had light brown eyes. *Like me* a voice inside her head whispered. *But loads of people have hazel eyes, don't they?* His clothes looked expensive; a well-cut dark suit and crisp white shirt. And she noticed that his hands were smooth and well-cared for.

'So . . .' He looked at the card in front of him. 'Miss Blake. What can I do for you today?'

'I – I've had a bit of flu,' she said. 'And I can't seem to get rid of this cough.'

'Maybe I should have a listen,' he said, smiling. He stood

up and picked up his stethoscope. 'Just to make sure you haven't developed an infection.'

She unbuttoned her top and stood patiently while he pressed the stethoscope to her chest, then repeated the process on her back. At last he smiled reassuringly and removed the instrument from his ears.

'Well, that sounds perfectly all right,' he said. 'No need for any antibiotics. I'll give you a prescription for some linctus. That should clear the cough up, especially now that the weather's improving.' He slipped on a pair of gold-rimmed glasses and filled in the details on his computer, then printed the form out. He tore it off and handed it to her with a smile. 'You're new in the area, are you?'

She nodded. 'Yes.' She swallowed hard, searching her mind for something to add. 'I – I'm hoping to go to art school here.' *Whatever made her say that?*

His eyebrows rose. 'Really? Why Haylesmere?'

She felt herself blushing. 'I – a friend studied here and – and she said it was – good.'

He laughed. 'Well, I hope for your sake that she was right.' He looked at her, frowning slightly. 'So – is there anything else troubling you. . . ?' He glanced again at the card. 'Danielle, isn't it?'

'Yes. I mean *no*, there's nothing else.' She picked up the prescription form and backed towards the door. 'Thank you, Doctor. Goodbye.'

He looked faintly amused. 'Goodbye. I hope your cough clears up soon. If it doesn't, come back and we'll try something else.'

Walking out through the door clutching her prescription form Danni felt dazed. It had all been so ordinary, just like any other visit to the doctor. But this man was her *father*! She had met him at last. It was hard to take in. The thing was, what did she do now? Should she have said something? But how could she have come out with it just like that? *'By the way, Doctor Naylor, I'm your daughter!'* The thought made her cringe with embarrassment. On the other hand, how else could she do it? Whatever had happened to feisty Danielle Blake; always in trouble for being too outspoken?

She went back to work after the weekend. Her cough responded to the prescribed linctus so there would be no excuse to go back to the doctor, but although her cough calmed down her thoughts grew more and more chaotic and she found it almost impossible to keep her mind on her work. By the end of the week she had received three warnings about putting items in the wrong section, occasioning complaints from customers. 'That's it,' she told herself. 'I've had it up to here!'

That evening on her way home she bought a local paper and over her evening meal she scanned the 'situations vacant' columns. Working in supermarkets was definitely doing her head in. She just had to find something more interesting or she would go spare.

In her room she scanned the columns, not sure of what she was looking for and although domestic work hadn't even occurred to her, one advertisement seemed to leap off the page at her.

An assistant/Girl Friday needed for Cavendish Interior Designs. General help around the house, some secretarial work plus dog-walking. No experience necessary but must be able to fit in with a busy working housewife.

The advert ended with a telephone number for application. On impulse Danni fished her mobile phone out of her handbag and punched in the number.

'Hello. Cavendish Interior Design.'

Danni took a deep breath. 'Oh – hello. I'm ringing in reply

to your advert in the *Gazette*,' she said breathlessly. Suddenly she knew that if she really wanted this job she had to be positive. 'I think I'm just what you're looking for,' she said.

'Really? Well, maybe this is my lucky day. Tell me a bit about yourself. Your name for instance.'

'My name's Danielle Blake. I've just moved to Haylesmere and I've been working in a supermarket. But I hate it.'

'How old are you, Danielle?'

'Almost eighteen. I had to leave school for – for financial reasons but I really wanted to go to Art College.'

'Ah – so you're interested in art?'

'Oh yes, very interested. I like dogs too. And I'm very domesticated.' Danni crossed her fingers, wondering what her mother would have made of the last remark. At the other end of the phone she heard a chuckle.

'Good! Well, Danielle, I think you'd better come round and see me. It's 64 Grafton Place. Do you know where that is?'

'I can find it,' Danni told her confidently.

'I have my studio in the basement and that's where I'll be. You reach it via the area steps. When can you come?'

'Now?' Danni said, holding her breath.

Again the chuckle. 'Well, you *are* keen. Yes, now would be fine. The sooner the better, I suppose. Would one hour from now suit you?'

'I'll be there,' Danni told her.

Mrs Bell told her how to get to Grafton Place. 'Very posh,' she said, nodding her approval. 'You get a job there you'll be mixing with the nobs!' She chuckled. 'Be tuppence to speak to you, eh?'

'I haven't got it yet.' Danni held up crossed fingers. 'Better wait and see.'

When she got off the bus she asked a passer-by for further directions and found that Grafton Place was a short walk away. Turning into the square, she was impressed by the elegant houses and the well-kept garden area in the centre of the square. She found number 64, walked down the area steps as instructed and knocked on the door beside which was a board with *Cavendish Interior Design* painted on it in a flamboyant script. The woman who answered was tall and blonde, dressed in a black skirt and white blouse over which she wore a loose smock.

'You must be Danielle,' she said. 'Come in. Forgive the mess but I'm working.'

In the studio a large easel stood near the window and a table nearby was littered with tubes of paint and other media. The other side of the room was set out as an office, with a computer, desk and filing-cabinet. Danni took it all in approvingly. It was just the kind of studio she had always dreamed of having. Her expression registered with Claire.

'You like my studio?'

'Oh yes,' Danni breathed. 'It's wicked.'

Claire laughed. 'Well, I'd hardly call it that. I'm not the tidiest worker. Now, please take a seat. Just put those drawings on the floor. And tell me all about yourself.' She swung her swivel chair round to face Danni and looked at her expectantly.

Danni shrugged. 'Not much to tell,' she said. 'As I told you on the phone I've been working in a supermarket but I want something more interesting.'

'You said you were interested in art,' Claire put in.

'Yes. I wanted to go to art school but we – Mum and I that is – couldn't afford it.'

'So there's just you and your mother?'

'Yes. Dad left years ago. I don't even remember him,' Danni said, thinking how strange it was that this wasn't strictly true. She had seen her 'father' only yesterday for the first time.

'So, you live with your mother?'

'No. She's with a new partner back in Meadbridge. I – we didn't really hit it off.'

'I see. So how do you come to be here in Haylesmere?'

'It was where the job was – and – and I was hoping to go to some art classes in my spare time; when I'd saved up some money.'

Claire's heart was touched by the girl seated before her. She was bright and articulate; attractive with her bright hazel eyes and mobile mouth. Yet there was something vulnerable about her. It must have taken guts to move to a strange town. Was there perhaps more to her than met the eye? 'What kind of art do you like?' she enquired, asking herself at the same time why she had put the question. It had no bearing on the job she was offering.

Danni's eyes lit up. 'All kinds,' she said. 'I love to draw and I like painting with watercolours; oils too.'

'In my job I work a lot with pastels,' Claire said. 'Very messy. The dust gets everywhere, hence the overall.' She cleared her throat. 'But I suppose we'd better get down to what the job is all about. I really need someone to help me round the house and walk Maddie, my Yorkie. I'll introduce you to her in a minute. I also need someone to answer the phone and take messages for me when I'm out or tied up down here. It's maddening to be interrupted when I'm working.' She shrugged. 'I suppose it's really the kind of job that will evolve as we go along, so who ever gets it will need to be flexible.'

'Sounds fine to me,' Danni said with a grin. 'I hate boring routine.'

Claire stood up. 'Would you like to see round the house and meet my little dog?'

'Yes please.'

When Claire opened the door that led directly into the kitchen a small bundle of brown fur hurled itself at them, barking excitedly. Claire bent down and picked the dog up. 'That's enough, Maddie,' she said. 'I normally have her with me in the studio when I'm working,' she explained. 'She likes company but she tends to be a bit over-enthusiastic.' She held the dog out. 'Say how do you do to Danielle.'

'Oh, she's gorgeous!' Danni took the little brown dog who licked her face, making her laugh.

'She obviously likes you,' Claire said.

Danni looked round the kitchen with its pristine marble surfaces and oak cupboards. 'This is nice,' she remarked. 'Really easy to keep clean.'

'I do have a woman who comes in once a week to do the heavy work,' Claire told her. 'I'd only need you to dust and vacuum and tidy up. Come and see the rest.'

Danni was impressed by the elegant house, spaciously laid out on three floors. She had never seen such beautiful furniture and lush carpets and she noticed that there were some stunning pictures displayed on the walls.

'Are these yours?' she asked.

Claire smiled. 'Not all of them, some are mine though. I like painting landscapes when I have time.'

Danni studied a woodland scene delicately painted in watercolours. 'What about this one?' she asked.

Claire nodded. 'That's mine, yes.'

'It's lovely. Just the kind of thing I'd like to do.' She looked at Claire. 'If I had your kind of talent.'

'I'm sure you have,' Claire said. 'You're certainly keen enough.'

'It's all I've ever wanted to do,' Danni said. 'All I've ever been any good at if I'm honest.'

'I wasn't always an artist,' Claire said. 'I was studying medicine to begin with, then I was ill and couldn't continue so I took up art, my second interest.'

Danni saw a shadow cross her face and said quickly, 'Well, you've obviously made a great success of it.'

Claire smiled. 'Yes. I suppose you could say that. I've been lucky. Well, Danielle, what do you think? Would you like to come and work with me?'

Danni noted the way she said 'with' and not 'for' She liked that. 'I'd love to, Mrs Cavendish,' she said.

'Oh, Claire, please. I hate formality. Cavendish is my maiden name anyway, so I'm only called that for business purposes.'

'I like to be called Danni.'

'Good! Well, Danni, shall we get down to business?' Claire named the salary she proposed to pay which made Danni's mouth drop open. It was twice what she earned at Savemore as a shelf-stacker.

'Where are you living at present?' Claire asked.

'Church Street,' Danni told her. 'I've got a bed-sit there.'

'Isn't that rather a long way away?' Claire asked.

'A bus ride and a bit of a walk, yes.'

Claire looked thoughtful. 'There are plenty of bedrooms here. How would living in suit you?'

Danni could hardly believe her ears. 'Here?' she said. 'Well, I . . .'

'I suppose I'd better check with my husband first,' Claire said. 'And the salary would have to be adjusted accordingly of course. But I'm sure it would be all right – if you would like to do that.'

'Well, yes. That would be fine,' Danni said.

'I'd like to offer you the job then, Danni,' Claire said with a smile. 'To begin next week if you can manage it.' She held out her hand and Danni took it.

'I'll give in my notice at Savemore right away.'

Claire walked up the area steps with her to the pavement. 'I think we're going to get along fine, Danni,' she said with a smile. 'Give me a ring tomorrow and I'll confirm whether it's all right for you to move in. We'll take it from there.'

As Danni was walking away a car drew up and stopped at the kerb. The man at the wheel looked familiar. A little way along the street she turned and saw that he was running up the steps to the front door of number 64. Then she realized where she had seen him before. It was Doctor Mark Naylor.

CHAPTER FIVE

A s he drew up Mark caught a glimpse of a girl coming up the area steps. She wore jeans and an anorak and didn't look much like Claire's usual clients. Just for a moment he thought she looked vaguely familiar, but he shrugged off the thought as he locked the car and ran up the steps.

It had been one of those days. Dad had been in during the afternoon, full of ideas and eager to inspect the builders' work, putting their backs up as usual with his interference and unwanted advice.

'When this extension is finished we'll be the most up to date, state of the art surgery in Haylesmere,' he said. Mark hadn't missed the 'we'. George still considered himself the senior partner in spite of the fact that he had retired.

'We can hardly be a state of the art surgery, Dad, if we refuse to give patients the latest treatments that they expect,' he pointed out.

George had shaken his head. 'They'll have to accept that as doctors we know what's best,' he insisted. 'And I'm sure that when Gerald joins us he'll agree.'

Mark had bitten his tongue to stop himself making a sharp retort. The prospect of his cousin joining the practice was becoming less and less attractive as the weeks went by.

In spite of the weather warming up there seemed to be a fresh outbreak of flu. Evening surgery had been full of coughing, sneezing patients; all expecting him to provide a miracle cure. When he explained – over and over again, his patience wearing thinner and thinner, that influenza was a virus and would take its course they looked at him as though he was some kind of quack. Some even implied as much, flouncing out of the consulting-room in a strop. He'd had four interruptions from pushy medical reps too, refusing to be fobbed off by the staff in reception and insisting that he order their latest revolutionary pills and potions. Evening surgery had taken almost twice as long as it should and now all he wanted was a long hot bath and his dinner.

Downstairs in the kitchen Claire was peeling potatoes. She looked up as he came in.

'Had a good day?'

'Don't ask.'

'I see. Like that?'

He took a bottle of wine from the fridge and poured himself a glass. 'Did you have a client?'

'No.'

'I thought I saw someone leaving as I drew up.'

'That was the girl who's going to be my new Girl Friday.'

'Your what?'

'I decided to advertise for some help. I'm finding it hard to manage now that the business is taking off. I'm always missing calls when I'm out.'

'You mean you're employing someone just to take your telephone calls? What's wrong with the answer-phone?'

'Nothing, but by the time I get round to ringing back a lot of people have gone elsewhere. This girl is going to help around the house too; walk Maddie, help in the kitchen and take calls too, when I'm out.'

'A general dogsbody, you mean?'

'A bit more than that, as it happens. I didn't expect someone as bright as Danni to reply. She's really keen on art and I've been thinking, I might even train her to help in the business if everything works out.'

The mention of art made Mark remember where he'd seen the girl before. 'What's her name?' he asked.

'Danielle Blake. She likes to be called Danni though. She's a nice girl; intelligent and funny. We got along really well.'

'Oh well, as long as you're satisfied. And as long as she doesn't get under my feet.'

Claire glanced at him, trying to assess his mood. He'd clearly had a stressful day. Maybe this wasn't the best time. In spite of her misgivings she heard herself saying, 'Actually, I thought it might be an idea for her to live in.'

He spluttered over his wine. 'You *what*?'

'Well, we've got plenty of room. I thought she might have one of the rooms on the top floor. If she had her own television she wouldn't actually be living with us. You need hardly see her at all.'

'Why the hell can't she come in to work each day like anyone else?'

'She's living right over on the other side of town in some grotty little bed-sit. It'd take her ages on the bus and you know how unreliable they are. She's a really sweet girl, Mark and it's not going to affect you in any way. I promise.'

'Have you actually offered her this live-in package?'

'Not yet. I did say I'd check with you first.'

He looked slightly appeased. 'Oh. Well, thanks for that, anyway.'

'So – is it OK? Can I tell her?'

'I don't suppose I've got any choice really, have I?' He finished his wine and stood up. 'I'm going up to have a bath. How long will dinner be?'

'Half an hour.'

Lying in the spicily scented water he felt himself slowly begin to relax. Odd that Claire's – what was the daft expression she'd used – Girl Friday should be the new patient he'd seen recently. She'd seemed a nice enough girl, though, and as long as it kept Claire occupied and he didn't have to bother with her he supposed it was all right. The business with the practice, on the other hand, was far more worrying. He could see everything falling from his grasp. If Dad got Gerald and his son on his side practice meetings were going to be hell. He'd be outvoted on everything. He wondered about Adam. Strictly speaking the practice wouldn't support four doctors, but Adam would be an invaluable ally. But even with Adam on his side it would be fifty-fifty and George would always have the casting vote.

As he was tying the belt of his bathrobe he heard his mobile phone ringing in the bedroom next door. He went through, fished it out of his jacket pocket and clicked the button, groaning when he saw who the caller was.

'What do you want, Fay?'

'Oh! Lovely to hear from you too!' She sounded miffed.

'Look, Fay, you know I don't like you ringing me when I'm at home.'

'How was I to know where you are? I have to see you, Mark.'

'Why?'

'I'll tell you when I see you. Can you come round this evening?'

'Can't it wait?'

'Not really. It's important.'

'Look, I've had a swine of a day. All I want is a quiet evening. Can't you give me some idea what it's about?'

'It's about Richard,' she snapped. 'What else did you imagine it would be about?'

He sighed. 'All right then. I'll be round after I've eaten.'

Downstairs when he announced to Claire that he was going out she was irritated. 'I thought you'd had such a bad day.'

'I have and it promises to get worse.'

'Why, where are you going?'

61

He laid down his knife and fork. 'OK, it's Fay.'

Claire groaned. 'What does she want?'

'I don't know. She wouldn't say, except that it's something to do with Richard.'

Claire shook her head. 'For God's sake, Mark. The boy's grown up now. Just how long does she think you can go on supporting him? You've seen him through university so what is it now?'

'I don't know that it's anything to do with support.'

'Well, I hope not. Right from the moment she knew you were never going to claim him as your son she's been doing this. It's nothing short of blackmail.'

'We don't know that.'

'Of course we do. She's been holding it over your head for years; threatening to go to your father. Why don't you just tell George about Richard. Tell him the truth and have done with it? She'll have to leave you alone then.'

'Oh yes, perfect timing!' he said sarcastically. 'When he's planning to make revolutionary changes at the practice this would be just what he wants to hear.'

'Why are you so scared of him, Mark?'

'I'm not *scared*. I just feel we let him down. I owe him my loyalty at the very least.

'You owe him nothing. We didn't produce a grandson to inherit the practice. It's not the end of the world. Who can say that a son of ours would have wanted to be a doctor anyway? The whole inheritance idea is archaic anyway. You could work anywhere, Mark. Why don't you tell him the truth and if he doesn't like it, tell him what to do with the senior partnership.'

Mark paled. 'I can't tell Dad about your abortion or the fact that I have an illegitimate son,' he said quietly. 'It would kill him.'

'So you'd rather your parents went on blaming me for letting them down.'

'Look, you're not the only one affected. It's a hell of a lot of hassle for me too. And Richard doesn't know I'm his father either.'

'Well, I'm sick and tired of being the scapegoat for you all. The whole thing is a complete mess.' Claire got up and began to clear the table. 'All right, go on. You'd better go and see what demands your mistress is making this time.' She began to load the dishwasher. 'But don't expect me to wait up!'

It was raining as Mark drove out to the suburbs. He parked the car in the driveway of Fay's bungalow. There was a light on in the hall and when he rang the bell the door was answered almost at once, as though Fay had been waiting for him. Her first words confirmed that she had.

'I thought you'd never come,' she complained as she closed the door behind him.

She had been a strikingly good-looking girl when Mark first met her, but now, at forty-five the years were beginning to take their toll. Her green eyes were carefully made up with shadow and mascara and although her wide mouth wore a generous coating of her favourite scarlet lipstick, it did not disguise the downward turn of discontent at the corners. She wore a pale-blue négligée and her auburn hair hung loose about her shoulders.

'I had to eat,' he protested, stepping over the threshold. 'And I haven't got all night, Fay so I'd appreciate it if you could get on with whatever it is you've got to say.'

She led the way through to the living-room. 'Well, sit down at least,' she said. 'You needn't stand there as though you're on the starting blocks!'

Reluctantly he sat down. 'All right, what is it?'

'As you know, Richard got his degree.'

'Of course I know, though what he's going to do with a philosophy degree I don't know,' Mark said. 'Except teach, of course, and I can't advise you on that, Fay. It's not in my . . .'

'He tells me he wants to be a gardener,' she interrupted. 'I ask you, a *gardener!* To think he spent three years of his life studying just to do some – some *menial* job like gardening! I'll never be able to hold my head up again! No one is going to believe he's got a degree when they see him digging up some old biddy's garden. They'll probably think he's doing community service! Can you talk to him, Mark? He refuses to listen to me. I just don't know which way to turn.'

He shook his head. 'I'm not sure that anything I could say would change his mind. After all, why should he listen to me?' He looked around. 'Where is he, by the way?'

'Out. He knows you're a good friend, Mark, and he likes you – always has. Surely that would hold some sway. You might at least try. I think you owe us that much.'

'Owe you!' Mark retorted. 'I don't know how you can stand there and suggest that I owe you anything.'

She rounded on him. 'I gave up everything for you, Mark. I could have been married. Goodness knows I had plenty of chances.'

'How did I stop you from marrying?'

'A woman with an illegitimate child? Who wants to saddle themselves with that? Especially when the boy's father refuses to acknowledge him.'

'As it happens you did pretty well financially out of it, Fay. Don't pretend otherwise. Perhaps that's the reason you haven't married. I've been a pretty good meal ticket for you all these years, so don't pretend to be the victim.'

'How can you say such a thing? I loved you, Mark,' she snuffled. She took a handkerchief from her pocket and slumped into a corner of the settee dabbing at her eyes. 'I loved and trusted you. I thought that when the son you longed for was born you'd leave Claire and make him legitimate.'

'I always made it clear to you that I'd never leave Claire.'

'But when Richard was born, when you held your son in your arms . . .' She choked back a sob. 'How do you think poor Richard feels?'

'Seeing that he has no idea I'm his father I don't see why he should feel anything. As far as I'm able to tell he's a perfectly normal young man who has never known his father,' Mark said. 'Along with about fifty per cent of the rest of today's young generation.'

'I see, so you think that makes it all right, do you?' She stood up, instantly recovering from her tearful outburst. 'I'm not concerned with fifty per cent of the rest of today's young generation. I only care about Richard's future – which is more than you seem to do.'

Mark rose from his chair. 'I think I've made adequate provision for Richard over the past years. If he wants to follow a career in gardening there's nothing either of us can do about it, Fay. I should let him get on with it if I were you. It's about time he started earning his own living.'

She drew in her breath noisily. '*Oh*! You wouldn't say that if he was your legitimate son,' she snapped. 'Oh no! You'd be pressing him to be a doctor to please your ogre of a father. And woe betide him if he went against you!'

Keeping his temper in check with difficulty, Mark moved towards the door. 'As far as I know Richard has never shown the slightest inclination towards medicine and I would be the last person to press anyone into it. There are enough indifferent doctors around as it is.' He walked into the hallway, Fay following close on his heels.

'Mark! Please don't go like this,' she wheedled. 'At least stay and have a drink. I didn't mean to upset you.' She caught his arm and turned him towards her. 'It's still there, Mark, what I feel for you,' she said softly, looking up into his eyes. 'It always will be. It's the real reason I never married. I think you know that, don't you?'

'Fay, please, I . . .' Whatever he had been about to say was lost as she suddenly threw her arms round his neck and pulled his head down, her mouth fastening on his voraciously. At last he took her arms from his neck and thrust her away. 'That's enough, Fay. I've had a bad day. I'm tired and—'

'Then stay the night. Why not, darling? It's been so long. Richard won't be back tonight. He's staying with a friend.'

'No, Fay. I can't.'

'Why not? I was good enough for you a few years ago, wasn't I? You couldn't get enough of me then. It's so typical that the moment a woman begins to lose her youthful appearance the man cools off. What's wrong, Mark? I've kept my figure, haven't I? I'm still attractive. There are plenty of men who think I am if you don't!'

He sighed. 'Then I suggest you invite one of them into your bed.' The moment the words were out of his mouth he realized he'd made a bad mistake.

He didn't even see the hand that struck him a stinging slap across the cheek. 'Sod off then!' she shouted. 'Go home to your snooty bitch of a wife.' As he turned away she grabbed his tie and thrust her face close to his. 'Don't you turn your back on me, *Doctor Naylor*.' Her eyes narrowed. 'There's something you should remember; as you said: it's time Richard started earning his own living now. Well, when he does we won't need *you* any more so there'll be no more reason for me to keep my mouth shut, will there?'

Mark pushed her back against the wall, none too gently. 'Don't think you can blackmail me, Fay. I've more than paid for my mistake over the years and now it has to end.' He straightened his tie. 'I'm going to do you a favour and forget the things you've just said. I suggest you do the same. You don't want to find yourself in a heap of trouble, do you? Just concentrate on Richard.' He pulled the front door shut behind him and made for the car.

He was backing out of the drive when she threw the door open again and screamed into the darkness at him.

'You haven't heard the last of this, Mark Naylor! You mark my words, when I've done with you you're going to wish you'd never been born!'

His headlights lit up her face. The green eyes were flashing venom and her mouth was twisted and ugly with rage. Mark shuddered. The woman whose passionate nature had seemed so irresistibly exciting to him all those years ago now simply looked like a fanatic. A dangerous one at that.

CHAPTER SIX

'I T'S ever such a posh house, Mum. Lovely furniture and other gear. And guess what – I've got my own room here. It's ever so pretty and I've even got my own telly.'

'Well, you do seem to have fallen on your feet, love. But housework – are you sure it's what you want to do?'

'Oh, I do all sorts of other stuff too.'

'So where are you, Danni – I mean what town?'

Danni held her breath. 'Haylsemere. It's in Suffolk.'

There was a pause at the other end of the line. 'I know where it is. What made you choose to go there?'

'I stuck a pin in the map,' Danni lied. 'Anyway, it's a very nice town, Mum. I'm sure you'd like it. It's nicer than Meadbridge.'

'I daresay. Danni . . .' Ruth sounded doubtful. 'You won't mess this one up by losing your temper and kicking off again, will you?'

'No problem, Mum. Not this time. It's a really interesting job. My new boss is an interior designer and I'm learning so much from her.'

Danni was sitting in her room at 64 Grafton Place, talking to Ruth on her mobile phone. She had waited until she moved in before letting her mother know her change of address because she could hardly believe it would really happen.

'I miss you, Mum. Are you all right?' she asked.

'I'm fine. I miss you too, love. Maybe you could come home sometime, for a weekend perhaps?'

'Yeah, maybe. Is Jim treating you OK?'

' 'Course he is. Danni, you will take proper care of yourself, won't you? I worry about you.'

Danni laughed. 'Mum! I'm a big girl now and I'm doing great. With the money I'm earning I'll even be able to afford to go to some art classes at night school.'

'I wish I could have afforded to let you go, love. I blame myself that you've missed out on so much – that you felt you had to leave.'

Hearing the catch in Ruth's voice, Danni said quickly, 'Oh, come on, Mum. It's not your fault. I don't blame you for what you did. If you hadn't kept me I'd never have known what a fantastic mum I'd got, would I?'

'Oh! Oh – Danni.'

Danni swallowed hard. 'Look, I'll ring you again soon, Mum. You're breaking up a bit and I think my phone needs charging. 'Bye.' She switched off her phone and sat looking at it. Mum hardly ever cried. When she did Danni never knew how to handle it. Was she telling the truth when she said that Jim was treating her OK? Or was it just that she missed their being together? Danni made up her mind there and then that she would try and go home sometime soon, even if it was only for the day. She could just about make it if she got a fast train.

Her room was quite large and on the second floor. Being under the eaves meant that it had an attractively sloping ceiling, which Claire had cleverly integrated into the built-in furniture. The bed was the most comfortable Danni had ever slept on and Claire had even moved in an armchair and a small table for her as well as the portable TV. A double dormer window opened on to a tiny railed ledge which, although there was barely enough space to step out, she already thought of as her 'balcony'. It looked down on to the communal gardens in the centre of the square. Right next door to her room there was a bathroom of which she had sole use. No more queuing up and sharing space with other people's discarded underwear, soggy towels and stale steam. She could hardly believe her luck. It was like a dream come true.

There was only one thing that made her slightly uneasy. On the day of her interview, when Danni had seen Doctor Mark Naylor arriving at the house she'd been surprised but she had assumed that he was merely visiting. It was a shock when she discovered that he actually lived there and that he was Claire's husband. She wondered what the Naylors would say if they knew who she really was, and, even more, what her mum would think if she knew it was the Naylors she was working for!

On her first morning when she passed Mark in the hall he'd smiled. 'Good morning. Danielle, isn't it? Small world eh?'

Danni smiled back. 'Yeah. Who'd have thought it?' Inwardly she longed to say. 'You don't know just *how* small, Doctor Naylor.'

But in spite of her plan to make herself known to her real father she had no intention of spoiling this new and wonderful job. Her plan would have to be postponed – probably indefinitely. Meantime it would be interesting to get to know what kind of man had been callous enough to keep her and her mum on the breadline for the past eighteen years whilst he lived in luxury. Was he was really the monster she had imagined? So far she had to admit that he seemed almost boringly ordinary.

Downstairs in the studio Claire explained how she worked. 'In the first instance I go to the client's house and take some measurements and photographs,' she said. 'Back here I do some drawings first. As I told you before, I like to use pastels or watercolour to try out different colour schemes. Then I go on to the computer and try it all out to scale, with the correct measurements. I've got the special software for that – don't know what I'd do without it. Would you like to see?'

'Yes please.' Danni watched with fascination as Claire switched on the computer and demonstrated the design she was currently working on, her eager questions tumbling out as she watched. At last she stopped in mid-question, her cheeks flushing. 'Sorry,' she said. 'I don't mean to be gobby. It's just that it's all so exciting.'

'Don't apologize. Ask as much as you want.' Claire was impressed by the questions Danni was asking. She looked at her. 'Tell you what, would you like to come along with me to visit a client some time?' she asked. 'I can see you're genuinely interested.'

Danni's eyes lit up. 'Oh! Could I really, Miss Cav – er – I mean Mrs . . .'

Claire laughed. 'I told you, Claire will do just fine.'

'OK, Claire. I'd love to go with you if you're really sure I wouldn't get in the way.' She looked around her. 'But shouldn't I be hoovering or something? I really came to get my instructions for the day.'

Maddie chose that moment to jump up with a shrill bark. As the little dog looked pleadingly up, her head on one side. Claire laughed. 'I think you're getting your instructions right now,' she said. 'Maddie usually has a run round the park after breakfast and it looks as though she already knows that you'll be taking her from now on. I'll be off out shortly. Are you sure you'll be OK?'

' 'Course I will. I'll just do the normal jobs, shall I? And answer the phone, of course.'

Danni enjoyed her first morning at Grafton Place. On her return from the park she cleared away the breakfast table and stacked the dishwasher as Claire had shown her, then she vacuumed and dusted the ground-floor rooms. When she heard the studio telephone ringing she ran downstairs and picked up the receiver. Taking a deep breath she assumed the voice she'd been practicing so carefully.

'Good morning, Cavendish Interior Design. Danni speaking, how can I help you?' Wouldn't do to let punters think they were dealing with a bunch of yobs, she told herself.

A male voice answered. He sounded surprised. 'Oh – hello. Is Claire there?'

'Miss Cavendish is out at the moment,' Danni said. 'Can I take a message, or get her to ring you back?'

'No, it's all right. I'll try again later.'

'Can I make an appointment for her to come out and see you?' Danni offered. After all, she was supposed to be here to stop people from going elsewhere. 'I'm Miss Cavendish's Girl Friday,' she added proudly.

'Are you really? Well, no. I'd rather ring later.'

'Well, can I at least give her your name?' Danni was getting desperate. What was the good of her being here if people wouldn't even talk to her?

The caller cleared his throat. 'No, it's all right. I'll ring later,' he said, and rang off.

Danni replaced the receiver, staring at it in disgust. What was the matter with people? Now what? Did she tell Claire that the man had rung or not? She decided she'd better mention it. After all, he said he'd ring back and Claire would think it funny if she said nothing.

Two more people rang the studio number during the morning. Both were far more co-operative than the secretive man. For the first Danni took a message and promised that Claire would ring back. For the second she made an appointment, using the book that Claire had left open on her desk. By the time Claire returned Danni was feeling quite pleased with herself.

'There was just this one caller who wouldn't let me help,' she told her employer when she came back. 'He kept insisting he'd ring back. I did try, really I did. He wouldn't even leave his name.'

'Oh well, never mind,' Claire said. 'Shall we have some lunch now?'

Danni made sandwiches and they ate companionably at the kitchen table. It was while Danni was making coffee that the telephone rang. She made to go and answer it but Claire stood up.

'I'll take it,' she said. 'It might be whoever it was who rang this morning.'

Danni filled the filter machine and stood waiting as the coffee slurped through into the jug. She could hear Claire's voice in the adjoining-room. She sounded slightly agitated. Danni could only catch the odd word here and there but it didn't sound much like a business call.

'Adam!' with one hand Claire reached out to push the door shut. She hadn't expected it to be him. 'Was it you who rang this morning?'

'Yes. Your new Girl Friday answered. It threw me a bit. I didn't know you had one.'

'She's new. It's not a good idea to ring here, Adam. You know that. If you had to call why didn't you use my mobile number?'

'I tried. You had it switched off.'

'I was with a client. What is it? I can't really talk at the moment.'

'OK, just listen then. It looks as though I'll be staying on.'

'Here – in Haylesmere you mean?'

'At the surgery. Mark has asked me. I think he feels a bit threatened by his cousin's appointment – needs someone to be on his side.'

'You said no, of course.'

'Actually I've accepted.'

'Adam! You promised. Staying on here – it's going to make things very difficult.'

'I know; which is why we need to talk. It's my day off tomorrow. The usual place?'

'We've already talked this through, Adam. I told you it had to finish. I haven't changed my mind. It's all too close to home; too complicated.'

'It needn't be. Just this once, Claire – please.'

'I – *can't*.'

'You can. You have to. Please, for my sake.'

'I've got a sale to go to at three o'clock.'

He sensed she was wavering and seized the opportunity. 'No problem. I promise I'll get you back in plenty of time.'

She sighed. 'Oh – all right then.'

Danni noticed that Claire looked flushed when she came back into the kitchen.

'Everything all right?' she asked.

Claire nodded. 'Yes, fine. Just a slight change of plan, that's all. Danni, I've got an antique sale to go to tomorrow. Would you like to go with me?'

'Antiques?' Danni looked surprised.

'Yes. You see, as well as working out colour schemes and so on, I have to search for the right fabrics and carpets and sometimes even furniture. This is for a Georgian house out at Mellbury that's being restored. I'm sure you'd enjoy seeing how it all comes together.'

Danni was spellbound. 'Ooh,' she breathed. 'I never knew it was all so – so . . .'

'Involved?' Claire laughed. 'Watch and learn, Danni. I think you'll be surprised. Tell you what: I'll lend you some books on style and architecture if you like.' She looked at Danni. 'Or would you find that boring?'

'Oh *no*! Thanks Claire. I'd love to see them.'

'I have to go out tomorrow morning,' Claire went on. 'I'll be out for lunch. Back here about half past two. I'll pick you up then. OK?'

'I'll be ready.'

'While I'm out just do the usual jobs and see to Maddie. And help yourself to some lunch of course.'

Danni was awake till after midnight that night, poring over the books Claire had lent her. She had never realized that there were so many different styles of furniture down through the ages. There was a book on fabrics too, beautiful colour prints of embroidered silks and rich velvets. Another book was on costume which had Danni enthralled. Then there was the big book about architecture. It was all there, from medieval halls that looked like cottage loaves with thatched roofs and just a hole in the roof instead of a chimney; Elizabethan manor houses with timber-beamed walls; Tudor palaces, elegant Queen Anne mansions and beautifully proportioned Georgian houses, right up to Victorian and Edwardian villas. There and then a new ambition dawned for Danni. This was what she wanted to do. She would learn as much as she could from Claire, hoping that maybe when she saw how keen she was she would take her on as an assistant. And one day, who knew? She might even be able to start a business of her own.

The antique sale was a revelation to Danni. She had never seen so much furniture in one place before: some plain and some ornately carved. Some of it was old and worn and some of it elegant and well-cared for. And when the bidding started she was amazed. It was all so frenetic. Claire waved her catalogue, challenging other bidders for the pieces she wanted. Impressed, Danni wondered if she would ever have the confidence to act with such ease and style?

Claire was successful in buying a walnut drum table for what seemed to Danni an outrageous sum, and then there was a lull in the bidding between lots.

'I have a budget from the client,' Claire volunteered during the brief interval. 'So I can work out how high I can go to for the various items.' She nodded towards where a porter was about to hold up a painting. 'See this one just coming up? It's one of the things I came for especially. A beautiful portrait;

not by a renowned painter, mind, but very well done. It will look spectacular hanging above the fireplace in the drawing-room.'

Danni watched, enthralled as the bidding progressed, hardly daring to move a muscle in case the auctioneer thought she was making a bid. Some people seemed to do it with the merest twitch of an eyebrow. Claire made the final bid and got her portrait. It was of a very pretty girl in a beautiful blue gown and picture hat. Danni had to agree that it was lovely. As they left the auction hall Claire was flushed with pleasure.

'One of my better days,' she said with satisfaction.

During the drive home Claire was quiet. Danni was busy with her own thoughts too. The sale had been a revelation to her; exciting and different. Her head was spinning with all the things she was learning, but at the back of her mind something was niggling.

Claire had been a little late returning after lunch and, to save time, Danni had put on her coat and gone outside to wait on the steps. She'd seen a car draw up at the corner of the street. It was driven by a man and Claire got out of the passenger side. For some reason she didn't quite understand Danni had moved back into the shelter of the doorway and from there she saw Claire glance round and then bend to speak to the driver through the window. She couldn't be sure but she thought she saw her briefly kiss him before straightening up to hurry down the street. Why hadn't the driver driven right up to the house? Could he be the man who wouldn't give his name over the phone this morning? Mmm – what was all that about, she wondered?

During the weeks that followed Danni learned a lot about interior design. Claire was generous with her knowledge, letting Danni go along with her to sales and letting her try her hand with the design software on the computer. She had encouraged Danni to enrol at night school for art classes, which she was thoroughly enjoying. Her weekends were her own too to do as she liked and she had spent the first few weekends in Haylesmere exploring the little Suffolk town, delighting in the winding streets lined with stone buildings; the attractive shops and cosy little tearooms of which there seemed to be an abundance.

Most of the streets in the town led down to the river. It was not a river like the one that ran through Meadbridge with its sluggish brown water and steep, muddy banks. She learned that this river was called the Hayle and the part that ran through Haylesmere had green banks lined with weeping-willows. It had dainty little wrought-iron bridges at regular intervals and a smart marina. The granary from where the barges that plied their trade between towns had once been loaded had been converted into a chic restaurant and the working barges had been replaced by smart cabin cruisers and sailing yachts. Now that spring was turning to summer all the boat owners were preparing for the season and Danni spent several Sunday afternoons perched on the bank, enjoy-ing the spectacle of white sails against a breezy blue sky, dipping masts and rippling water. Her pencil sped over the pages of her sketch pad as she tried to capture thumbnail sketches of the bustling atmosphere.

'Do you ever draw anything other than boats?' a voice enquired one afternoon just as she was thinking of packing up. Suddenly she was aware of a young man looking over her shoulder and blushed furiously. She hated anyone watching her work.

'What's it to you?' she asked rudely.

'Nothing. Actually you're very good.' He reached over her shoulder to point. 'You've really captured the movement of the water and the sails. I can almost hear them flapping.'

'Oh, good for you! What are *you*, then – some kind of expert or something?' Danni slapped down the cover of her sketch pad and stood up. Brushing the grass off her jeans, she pushed past him and began to climb up the bank to the path.

'Fancy a cup of coffee?' Oblivious to her snub he was walking behind her. 'They've put the tables outside at the Granary coffee shop. First time this year, see?'

A withering refusal on her lips, Danni turned to look at him properly for the first time and the words died on her lips. Actually he wasn't bad-looking, quite tasty in fact; tall slim figure in jeans and T-shirt, brown hair and smiling dark eyes. She swallowed the sharp remark she had been about to make. 'Well – I don't know.'

'Oh, come on,' he said, 'Sitting there sketching all afternoon – you must be spitting feathers by now.'

She laughed in spite of herself. 'Oh, go on then. I am a bit thirsty.'

It was pleasant, sitting under the striped umbrella, sipping cappuccino with this new companion to talk to. He told her his name was Rick and that he was twenty-one.

'What do you do for a living?' she asked him.

'Nothing – yet. I've just finished at uni. Still looking round.'

She cocked an eyebrow at him. 'I see. The brainy kind, eh? Well, with an education like that they'll be falling over each other to give you a job.'

'Now you're laughing at me.'

'Yeah. Now you know what it feels like.'

'I wasn't laughing at you,' he protested. 'I really do think you're good.'

'So, you're an art critic too, are you?'

'No. Don't know anything about it really, but how else was I going to get to talk to you?' He took a sip of his coffee, grinning cheekily at her over the rim of the cup. 'You haven't told me your name yet.'

'You haven't asked.'

'Well, I'm asking now.'

'It's Danni,' she told him.

'Short for Danielle?'

'How *did* you guess?'

'Rick.' He held out his hand and she touched it briefly. 'So – what do you do for a living? Or are you an art student?'

'Don't want to know much, do you?' She spooned up the froth on her coffee. 'Actually I'm training to be an interior designer.' The words came out suddenly, surprising her so much that she was obliged to lift her cup and bury her face in it to hide the hot colour that rushed to her cheeks.

'That sounds interesting.'

'It is. We have to do everything; soft furnishings and décor; furniture, even ornaments and lighting.'

'How long have you been doing that?'

Danni bit her lip. 'Not long, but I've learned a lot already.' She tucked a strand of windblown hair behind her ear. 'I live in where I work, you see; help out with lots of other things as well as the design stuff.'

'You mean you're a bit of a dogsbody.'

'*No!*' she said hotly. 'Not all of us have got parents who can afford to let us go to uni!'

'Sorry. I didn't mean it like that. So you're sort of working your passage, are you?'

'Something like that.'

'Well, sounds like a good arrangement anyway.' Rick swallowed the last of his coffee and looked at her. 'Like another, Danni?' She shook her head. 'Ice cream then – cake?'

'No. I really should be getting back.'

'I'll walk with you if you like. I've got my bike but that doesn't matter.'

'It's OK. I'll get the bus. It's quite a long way.' She stood up. 'Thanks for the coffee, Rick.'

He jumped up. 'I'll walk you to the bus stop.'

'Don't put yourself out.'

He looked at her. 'You're a bit spiky, aren't you?'

She smiled shamefacedly. 'S'pose I am. Sorry.'

As they walked he asked, 'Will you be here next Sunday?'

She shrugged. 'Don't know. It's getting a bit busy now. Too many people.'

'Tell you what; I know a place where you could do some fantastic sketching.'

'Where's that then?'

'Do you like gardens?'

'Well, yes. Where is this garden?'

'It's sort of hard to describe to you. If you were to meet me I could take you there.'

She raised an eyebrow at him. 'Oh yeah?'

He grinned. 'You're doing it again. I'm serious. Not many people know about this place and I'd like to keep it that way. It's somewhere I like to go.'

'Why? What's so special about it?'

'There are some interesting plants there. I like botany – horticulture – that kind of thing.'

She laughed. 'Whatever floats your boat, I suppose.'

'No. There isn't a lake,' he said innocently.

They both laughed and Danni said. 'OK then. I'll try anything once. Next Sunday?'

'Next Sunday it is. Shall we say three o'clock outside the town hall?'

'Is it far?' she asked. 'Do I need to borrow a bike or anything?'

'No, easy walking distance,' he told her.

The bus came and Danni jumped on to the platform. ' 'Bye, Rick,' she said with a wave. 'See ya.'

'Next Sunday,' he called. 'You will come, won't you?'

'I'll be there,' she called as the bus moved away.

Settled back in her seat, Danni thought about Rick on the ride back into town. He was nice, she decided: on the level, or so he seemed. All the boys she'd met so far were either geeks or randy little gits with only one thing on their tiny minds. She'd kept well clear of them at school. Too many of her classmates had been up the duff by the time they were fifteen. She'd decided at thirteen that that kind of thing wasn't for her. You heard a lot about feminism and equality but as far as Danni could see there wasn't much equality about being stuck in a council flat fourteen floors up with only a screaming baby for company. Most of the lads responsible were long gone by the time the kids were walking. She couldn't believe those girls could be so thick. Because of all this she'd never had a boyfriend. Never allowed herself to trust anyone of the opposite sex, specially after what Mum had been through with the two men in her life. But this Rick seemed different; genuinely friendly and interested in her as a person. Well, she'd meet him next week, she decided; give it a go. But let him try anything, that's all, she told herself. One chance was all he was going to get!

CHAPTER SEVEN

Fay pulled down the blinds and locked up the shop with a sigh of relief. It had been a long day and she was tired as she made her way round to the car park. All the new summer stock she had ordered weeks ago had arrived today in one fell swoop and she'd had to deal with it and her customers single handed. Her only assistant, Tracey, had called in sick yet again. She really would have to sack the wretched girl and find someone more reliable, she told herself as she unlocked her little Ford Ka and eased her aching back into the driving seat.

She'd been running *Style and Grace* for the past sixteen years; ever since she had first followed Mark to Haylesmere. He would have preferred to keep her at a distance, she knew that, but Fay didn't intend to let him out of her sight and she certainly wasn't going to let him fade out of her life and Richard's just like that. He had a commitment to her and her son and she wasn't going to let him forget it; even though he refused to acknowledge Richard as his.

She had first met Mark when he had been a junior house-man at Meadbridge General Hospital and she had been secretary to his boss, Jack Kendal, the orthopaedic consul-tant. They'd shared a table in the canteen for lunch a few times and she'd learned that he was newly married and that his wife was unable to have children because of a botched termination. Apparently she'd been studying medicine at the time and didn't want to give up her studies to have a baby. Fay was sorry for Mark. It was clear that he desperately wanted a child. High-flying career women could be so selfish.

Although she was aware that he was eight years her junior Fay soon became aware that Mark was becoming attracted to her. She did not draw his attention to the age difference, neither did she discourage him. Once, in an unguarded moment he confided that he'd married Claire, his wife, partly out of pity and guilt. After all, it had been his carelessness that had resulted in the pregnancy and due to the disastrous operation she'd had to give up her medical studies. Privately Fay thought it served her right.

She'd asked Mark to give her a lift home one evening when her car was out of action, (she'd purposely left it in the garage that morning) inviting him into the flat for a drink as a thank you. They'd ended up in bed and that had been the start of their affair.

When she gave him the news that she was pregnant a few months later she thought he would be thrilled and immediately decide to divorce Claire and marry her. Instead his reaction shocked her. He explained that he planned to do a GP course and join his father's practice in Suffolk. It appeared that his father was against divorce and illegitimacy and would sever all ties with him if he knew the truth about Claire's abortion. He would certainly never accept an illegitimate grandchild into the family. Fay tried everything: tears, hysteria, pleading; finally in desperation resorting to threats, but Mark was adamant. She saw another side of him, a hard, unbending, self-seeking side. He told her that he would pay her maintenance for the child but warned her that he would never acknowledge it as his own. All her ranting was to no avail and eventually she was forced to agree to Mark's terms. He would see that she and the child went short of nothing, but if she ever breathed a word to anyone about their connection she would be on her own.

'If I don't join my father's practice I won't be able to afford to pay you a penny,' he told her. 'It's as simple as that. And by the way, Claire knows about us just in case you have any plans to go to her with your story.' The revelation took the wind out of her sails but she had to acknowledge at that point that he'd won.

When she went into labour she was completely alone. She telephoned him at home but he hung up the moment he heard her voice. She called an ambulance and went into hospital where Richard was born the following day by Caesarean section. She vowed then that if Mark stuck to his resolve to keep her a separate part of his life she would make sure he paid for her suffering – one way or another and however long she had to wait.

Mark visited her and baby Richard whenever he could after the birth. She decided to bide her time, sure that he would grow so fond of the baby that he would change his mind eventually, but further disappointment was to come. When Richard was two and a half Mark dropped the bombshell that he and Claire were expecting a baby of their own. At first Fay refused to believe him.

'You told me she'd never be able to have children,' she said. 'Because of the termination she had. This is just a trick to get rid of me, isn't it? Maybe I should write to your father? I'm sure he'd be interested to see a photograph of his grandson!'

To her gratification he looked alarmed. 'Oh, all right, if you must have the truth . . .'

He'd sighed, running a hand exasperatedly through his hair. 'If I tell you you'll have to promise it will go no further.

If it does you and I will be finished once and for all.'

'Naturally.'

'We – that is Claire and I have found a woman who is willing to have a child for us.'

She stared at him. 'You mean you're going to get some *other woman* pregnant?'

'Basically, yes. In fact it has already happened.'

'And you're telling me that Claire is happy with this?'

'Everything has been done clinically,' he said. 'When the child is born it will be ours.'

'Is this legal?'

'It's the same as adoption,' he hedged. 'Except that the child will be mine biologically.'

She was stunned. 'And your father will accept this?'

'He will never know. That's the whole point.' He looked at her. 'He must never know which is why you have to guarantee to keep your mouth shut.'

They spent the rest of that evening talking about the future. Mark had agreed to keep up his visits until the child was born. After that he would keep up the maintenance payments throughout Richard's childhood and education. Apart from that their relationship must cease. When she argued he threatened to withhold maintenance and deny that Richard was his. He left her little choice but to comply.

When she heard some months later that the surrogate child was a girl and that the mother had refused to give the baby up she'd gloated inwardly. But she forced herself to be sympathetic. Mark was clearly angry and deeply disappointed, but Fay felt that it was a judgment on him. Even if they'd been able to keep the child it was a girl and not the son he wanted so badly. She'd hidden her triumph however, holding Mark close and murmuring soothing words, reminding him that he still had her – and that Richard would always be his son.

When he moved to Haylesmere to join his father's practice

she moved too, finding a bungalow to rent in a discreet little village on the outskirts of the town. Mark visited occasionally, always bringing a toy or sweets for Richard who came to regard him as a family friend. Fay usually managed to seduce Mark into bed before he left. She felt he owed her that much at least. Life was bleak bringing up a child alone with no prospect of love or marriage.

When Richard started school she decided that she would like to go into the fashion business. Walking round the little town she saw that there were no high-class fashion boutiques. Women who liked good clothes were obliged to travel to Ipswich or even further to Norwich to find what they wanted.

She found the little premises in a good position close to the market place. It had been a stationer's shop and Mark reluctantly agreed to pay the cost of the refurbishment and the initial advertising, providing that she stood on her own feet from then on. To her relief and satisfaction her gamble paid off. She had good taste in clothes and an eye for colour and fashion and the word had spread among the better-off women of Haylesmere. *Style and Grace* had been making a comfortable profit ever since. But as the years went by and Richard grew to manhood and needed her less Fay began to worry about the future. As the only child of elderly parents she had been on her own since her late teens and she'd already had a taste of solitude while Richard was at university, but she recognized now that her son would soon want to spread his wings – move into a place of his own, perhaps with a steady girlfriend. What would become of her then? She had lots of acquaintances but no real friends. She had always worked too hard – been too single minded to get to know anyone properly. Anyway most of the women she knew had husbands and families – busy lives with weddings to plan and grandchildren to look forward to. No time to befriend ageing single mothers with doubtful pasts.

Long years of being alone stretched ahead of her. Yes, she would eventually sell the business and make a good profit, but what then? Taking holidays on her own? Sitting alone each night with only the television for company while Mark and Claire enjoyed sharing a home; going to parties as a couple; spending their holidays and evenings together. To Claire she was just a mistake in her husband's past, forgiven and forgotten long ago. The thought made Fay's blood boil. Mark had stolen her life and somehow or other he was going to have to pay for it. Pay in a way that would hurt. She would think of something. From now on she'd have plenty of time.

Richard was already home when she arrived, making his favourite spaghetti Bolognese in the kitchen. He looked round from the cooker as she came in.

'Hi, Mum. Good day?'

'Hellish,' she said, kicking off her shoes. 'That wretched Tracey was off sick again and all the summer stock came in.'

'Poor you.' He reached for the bottle of sherry and took a glass from the cupboard. 'Sit down and have a swig of your favourite tipple. Supper'll be ready in a couple of ticks.'

Fay took the glass from him with a smile and sipped from it gratefully. 'What would I do without you?' She watched him as he tested the spaghetti. He was a lovely young man and a credit to her if she did say it herself. His shoulders and chest had broadened over the past couple of years. He was almost six feet tall and handsome, with his dark good looks. He took after Mark of course. He hadn't inherited her fair colouring and the auburn hair, now helped weekly to retain its colour by a skilful hairdresser. Some girl was sure to snap him up soon. She sighed, hating the idea. Not that she would ever let him know how she felt of course. Didn't want him sneaking off to meet some highly unsuitable girl she hadn't vetted. No, she would encourage him to bring any girl he met home to meet her.

'Have you had any more thoughts about a career?' she asked him.

He glanced round at her. 'You know what I want, Mum.'

She sighed. 'Surely you can do that as a hobby, darling.'

'It's not what you seem to think it is,' Richard protested. 'I don't intend to spend my life as a jobbing gardener. I want to study landscaping.'

'I still don't think it's a career,' Fay insisted.

He turned to look at her. 'No? Ever heard of Capability Brown?'

She laughed. 'Oh! You're planning to landscape stately homes, are you? I think you'll find those jobs a bit thin on the ground nowadays. Really, darling, I can't think why you took a degree in philosophy just to do manual work.'

'Philosophy can be applied to almost anything,' he said. 'And there's a lot more to landscaping than digging someone's cabbage patch.'

Fay sighed, deciding to leave the argument for now. 'What have you been doing today?' she asked.

He shrugged. 'Nothing much.'

'Well, if you're at a loose end I can find plenty of jobs for you at the shop,' she said.

'Me?' He laughed. 'Working in a ladies' dress shop. Do you want all my mates to think I'm gay?'

'You needn't let anyone see you if you're worried about that,' she said. 'Plenty of lifting to do out at the back.'

'I'll think about it.' He piled the sauce on to the cooked spaghetti and brought the plates to the table. They ate in silence for a few minutes, then he said: 'I met a really nice girl last Sunday afternoon.'

'Girl?' Fay's heart gave a lurch. 'What sort of girl? Who is she? Where did you meet her?'

He laughed. 'Which one shall I answer first? I met her down at the marina. She was sketching the boats. Her name's Danielle. She's different; funny and a bit quirky.'

Fay sniffed. 'What's "quirky" when it's at home?'

'You know, slightly spiky. Not giggly and daft like some girls her age.'

'Her age. How old is she then?'

'I don't really know. I didn't ask her, but I reckon she's probably about nineteen.'

'When I was that age I was already alone in the world, earning my own wage and living in a bed-sit,' Fay told him. 'No chance to be giggly. I had to work for survival.'

'She's on her own too from what I could make out. And she works.'

She looked at him. 'What work? Where does she live?'

He laughed. 'For God's sake, Mum. I've only just met her. I didn't give her the third degree!'

'Are you seeing her again?'

'Probably. I wondered if I could borrow the car on Sunday?'

'The car? Why? Where are you planning to go?'

Richard bowed his head over his plate as he curled spaghetti round his fork. Why was Mum always so intense? And then she wondered why he didn't confide in her more! 'It doesn't matter,' he said. 'Forget it. It was just an idea.'

'Have you got her phone number – address? Why don't you bring her here?'

'Oh, give it a rest, Mum. She's just a girl. We had a coffee together, that's all. I haven't asked her to *marry* me!'

'You'll be lucky if you ever earn enough to marry anyone if you insist on pursuing this ridiculous gardening idea,' she said. She knew as she was saying it that she was going too far but as usual she ploughed on regardless, unable to stop herself.

Very carefully he put down his fork and stood up. 'OK, Mum. Have it your way,' he said levelly. 'I'm going for a walk. I'll probably drop in at the pub later. Don't wait up.'

'*Richard*! You haven't finished your . . .' She bit her lip as the kitchen door closed firmly behind him. Quick tears sprang to her eyes. *Damn*! She'd done it again! Oh why couldn't she leave him alone to work things out for himself? She always knew when she was going too far so why couldn't she keep her stupid mouth shut?

CHAPTER EIGHT

H<small>E</small> saw her as the car turned the corner into the High Street. She looked a bit different today. She still wore jeans but instead of the T-shirt she'd worn last week she had on a pretty top; a pale primrose colour with some kind of embroidery round the scooped neckline. She wore her tawny brown hair loose around her shoulders instead of tied back and he suspected that she was wearing a little make-up. He felt flattered. Had she gone to all that trouble for him? She was carrying her sketching equipment but it was only as he drew up that he noticed the dog: a tiny dog on a lead. He leaned across and opened the door.

'Hi! You came, then.'

'Looks like it! Wasn't expecting the VIP treatment though. I like the wheels.'

'Get in. It's my mum's,' he said. He nodded his head towards the dog. 'Who's your friend?'

'This is Maddie,' she told him. 'Hope you don't mind. She's no trouble only everyone else is out and I didn't want to leave her on her own.' She scooped up the little dog and climbed into the passenger seat.

'That's OK. I love dogs,' he said, ruffling Maddie's head. 'Always wanted one of my own when I was a kid but Mum wouldn't let me. She said it wasn't fair when we were out all day.'

Danni looked at him. 'What about your dad?'

He shrugged. 'Never had one of those around I'm afraid.'

Her eyes widened. 'No kidding? Neither have I.' She looked out of the window. 'Where is this garden? I thought you said easy walking distance.'

'It is really. On the outskirts of town, but I thought it might be nicer to have the car. After all, it might rain.'

Danni glanced up at the clear blue sky and grinned to herself. He'd borrowed his mum's car to impress her. That was nice. *He* was nice. She liked his sincere brown eyes and his warm smile – his way of talking: open and frank.

'Do you live in town?' she asked as they drove.

He shook his head. 'Kaisley. It's about two miles out; a suburb, I suppose you'd call it. We've got a bungalow there.'

'Just you and your mum?'

He nodded. 'Mum has a little dress shop just off the market place. It's called *Style and Grace*.'

'Oh yes. I've seen it.' Danni pulled a face. 'A bit out of my price range though. Quite posh.'

He laughed. 'Not for anyone your age anyway. More for Haylesmere's fashion-conscious ladies who lunch.'

'No! Don't knock it,' Danni said. 'Lovely designer stuff. Classic, well-cut suits and dresses. I want to dress like that one day.'

He looked round at her. 'Well, I like the way you look now.'

She smiled. 'Right – thanks.' She looked out of the window and saw that they'd left the built-up area behind and were driving along a country road.

'We're almost there,' he told her. 'Not many people know about this place. No one ever seems to come here anyway.' He turned into an overgrown driveway. 'I don't like people to know I'm here,' he said. 'I suppose you could call it my secret hideaway.'

'And you're bringing me here! I'm honoured. Aren't you afraid I'll blab to everyone?'

'No. You're not like that.'

'How do you know? You hardly know me. I could be a junkie for all you know. Some girl who goes out clubbing every Saturday night, drinking till three in the morning.'

He laughed. 'What, *you*?'

She coloured. 'Well why not? Do I seem so tame to you that I couldn't behave like that? What do you think I am – some kind of nerd?'

He looked hurt. ' 'Course not! Are you always this prickly?'

Danni bit her lip. 'Sorry. I didn't mean to snap.'

'Doesn't mean you're a nerd just because you don't behave like a tart.'

'I know, sorry. Sometimes I'm too quick off the mark.' She opened the car door. 'Come on then, what are you waiting for? Are you going to show me this secret place of yours then, or aren't you?'

He was still smarting as he got out of the car. Why did she have to bite his head off just because he thought well of her? She was a strange mixture, this girl.

At first glimpse the place looked derelict and neglected. In the centre of the plot were the ruins of an old house. The roof was missing and what was left of the walls was covered with ivy. All around was tall grass, trees and overgrown shrubs, Rick took her hand and led her through a gate to what had been the back garden. Danni gasped. Rhododendrons and azaleas were bursting into flower, a mass of glorious colour, late narcissi, grape hyacinths and tulips bloomed in the long grass under the trees and forsythia provided a splash of brilliant yellow backdrop against the garden wall. A circular summerhouse stood in one corner, its disintegrating thatch slipping sideways, half on and half off.

'Oh, Rick, it's gorgeous!' she said. 'I wish I'd brought the paints now. Who does it belong to? Do you know?'

'An old chap used to live here,' he told her. 'Someone told me he was a keen gardener. This place was his pride and joy.

He got too old and sick to look after it properly in the end, but he wouldn't leave. One night some louts broke in and found him in the garden. No one knew how long he'd been dead.'

Danni shivered. 'Poor old guy. That's awful.'

'Not really. He stayed where he wanted to be and died among his precious plants. I reckon that would have been what he wanted.'

'All the same, he must have been lonely.'

'Maybe.' Rick pointed to the house. 'Vandals set fire to the place a couple of years ago. There's only a shell left now so no one will buy it. One of these days they'll pull it down and build something hideous, I shouldn't wonder. Till then I'll come and enjoy it while I can.'

Danni let Maddie off the lead and she bounced around the garden, in and out of the shrubs, pouncing on imaginary rabbits. Rick went back to the car and produced two garden chairs from the boot and Danni sat down to sketch the ruined house. For a while Rick watched her with fascination. After a while he went back to the car and returned with a packet of sandwiches, a bottle of lemonade and two plastic cups.

Danni laughed. 'You're full of surprises, you!'

'As a matter of fact I was going to ask you back home to meet Mum,' he said. 'But she's stocktaking at the shop this afternoon.'

They ate and drank in silence for a while, then he held out his hand and said. 'You haven't seen all of it yet. There's something else you might like to draw. Come and see.'

He led her through the long grass and opened a rusting wrought-iron gate in the wall. Holding back the trailing briars with one hand he said, 'There. How about that?'

It was a delightful little Italian garden. Two steps led down into a paved area with broken columns and tall urns at each corner planted with trailing ivy and pansies. In the centre was a pool with a little statue on a plinth to one side. It was of a girl, carrying a ewer on her shoulder and looking down into the water.

'All this was completely covered in weeds and algae,' Rick told her. 'I thought it was too nice to be allowed to rot so I cleared it and planted up the urns.

'On your own? It must have taken you ages.' Danni looked at him, her head on one side. 'You're a bit of a loner, like me, aren't you?'

He shrugged. 'Once I went off to uni I lost touch with a lot of my schoolmates,' he said. 'When I came home they'd all moved on with their lives. It's OK though, I've never minded my own company.'

'Me neither.' She admitted. 'I suppose it comes of being an only child.'

'There's a fountain in the pool,' he told her, pointing. 'But I haven't figured out how it works yet. I daresay there's a pump for it somewhere; probably rusted up.'

Danni sat down on the top step and patted the space next to her. 'Tell me about yourself, Rick,' she said.

He smiled and sat down beside her. 'Not much to tell really. Got born, went to school, then uni. Got my degree and now I'm wondering what to do next. What I really want is to be a landscape gardener, but Mum doesn't approve.'

'Have you always lived with your mum?' He nodded. 'You said you never knew your dad. Did he die or just take off, like mine?'

'No idea. Mum won't talk about it – won't even tell me his Christian name. All I know is that she's never been married. My name is the same as hers – Scott. I suppose I was some kind of mistake she made a long time ago.'

'Don't say that.' She slipped her hand through his arm and gave it a squeeze. 'I used to feel like that too, but I reckon when it comes down to it it's up to us. We're whatever we make of ourselves. You're nice and you've worked hard at your education and done well. Not like me. I've been a bit of a rebel.'

He grinned at her. 'I'd already sussed that out.'

'Not any more though. You can't blame your parents for what you are. You can't let something that happened years ago to two other people mess up your life. The only thing I was any good at at school was art,' she told him. 'Mum couldn't afford to support me through art college, though, and I did a dead-end job in a supermarket. It was really minging. It was a real stroke of luck, finding this job I've got now and I mean to get the best I can out of it.'

'Good for you. So – you never knew your father either?'

'No. The man Mum was married to took off before I was born, but I found out recently that he wasn't my dad anyway.' She shook her head. 'That's not the way it sounds. My mum worked hard to bring me up. She's one of the best.'

'Where does she live?'

'Meadbridge. That's where I grew up. She's met this bloke now though – moved in with him.'

'And you and he don't hit it off?'

She shrugged. 'I decided the time had come for me to move on. It's time she had a life of her own.'

'Why did you come to Haylesmere?'

'It's where . . .' Danni hesitated, 'where the job is,' she said.

He sighed and for a few moments they were silent. Rick selected a blade of grass and began to chew it. 'Do you ever wonder about your father?' he asked after a minute.

She looked at him. 'Do you?'

He nodded. 'I think I have a right to know who he is. I don't feel complete, not really knowing who I am. Do you feel the same?'

'Oh, I know who my dad is all right.'

'You do?'

'Yes. I found out by accident. Can't do anything about it though. It'd mess up too many lives.'

'Still, at least you know. I'd give anything to know who he is, but Mum won't even talk about it. I can't make her understand how important it is to me.'

'You're still *you* though. Nothing can change that.'

'I know but it'd help me to understand the way I am – the way I feel about things. I look in the mirror sometimes and wonder if I look like him; whether I've got any half-brothers or sisters. I could have a whole family out there somewhere that I don't know about. It drives me mad at times.'

Suddenly she looked round. 'Where's Maddie? Oh God, I'd forgotten all about her!' She stood up and looked round. '*Maddie!*' she called. 'Oh no! If I've lost her I don't know what Claire will say.'

'I'll help you find her, come on.' Mark took her hand and they went back to the main garden, calling the dog's name as they went.

They found her finishing off the sandwiches where they'd been sitting, her whiskers covered in mayonnaise. Danni stopped short when she saw her and burst out laughing.

'Oh, Maddie, you clown!' She picked her up and kissed the top of her head. 'Thank goodness!' She looked around at the lengthening shadows. 'What time is it?'

Rick looked at his watch. 'Five o'clock. You're not in a hurry to get back, are you?'

'I think I'd better,' she said, gathering up her sketching pad and pencils. 'Claire will wonder where Maddie is when she gets home. I didn't say I'd take her.'

'Which evening is your art class?' he asked.

'Wednesday, at the adult education centre.'

'How about meeting me for a drink afterwards?'

She smiled. 'That'd be nice. Something to look forward to.'

He smiled, reaching for her hand. 'Do you mean that? Would you really look forward to seeing me again?'

She shook her shoulders. 'Oh come on – fishing for compliments?'

'No – 'course not.' He let go of her hand and walked ahead of her to the car.

'*Rick,*' she called, realizing that she'd upset him. 'Rick – don't be daft. I'm only teasing. Of course I'll look forward to seeing you, you daft wuss.'

He turned to her with a wry smile. 'I never know when you're joking. And don't call me a wuss!'

She caught up to him and put her arms round his neck, planting a kiss on his cheek. For a moment he stared at her in surprise then he drew her close and kissed her hard. When he let her go she was flushed.

'Wow! That was unexpected,' she said shakily.

Still holding her he looked into her eyes. 'Unexpected and. . . ?'

'OK, unexpected and nice,' she said, giving him a little shake. 'So nice in fact that I think I'd like you to do it again.'

'Just as long as you promise not to call me a wuss again.'

Danni laughed. 'You'll get used to me and my mouth,' she said. 'Mum used to say it'd be the death of me.'

Fay locked the shop door securely and dropped the keys into her handbag. She'd completed her check on the stock and now she looked forward to a nice hot bath and putting her feet up in front of the TV for the evening.

The street was empty as she walked round to the car park. It was a warm evening. Summer would soon be upon them and her customers would be shopping for holiday clothes any week now. At least, she hoped they would after what she'd spent on the new summer stock.

As she unlocked the car she was deep in thought, wondering whether the colours she had chosen this year would be popular. The ones she had picked were the trendiest for the coming season but you could never tell with provincial women. She would try them out when she re-dressed the window tomorrow, she decided.

There was a handful of cars in the car park, but one caught her eye as she slipped into the driving seat of the Ka: a racy little blue sports car on the other side of the parking space. She was pretty sure it was Claire Naylor's. Then she noticed the occupants of a dark-blue saloon nearby. There was a couple sitting in the front together, deep in conversation, and Fay was almost certain that the woman was Claire.

Well, well! Fay reached into her bag for her sunglasses and slipped them on. Better if Claire didn't recognize her. Not that she had eyes for anyone but the man beside her at the moment. What was she doing out with another man on a Sunday afternoon? Did Mark know? It was intriguing to say the least. She picked up the Sunday newspaper she had bought on her way to the shop and opened it, peering over the top at the couple. After a few minutes the woman got out, confirming without a doubt her suspicion that it was Claire. She watched with a *frisson* of excitement as Claire leaned in through the window and kissed the driver, then after walking quickly across the car park she got into her own car. As the sports car drove towards her Fay buried her face in the news-paper. *Well, well*, she told herself gleefully. *What did you make of that?*

CHAPTER NINE

'As you see the new extension is almost finished,' Doctor George Naylor swept an arm proudly round the reception area of the Charlesworth Avenue Medical Centre, while his nephew, Gerald Naylor looked on. 'There will be access to it through there. We'll have two new consulting-rooms, a sister's room and a minor ops theatre, not to mention a new office and toilet facilities.'

'Very nice,' Gerald said politely. 'I'm sure it will be a great improvement.'

'An improvement?' George looked at him, a slight frown creasing his brow. 'Charlesworth Avenue practice has always been streets ahead of other surgeries in the town. When this expansion is complete we shall be as good as anything Ipswich or any other city has to offer. State of the art, as they say.'

Gerald's son, Paul leaned forward. He was a tall, thin young man with hornrimmed spectacles and an earnest expression. His shoulders were slightly stooped through years of studying and although still in his twenties his dark hair was already thinning. 'Did you say there was to be a minor ops theatre, Uncle George?' he ventured. 'That would be extremely useful.'

'Well, we hope so,' George said. 'We're doing all we can to prevent the closure of A and E departments. I'm chairman of the local protest group.'

Gerald looked at him. 'I'd have thought you'd be enjoying your retirement now, Uncle,' he said. 'I daresay Aunt Mary would rather you spent more time with her.'

George shook his head. 'Can't leave everything to the youngsters,' he said. 'Experience is everything, especially in our profession, as I'm sure you agree.'

'Mark is hardly a youngster though, is he?' Gerald pointed out.

George laughed. 'Might as well be, Gerald,' he said enigmatically. 'Might as well be. Speaking of Mark, shall we look in on him?' He strode down the corridor, Gerald and Paul following and after a brief tap on the door marked DR M NAYLOR, he marched in, to the surprise and consternation of an elderly man who was having his chest sounded. Mark removed his stethoscope from one ear and looked round in annoyance.

'I'm with a patient, Father,' he said. 'Can you wait outside a moment?'

Unrepentant, George rubbed his hands together. 'We're all doctors here,' he said, addressing the patient. 'No need for embarrassment. Not every day you see four doctors all at once, is it?' He laughed heartily at his own joke. Gerald cleared his throat.

'I'm so sorry, Mark,' he said. 'We'll wait for you in reception.'

When Mark joined his father and cousins ten minutes later in reception he looked annoyed. Gerald stepped forward.

'I'm so sorry about that, Mark,' he said. 'We thought your surgery was over.'

'Don't worry about it.' Mark brushed the apology aside. 'Father mentioned that you were all coming down for a visit this weekend.' He looked at his father. 'It would have been nice if you'd telephoned to say you were looking in this afternoon.'

George bridled. 'Have to make an appointment to visit my own surgery now, do I?'

Mark bit back the reply he longed to make and adjusted his expression, holding out his hand to Gerald. 'Forgive me,' he said. 'I haven't had the chance to say hello.' He shook Gerald's hand. 'How are you – and Anita of course?' He looked at Paul. 'And I understand that congratulations are in order.'

Paul smiled and nodded. Gerald said, 'We're all very well, thank you.' He glanced round and saw that George was behind the reception desk, having an earnest conversation with the practice manager. He lowered his voice. 'I wondered if Anita and I could come round and see you and Claire while we're here,' he said. 'I think there are things we should talk about.'

'Of course,' Mark said with an enthusiasm he didn't feel. 'Just give Claire a ring. You must come for dinner; Paul too of course.'

A dinner appointment was hastily made between Claire and Anita the following morning for that evening. It was short notice and Claire was put out. She voiced her concerns to Danni when she replaced the receiver.

'Three of them to dinner this evening! What on earth am I going to give them? I'll have to drop everything and go to the supermarket now,' she said. 'It's a nuisance. I was hoping to work on those designs for the Frobishers' house. I'm really keen to land this job, if only I can come up with something that appeals to them.' She looked at Danni. 'Can you hold the fort for me here? I know it's your day off but if you've got nothing planned . . .'

'Of course. You go. I'll be fine,' Danni assured her. 'Can I ask you a favour?'

Claire was pulling on her jacket. 'Yes, what?'

'Can I have a go at the designs? I've been playing around with some ideas since you took me to see the house. All the measurements are on the computer. Can I – just for a laugh of course?'

Claire smiled. 'Be my guest! Look, I'll be about an hour. Mark will be back from his emergency surgery at twelve. If you wouldn't mind making him a coffee and telling him where I am.'

'Sure. Don't worry about a thing.'

When Claire had gone Danni fetched her sketch pad and opened it. She had already done some sketches of the house they'd visited a few days before; a newly built, architect-designed house in a beautiful wooded location on the outskirts of Haylesmere. She'd done some pastel drawings of her own ideas for the hall, lounge and dining-room as she'd seen them. She switched on the computer, found and inserted the design disk and located the house in question. Then she set about trying out her colour schemes. She'd been particularly taken with the house, loving the layout and design, and she'd given a lot of thought to it. It had been a sunny day when she and Claire had visited earlier in the week. Large windows overlooked a green area with beautiful trees and shrubs and Danni had the idea of bringing the natural colours into the house. She had chosen yellows of every shade, from palest lemon through to rich gold. As contrast she'd chosen splashes of natural green and pale earthy shades for carpet and curtains. She told herself that a colour scheme like this would retain the colours of summer through the winter and give the house a warm feel.

She was so engrossed that she didn't hear the front door and when Mark spoke behind her she jumped.

'Does Claire know you're playing around with her computer?'

She spun round. 'Yes. I asked her if I could. It's work,' she said.

'Where is she by the way?'

'She had to go to the supermarket to get stuff for the dinner party this evening.'

'Right.' He peered at the computer screen and sniffed. 'I don't know anything about designing but that looks a complete mess to me. Did you say it was Claire's work?'

Danni coloured. 'No, it's mine.'

'That explains it then.' He chuckled. 'All I can say is, don't give up the day job!' he looked around the room. 'Speaking of which, it seems to me you'd be better employed giving this place a good vacuuming.'

'It is my day off,' she told him.

He raised an eyebrow. 'I'm sure I don't have to remind you that you have a free room and board here. Young people like you don't realize when you're well off,' he said. 'Surely it's not too much to ask to use your own initiative and offer help where you can see it's needed.'

Stung, Danni switched off the computer and went out of the room, returning a few minutes later with the vacuum cleaner. She was plugging it in when Mark said,

'Would it be beneath your dignity to make me a cup of coffee on your day off?'

'Well, make your mind up!' Danni snapped, her cheeks pink. 'What do want me to do first, hoover or make coffee. P'raps you'd like to stick a broom up my jumper so that I could . . .'

'*That's enough*!' Mark glared at her. 'How dare you speak to me like that? It's easy to see how you were brought up. If any daughter of mine spoke to her employer like that I'd . . .'

'*Any daughter of yours*? Huh!' Her temper was well and truly up now. He was talking about having a daughter when he knew less than nothing about being a parent. How would he feel if he knew that he was actually speaking to his daughter? She was on the brink of blurting out the truth, imagining the shocked look on his face. Well, why not? What did she have to lose? *Except this job and a decent future*, said an urgent little warning voice inside her head. She swallowed hard and bit down on her lip.

'Sorry,' she said, looking down at her feet.

'I should bloody well think so! You can forget the coffee and I advise you to keep out of my way in future!' He strode past her and out through the door, almost colliding with Claire who was coming in loaded with bags of shopping. She paused to look at Mark's crimson face then at Danni's pink one.

'Oh dear. What's the matter with him?'

'My fault,' Danni said. 'I was rude to him.'

Claire frowned. 'That's not like you. What did he say?'

'Oh nothing.'

'And why are you cleaning on your day off? Did he. . . . ?'

'It's OK,' Danni said. 'Honestly. It's fine.' She picked up the carrier bags and carried them through to the kitchen. 'Wow, smoked salmon,' she said, unpacking the bags. 'And chicken.'

'I thought I'd make a starter with the salmon while the chicken is cooking,' Claire said. 'You can help me if you've nothing else you want to do.'

'Great. Just tell me how.' She looked at Claire. 'Will you show me how to lay a proper dinner-party table too?'

They worked together all afternoon. Danni learned how to make smoked salmon and cream cheese roulade and how to roast a chicken with cream and herbs. Claire had bought a gateau for dessert, but she made a fruit salad as an alternative. Upstairs in the dining-room they laid the table together and Claire showed Danni how to set out the glasses and cutlery. At last, with the small floral centrepiece and the candelabra in place she stood back.

'It looks lovely,' she said.

'Why don't you act as our waitress for the evening?' Claire suggested.

'Oh, I'd love that.' Danni's face suddenly dropped. 'Oh, but what about Doctor Naylor? I don't think he'll want me to do it.'

'Well, that's hard luck,' Claire said. 'I'm your employer, not him, and I'm asking you. Unless you planned to go out, that is.'

'No. I'd love to do it.'

'And you must have some dinner too. You must have some of everything. After all, you've helped to make it.'

Danni was nervous when the time for the dinner party drew near but everything went without a hitch. She and Claire had dished up previously and all Danni had to do was serve each course to the guests. She avoided Mark's eyes as she served him but she couldn't help noticing that the gangling young man with the glasses watched her every move. He seemed unable to take his eyes off her as she circled the table dressed in her best black skirt and a white top, her hair tied back with a black ribbon.

As she was clearing away the dessert plates Claire said: 'I think we'll have our coffee in the drawing-room.' She smiled at Paul. 'Perhaps you'd like to help Danielle with the coffee, Paul.'

Scarlet-faced, he sprang up, dropping his napkin on the floor. 'Oh yes please. I mean, of course – glad to.' He followed Danni out of the room and down the basement stairs.

I hope he doesn't want to stay and chat me up, Danni said to herself Serving the food had made her hungry and she couldn't wait to get her teeth into that delicious chicken.

When Paul and Danni had gone Claire invited Anita to go with her to the drawing-room.

'Don't sit there talking all night, you two,' she said to Mark as she stood up. 'The coffee will be cold.'

'We won't,' Mark promised.

As the door closed behind their wives Gerald looked at Mark. 'I really wanted to see how you felt about this idea of your father's,' he said. 'Uncle George can be a little – shall we say – intractable when it comes to his precious practice.'

'Pig-headed, you mean.' Mark stretched his back. 'The

thing is it isn't his practice any longer. He retired almost a year ago. He just can't let go.'

'Does that mean you're against Paul and me joining you?' Gerald asked.

'Not necessarily. It just means I haven't been consulted,' Mark said. 'Dad is paying for the new extension out of his own pocket, so he feels that he has the right to the first and last word on the way things should be run.'

'And you. . . ?'

'My opinions don't matter – apparently.'

'Oh dear. This makes things very difficult.' Gerald looked uncomfortable.

'He isn't the easiest man to work with,' Mark said. 'He can be very manipulative. There were four of us in the practice before Dad retired. I already have two other partners, counting Dad, and we're quite hard pressed. He just can't stop dropping in and interfering. You saw the way he barged in yesterday afternoon. He wants to lay down rules about treatments we can and can't provide now too.'

'Such as?'

'Terminations and IVF treatment to name but two,' Mark said. 'He's dead against what he refers to as "messing with nature".'

'That rules out a hell of a lot of things in this day and age.' Gerald cleared his throat. 'For me the job of taking over minor ops here would be semi-retirement,' he said. 'And although at the moment I'm thinking about taking things easier I'm not at all sure if I'm quite ready for it yet.'

'Did Dad pressure you?' Mark asked.

Gerald sighed. 'More or less. He came up with this idea when he and Aunt Mary came up to visit us. He seemed to think that the main incentive was the prospective partnership for Paul. The boy is brilliant – passed all his exams with flying colours and I wouldn't want to stand in his way, but I'm not altogether convinced that he's GP material, at least, not at the moment.' He looked at Mark. 'I feel uncomfortable about this, Mark. You're the senior partner. You should be the one to make the final decision.'

Mark smiled wryly. 'You'd think so, wouldn't you? The trouble is that Father thinks I've let him down by not producing a son to carry on the tradition.'

Down in the kitchen Paul watched Danni as she filled the kettle.

'Are you the maid?' he asked.

Danni spun round and gave him a withering look. 'No, I'm *not*!' she said. 'I help out round the house but basically I'm training to be an interior designer with Claire. As it happens today is my day off but I offered to help.'

Paul blushed. 'Oh, I'm sorry. I didn't mean to offend you.'

'That's all right.' Danni felt a little deflated by his shamefaced expression. 'I s'pose it's a natural mistake.'

'I'm always putting my foot in it.' He glanced at her. 'I might be coming to work here. If I do perhaps you and I could see a bit of each other?'

Danni smiled to herself. He didn't waste any time, even if he did look like a bit of a geek. 'I don't think my boyfriend would like that,' she said, pushing him gently out of the way as she set out the coffee cups on the tray.

'Oh! Sorry, I didn't know.'

She looked him up and down speculatively. 'Is it really what you want then – coming here to work?'

He sighed and sat down. 'To be completely honest, no,' he said. 'What I really want is to go on and study pharmacology, then tropical diseases – work abroad.'

Danni pulled a face. 'Sounds yukky! Rather you than me.'

'Uncle George seems dead set on me coming here, though, and eventually taking over the family practice when Mark retires, so that's probably what I'll end up doing.'

'Because Mark hasn't got a son of his own to take over?'

'I suppose that's the idea.'

'Well, it's none of my business but I don't think you should let them shove you around, 'specially after all those years of studying.'

'You don't know Uncle George,' he said.

'I've heard plenty about him and how he wants all his own way,' she said. 'Sounds to me as if he wants putting in his place. After all, he's had his life, hasn't he?'

'Yes, but—'

'I think you should do what *you* want to do. Tell them what you just told me – that you've got your own plans. I would.'

'Would you?' He gave her a wistful smile. 'Yes, I guess you would. You're that sort of person, aren't you?'

'What makes you think you know what sort of person I am?' She put the coffee pot on to the tray and lifted it, nodding towards the door. 'Go on then – make yourself useful. It won't open itself, will it?'

Galvanized into action he sprang up to open the door. 'Look,' he said as she went past him. 'I don't like coffee so can I come back and help you with the washing-up?'

'No,' she said firmly, thinking of her dinner drying up in the oven. 'Anyway, there's a machine for that and you've got more important things to do. You want to go back up there and put your cards on the table; tell them you don't want to come and work here. Tell them what you really want.'

He stared at her. 'Do you think I should?'

'I do. Tell them what you've just told me. If you don't you'll regret it for the rest of your life. You know I'm right, don't you?'

He stood for a moment, chewing his lip indecisively, then suddenly he smiled. 'Thanks for that, Danni. I think you're right.'

As Mark closed the front door behind his departing cousins he turned to Claire. 'Well, what do think of all that?'

She gave him a rueful smile. 'I think they've made up their own minds,' she said. 'But I'd like to be a fly on the wall when they tell your father their decision.'

'Mmm.' Mark sighed. 'I've got a nasty feeling that it'll be me who comes in for the flak though,' he said.

He was right. A bristling George Naylor presented himself at the surgery at nine o'clock on Monday morning.

'I wish to speak to my son,' he told the receptionist.

'He's about to start his surgery,' she told him. 'Can you come back at eleven?'

George's face took on a deep purple colour. 'No I *cannot!*' he said loudly. 'I've no intention of returning at eleven. This is *my* practice and I need to speak to my son *now*! Please ring through and tell him I'm here.' He leaned forward and peered keenly at the girl. 'You're new, aren't you? What is your name, girl?' he demanded.

The girl shrank visibly. 'Sarah,' she said. 'But . . .' She broke off as George turned to march purposefully off in the direction of Mark's surgery.

'What did you say to them?' he demanded as he burst into the room.

Mark looked up. 'Say to whom?'

'You know perfectly well who I'm talking about,' George shouted. 'Gerald told me calmly yesterday before they left for Edinburgh that neither he nor Paul intend to come and work here.'

'Surely it's their choice,' Mark said. 'I certainly did nothing to dissuade either of them.'

'It was a golden opportunity for that boy,' George railed. 'Having a flourishing practice handed to him on a plate. Someone must have put him off. If it wasn't you then it must have been Claire getting at Anita.'

'No one got at anyone, Father,' Mark said patiently. 'Paul wants to study further. He wants to work abroad with tropical diseases.'

'Why ever would he want to do that when he has the opportunity of a comfortable life here as a GP?'

'Well, it seems that he does.' Mark looked at his watch. 'I'm sorry, Father but I have a waiting-room full of patients out there so if you wouldn't mind . . .'

George let out his breath in an explosive snort. 'Huh! It's impossible to help you,' he said. 'And you want to get rid of that stupid new girl in reception. She's an idiot!' At the door he turned. 'This practice has been going rapidly downhill since I retired and I just have to stand back and watch with my hands tied. I give up!'

Mark gave a sigh as he watched his father storm out of the room. 'If only you would,' he muttered. 'If *only* you would!'

CHAPTER TEN

'DID you do this, Danni?' Claire was sitting at the computer.

Danni turned to look at the screen. 'Oh, yes. I was having a go at the Frobishers' house last Saturday. I did ask you if I could.'

'I know. These ideas are very good,' Claire said. 'I love the colour schemes.'

'I thought it would be nice to bring the natural colours indoors,' Danni explained.

'Yes, I can see that.' Claire turned with a smile. 'Tell you what, with a few minor changes I think we should let them see these.'

'Really?' Danni flushed with pleasure.

'At the moment I think there might be just a tad too much yellow,' Claire went on. 'Maybe we could introduce some blue – a very soft cerulean blue like a summer sky – just the merest touch, maybe on the ceiling mouldings.' She clicked the computer mouse and instantly showed Danni what she meant.

'Oh yes, that's perfect,' Danni said. 'I love it.'

Claire smiled. 'Well, let's hope that the Frobishers think so too, eh? Let's print these out and fax them off.' While she was waiting for the printer she glanced at Danni. 'Your evening classes are really beginning to pay off, aren't they? Are you enjoying them?'

Danni nodded. 'I love them. It's what I've always wanted to do.'

'Good. How did you get on with Paul on Saturday evening? I could tell he was taken with you.'

'OK,' Danni said, hoping that Paul hadn't said anything about her voicing her opinion about his future career. 'He's a bit shy, isn't he?'

Claire laughed. 'I used to think so, but he surprised us all on Saturday evening. Mark's father wanted him to come and join the practice here but he made it very clear that he has no intention of falling in with the plan. He was quite firm about it; adamant, almost.'

'I see. Did that upset things?' Danni asked.

Claire shook her head. 'Far from it. His father was obviously relieved. The plan was for him to come too and run the new minor ops room. He didn't really want to come either, so Paul's decision rather let him off the hook too.'

'It would have been confusing, wouldn't it – having three Doctor Naylors at the surgery?'

'I suppose it would. They would have had to go by their Christian names.' Claire sighed. 'If life had panned out the way it should Mark and I would have had our own son or daughter working towards becoming a doctor by now,' she said.

Danni paused. 'But you – never had children?'

'No. Anyway even if we had there's no guarantee that he or she would have wanted to be a doctor, is there? Life's not that simple.' She got up from her desk. 'I think it's about time for coffee. Let's go and make some, shall we?'

She was reaching for the jar of instant coffee in the kitchen cupboard when she suddenly said: 'I almost had a baby once.'

Danni held her breath. 'Did you?'

'Yes. It was a case of the wrong place and the wrong time,

though,' Claire said wistfully. 'I was still at university. Mark and I were both studying hard and he – we decided that we should postpone our family.'

'So you had an . . .'

'A termination,' Claire put in. 'The trouble was that it turned out not to be a postponement but an end to all our hopes of ever having a family.'

Danni was shocked. She was sure that Ruth had never known this. 'There were complications?' she said.

Claire smiled wryly. 'You could say that.' The kettle boiled and she shrugged her shoulders. 'But there, I'm sure you're not interested in my personal problems. I sound like one of those awful women who drone on about their operations!'

'Did you never think about adoption?' Danni asked, reluctant to let the subject drop.

Claire hesitated. 'In a way, yes. As a matter of fact we might have had a little girl if things had worked out. As it happens they didn't.' She looked at her watch. 'Heavens! Look at the time. I have to go out for a while.' She hastily drank her coffee. 'I'll be back after lunch. Have another session with the design software if you like.'

'I'll take Maddie for a walk and then do a bit of housework, shall I?' Danni said. 'If there's time after that I'd love to have a go at the designs if that's all right.'

Claire had been gone about ten minutes and Danni was putting Maddie's collar and lead on when her mobile rang. She fished it out of her pocket and saw that it was Rick calling.

'Rick! What are you ringing me here for?' she asked. 'I asked you not to ring me during working hours.'

'I know but I couldn't resist it. I've got some good news.' He was bubbling over with excitement. 'Guess what? I had an interview with Phil Rowlands of Rowlands Landscapes yesterday and I've just had a call from him. He's offered me a job!'

'Oh, Rick, that's brilliant!'

'Not fantastic money. I'll be training on the job. But Rowlands has a terrific reputation. He goes all over the county and he's done some really big jobs. And guess what, Danni?'

'Don't know – tell me.'

'He's got a degree in philosophy too! That'll be something to shut Mum up.'

Danni laughed. 'I expect she only wants the best for you.'

'Yeah, I know. Danni, you haven't met Mum yet. Why don't you let me take you home next Sunday? I think you and she would get on OK.'

'I don't know.' Danni chewed her lip. 'Am I being taken home for Ma's approval?'

Rick chuckled. 'Nothing like that. I just want you to meet her, that's all.'

'And if she doesn't like me?'

'Tough! But I know she will.'

Claire slipped into the passenger seat of Adam's car in the place where they usually met, in the car park at the back of the market place.

'Darling, how are you?' He leaned across and kissed her.

'I'm fine.' She sighed. 'But I do hate meeting you in this hole-and-corner way. I told you some time ago that we should stop—'

'We can't stop,' he interrupted. 'You know that as well as I do. What we have to decide is what we're going to do.'

'What *can* we do?'

'We can be together. You can leave him.'

She sighed. 'I don't think I can, Adam. I'm not sure that I can face it.'

'You think I'm not worth it?'

'You know that's not what I think.' She looked around. 'Let's get out of here. I hate this place. I can't think straight.'

He drove out into the country and they stopped at a tiny pub on the edge of a village. At a table in the corner of the bar Adam reopened his argument.

'I was going to leave anyway. I know Mark asked me to stay on but I gave him to understand it would only be temporary. I couldn't stay here if you said you didn't want to see me any more.' He leaned across and took her hand.'There's a partnership going in a large practice up in Scotland – Edinburgh. I've already applied. You'd love it up there. You could start your design business over again. I know we'd be happy.'

'I'm not sure.'

'Why? What are we waiting for?' Adam pushed a frustrated hand through his hair. 'Darling, what do you owe him? Nothing! It's he who owes you – for all the years of misplaced loyalty. He's barely civil to you. I've seen that.'

'I know.'

'For God's sake, you don't still love him, do you? You're not still hanging on to something that dead?'

She shook her head, miserable with uncertainty. 'It's just that it's been so long.'

'All you have to do is tell him you're leaving,' he said gently. 'Tell him we love each other and you need to have a life and some happiness before it's too late.' He looked into her troubled eyes. 'Listen, come away with me – next weekend. I'll book us into a hotel, somewhere nice and quiet. Somewhere where we can take our time; talk; make up our – *your* mind.' He looked at her enquiringly. 'Well, will you come?'

'Adam – I'm older than you. You know the situation. I couldn't give you a child. It would be doomed to failure and—'

'You've told me all that a hundred times. It makes no difference. I know it *would* work.' He took her hand. 'Just tell me one thing: Will you come away with me next weekend?'

She smiled tremulously. 'All right, Adam. God help me, but I'll come.'

The following Sunday Rick had the car again and he and Danni drove out to the old house, which Rick referred to as Manderley after the house in *Rebecca*. Danni had brought her watercolour paints and she did a sketch of the Italian garden, which she gave to Rick.

'Maybe your mum would like this,' she said. 'It wouldn't look too bad in a frame.'

They ate their picnic and then Rick drove them both back to Kaisley. As they drove into the bungalow's drive Danni asked, 'Does she know you're bringing me back with you?'

He nodded. 'I said we might look in.'

'It's a good job I didn't bring Maddie then,' Danni remarked. 'She probably wouldn't approve of a strange dog in the back of her car.'

As she began to pack up the picnic things Rick sat back on his heels, looking at her.

'Danni, I've been meaning to tell you something.'

She looked up with a grin. 'OK – so tell me.'

'I'm seriously thinking of leaving home.'

She opened her eyes wide. 'Wow! What will Mummy say about that?'

Catching the teasing note in her voice, he coloured. 'I know what you think – and what everyone else must think, but I'm not a mummy's boy. I hate the idea that anyone should think I am. I'm grateful for the support she gave me while I was at uni but now that I'm going to be earning my own living I'll be able to afford a place of my own. It's high time I moved out, anyway. I won't be able to afford anything posh, mind, but . . .' He paused and looked at her, trying to assess her mood. 'The thing is – I could afford something better; a little flat maybe – if there were someone to share it with me.'

Danni pushed a teacloth into the basket and tucked it

round the crockery. 'So – do you know anyone who'd be likely to put up with your freaky habits?' she teased without looking up.

He reached out to touch her shoulder. 'Oh come off it, Danni, you know what I'm trying to say. How would you feel about sharing a place with me?'

Seeing that he was serious she looked up. 'I don't know,' she said. 'I'm OK where I am. If I moved out Claire would have to pay me a bit more. I don't know how she'd feel about that. It'd be nice, I suppose, to be independent.'

'But what about *me*, Danni? How do you feel about sharing with *me*? That's what I really want to know.'

She gave him a rueful smile. 'You're not too bad,' she said. 'I daresay I could probably put up with you.'

He moved closer to her. 'For heaven's sake, Danni! I never really know what you're thinking,' he complained. 'You keep things very much to yourself' He took both her hands. 'What if I were to tell you that I *love* you? Would that make a difference?'

The words hung between them on the summer afternoon air. Danni's face lost its impish grin and she lowered her eyes. 'You shouldn't say things like that unless you're sure you mean them,' she said.

'I *am* sure. I *do* mean it. I've known for ages; since soon after we first met, if you really want to know.' He reached forward and cupped her chin in his hand to kiss her, and Danni knew immediately that he was sincere. Everything was in that kiss. It was soft and gentle but at the same time there was a hint of suppressed passion. Before he had kissed her like a boy. This was the kiss of a man – a man in love. She felt herself melt and in that moment she allowed herself to admit something she had known for weeks – that she shared his feelings. Winding her arms around his neck she clung to him and returned the kiss.

'I love you too, Rick,' she whispered. 'And I'd love us to

share a place if we can find one. Maybe not just yet but when you've settled in your new job, eh?' She leaned back to look into his eyes. 'We can wait a little while, can't we? After all, I'm not going anywhere.'

Fay met them in the hall. She was wearing jeans and a white top which showed off the tan she had acquired working in the garden at weekends. She smiled and held out her hand. 'So you're the famous Danni I've heard so much about,' she said, shaking Danni's hand. 'Come and sit in the garden. Richard, get two more chairs out.'

Danni hadn't heard him called Richard before. She glanced at him and he gave her a sly wink. 'OK, Mum.'

It seemed to Danni that Rick's mother was very pleasant. She chattered about the garden and was delighted with the watercolour sketch that Danni had done of the Italian garden. 'Richard seems quite obsessed about that old place,' she remarked. 'But looking at this makes me wonder if I should go and have a look at it myself. Thank you dear. I'll have to get it framed.' Fay smiled. 'Richard tells me that your mother brought you up single handed, just as I did with Richard. It's very hard.' She reached out a hand to Rick. 'But well worth it. He's a credit to me and I'm sure you are to your mother too.'

'It's great about Rick – er Richard's new job, isn't it?' Danni remarked.

Fay's eyes clouded. 'I suppose so – if that's what he wants. I can't say I'm not disappointed though, after all the years of study, not to mention the sacrifices involved.'

'I keep telling you, Mum. The prospects are very good. It's not what you think. You'll have to let me take you to see some of Mr Rowlands's work.'

'One day he'll have his own business, won't you?' Danni said. 'That's what I'm hoping for too. Hey, tell you what, we could work together; you on the gardens and me on the houses.'

Fay laughed. 'There's ambition for you.' Privately she thought the girl was being outrageously presumptuous. They were just kids after all, weren't they? Their relationship wasn't a permanent thing. At least she hoped not. She had visualized a better-bred girl for him than this little comprehensive-educated nobody. She made up her mind to find out as much as she could about the girl. It wouldn't do for Richard to get trapped into an inappropriate relationship. If the girl wasn't suitable she would make sure she nipped it in the bud before things went too far.

'Richard tells me you're training to be an interior designer,' she said.

'Yes, at Cavendish Designs. You might have heard of it,' Danni said. 'It's in Grafton Place.'

Fay's heart gave a leap and her eyes narrowed. 'Isn't that Claire Naylor?'

'Yes.' Danni was surprised that Fay knew Claire's married name. 'Do you know her?'

'I know *of* her,' Fay said.

'She's very talented. I've learned such a lot from her.'

'Richard says you have a room in the house.'

'That's right. I'm very lucky.'

'And you're taking evening classes too?'

'Yes. I love it.'

'Well, that's nice for you then, isn't it?' Fay stood up. 'I'm sure you'd both like some tea. Excuse me while I go and make some.'

When she had disappeared into the house Danni looked at Rick. 'You never said your name was Richard,' she said.

He pulled a face. 'It sounds so stuffy. All my mates call me Rick.'

'Your mum seems nice.'

He nodded. 'The trouble with single mums is that they tend to be over-protective. It's a bit embarrassing.'

'I guessed that,' Danni said with a grin. 'If anything it's the other way round with mine. I worry about Mum and what'll happen to her now I'm not there.'

He grinned. 'Mums, eh?'

In the kitchen Fay waited thoughtfully for the kettle to boil. So this girlfriend of Richard's worked and lived in the same house as Mark! Who would have thought it? Ever since she'd spotted Claire in the car park with another man she'd been itching to know what was going on. If she played her cards right she could get to know a lot about what went on in that house. This girl could make a useful ally – especially if she remained unaware of the fact. She decided not to nip Richard's friendship with the girl in the bud just yet after all. She poured boiling water into the teapot and picked up the tray, determined to turn on the charm and gain the girl's confidence.

The three of them drank tea in the garden and Fay made small talk until suddenly she said, 'Richard, darling, we're almost out of milk. You wouldn't run down to the village shop and get a pint, would you? They're open till five.'

He stood up at once. 'OK. Do you want to come, Danni?'

Before Danni could reply Fay said, 'Danni and I will wait here – have a cosy girl chat while we wait for you.' She reached out to touch Danni's hand. 'Won't we, dear?'

Danni shrugged. 'I should be getting back soon anyway.'

'I'll take you when I get back,' Rick said.

Fay was silent for a moment when they were alone then she looked at Danni. 'I expect your mother misses you,' she said.

Danni nodded. 'She moved in with a new partner not long ago,' she said.

'So – how do you feel about that?'

'To tell you the truth I don't think it will work out.'

'Really? What makes you think that?'

'I don't know. I just don't trust the man. He's got a nice house and he's promised her all sorts of things but . . .' Danni shook her head. 'There's just something – a feeling.'

'You're obviously a very shrewd girl,' Fay said. 'Is your father still around? Are you in touch with him?'

'No.' Danni shook her head. 'Is Richard's?'

Fay bridled. What an impudent question. 'No,' she said shortly.

Danni shot a look at Fay. 'It's – complicated, about my father.'

'I see.' Fay decided not to pursue that line of enquiry for the moment. 'So are you happy, living and working under the same roof as your employer? I imagine there could be a downside.'

'Oh no, it's fine. I've got my own room and everything; on the top floor right away from everyone else.'

'Don't you get lonely?'

'No. Claire, my boss, is lovely. We get on really well.'

'And – her husband. You like him too?'

Danni paused just long enough for Fay to draw her own conclusions. 'He's OK,' she said. 'We don't really have much to do with each other. He's a doctor.'

'Do I detect a little friction?' Fay cocked an eyebrow at her.

'Only a bit. I keep out of his way.'

'I'm sure that's wise.' Fay regarded her for a moment. 'There are rumours that the Naylors' marriage is on the rocks,' she said.

'Really?' Danni looked at Rick's mother. If she was hoping she was going to gossip about her employer she was mistaken. What a cheek. 'Are there?' she said. 'I wouldn't know.'

Fay raised an eyebrow. The girl wasn't going to be as much of a pushover as she'd hoped. 'So – your father abandoned you and your mother?'

Danni hesitated. 'Yes.' she said. 'I do know who he is, as it happens but that's as far as it can go. Bringing it all out into the open would upset too many people.'

'It sounds intriguing.'

'Not really. I know and that's enough for me.'

'You're letting sleeping dogs lie.'

'Something like that.'

'Well, I'm sure you're doing the right thing.' This girl wasn't going to be as easy to pump as she'd thought. Fay reached out to cover Danni's hand with her own. 'I can see that you and Richard have a lot in common,' she said. 'He's a sensitive boy and I can see that you are a very thoughtful girl. But you're both very young, of course; far too young to be thinking of anything serious.' She switched on her warmest smile. 'Try not to worry too much about your mother,' she said. 'She sounds a really strong woman. I'm sure she can take care of herself, and if ever you want to talk about anything – ask advice from an older – from someone impartial, for whatever that's worth, I'd like to think you'd feel you could come to me.'

Danni looked at her in surprise. 'Thank you.'

'Not at all. I've been lucky in a way. Richard's father has always made sure that we never went short of anything and that Richard had a good education. I've made sacrifices, of course, but the hardships your mother must have had to suffer with no help at all are unimaginable.'

'It's been hard for her, yes but we've managed. She's a brilliant manager, my mum.'

'How loyal of you. Men are such selfish brutes,' Fay went on. 'I hope I've brought Richard up to be different.' She gave Danni's hand a light squeeze. 'I expect you know my little shop, *Style and Grace*. If ever you want any clothes do pop in.'

Danni laughed and shook her head. 'Out of my league, I'm afraid. I often look at the things in the window but I couldn't afford to buy any of them on what I earn.'

Fay gave her a reassuring smile. 'Nonsense. Just come in next time you see something that takes your fancy,' she said. 'You'd be surprised at how cheap some things can be – to my friends.'

Fay stood in the window waving them off. But behind her bright smile her mind was working overtime. The girl had been polite enough. But clearly she was no fool. It wouldn't be easy to prise any information out of her. Fay'd had the distinct feeling that she had no intention of talking about Claire – or her precious husband. Maybe she had already sensed that theirs was a flawed marriage. Still, a sense of loyalty was no bad thing and it was early days. Perhaps she'd open up more once Fay had had time to break down her reserve.

'Do you ever wonder about your dad?' Danni asked as Rick drove her home.

He looked at her. 'Yes; more and more as I get older. Mum is adamant about not telling me his name. I think I have a right to know who fathered me but she sticks to her guns.'

'Your mum says that he's always done the right thing by you.'

'Except stuck around to get to know me,' Rick said.

'What about your birth certificate?'

He shrugged. 'That bit is just left blank.'

'Same as mine.'

'Frustrating, isn't it?'

'At least I know who my dad is,' she said. 'I found out. The frustrating part for me is that I can never tell him who I am.'

'Why not?'

'It's like I was telling your mother this afternoon. It would upset too many lives.'

'He's married, you mean?' When she nodded he asked, 'Other children?'

'No.' She bit her lip. 'Look, Rick, I'd rather not talk about it any more if you don't mind.'

'OK.' He coloured. 'I wasn't trying to pry.'

'I know you weren't. It's just . . .'

'A difficult subject,' he finished for her. 'I know what you mean, but I'll tell you one thing; I mean to find out who my father is, 'specially now that I've found someone I want to be with. Mum can't keep it from me for ever. I'll get to know the truth sooner or later.'

He drew the car up at the end of Grafton Place. Leaning across he pulled Danni close and kissed her. ' 'Bye, Danni. Meet you after your class on Wednesday?'

She nodded. 'Great. And thanks for a lovely day, Rick.'

'You and Mum – did you like her?'

'Yes. I think she's really cool.' She got out of the car. 'See you on Wednesday.'

She was getting ready for bed when her phone rang. It was Ruth.

'Hi, Mum'

'Hello love. I was thinking – would it be OK if I came over to see you next weekend?'

'For the day, you mean?'

'Well, no. I thought I might come Friday evening and stay till Sunday afternoon.'

Danni's mind worked fast. It meant she wouldn't be able to see Rick, and if Ruth came here to Grafton Place the cat would be out of the bag. That was the last thing she wanted. 'Yeah,' she said, trying hard to sound enthusiastic. 'That'd be great. The only thing is . . .'

'Just say if you'd rather I didn't come,' Ruth said hastily, picking up on Danni's hesitation.

'No! It isn't that. I just wondered where you'd stay.'

'Well, of course I wouldn't expect to stay with you. That would be an imposition and I don't want to put you in an awkward position. Isn't there a B and B anywhere near?'

Danni suddenly thought of Mrs Bell and her heart gave a leap. It was far enough away not to arouse Ruth's suspicions. 'Leave it with me, Mum. I'll book you in somewhere. It'll be lovely to see you. You are all right, aren't you? There's nothing wrong?'

Ruth hesitated on the other end of the line. 'Well – there are one or two problems, but I'll tell you about them when we meet,' she said. 'Nothing for you to worry about though.'

'Right. See you next weekend then, Mum. 'Bye.'

The following evening Danni caught a bus and went along to 28 Church Street. It seemed an age since she had lodged there and as she looked up at the shabby little house she thought of Crane Row and how far she had come since she and Ruth had lived there. Mrs Bell answered her knock on the door and her face lit up in a smile when she saw who her visitor was.

'Well, well! Look what the wind's blown in,' she said. 'Thought I'd never set eyes on you again once you'd moved in with the nobs!' She cackled heartily. 'Come on in, duckie and tell me all your news.'

Sitting in the kitchen over a cup of strong tea Danni told her ex-landlady all about her job and the evening classes while the old lady smiled her approval.

'Well, I reckon you've landed on your feet and no mistake,' she said, refilling Danni's cup. 'Good luck to you, lovie. You've done really well.'

'As a matter of fact my mum is hoping to come and stay next weekend,' Danni said, coming to the point of her visit. 'I was wondering if you could put her up for a couple of nights?'

'Well, my first floor front is vacant at the moment as it happens,' Mrs Bell said. 'It's a bit better than the room you had but it ain't posh and I couldn't do her any food apart from a bit of breakfast.'

'That's all right,' Danni said quickly. 'It's only for the two nights. We can eat out.' A thought suddenly struck her. 'That's a double room, isn't it? I could come and stay with her.'

Mrs Bell looked surprised. 'Don't see why not, love.'

'If that's all right we'll be with you Friday evening then.'

When she got back to Grafton Place Danni went in search

of Claire, whom she found in the studio. 'I've just fixed some-where for my mum to stay next weekend,' she said. 'Would it be OK if I went and stayed with her? It'd only be for Friday and Saturday nights.'

Claire nodded. 'As a matter of fact I'll be away next week-end myself,' she said. 'I've been meaning to tell you. So as it happens it will work out quite well.'

Danni was surprised. 'Are you going somewhere on a job?' she asked.

Claire shook her head. 'No. It's just a little break.'

'I see, so you'll want to lock up the house.'

'No, Mark – Doctor Naylor will still be here.' Claire smiled. 'Oh, by the way, I've got some interesting news. The Frobishers love the designs we submitted. We've got the go-ahead, thanks to you!' She patted Danni's shoulder. 'That'll be something good to tell your mother, won't it?'

CHAPTER ELEVEN

'WHAT do you mean, you need a break?' Mark stared at his wife. 'I was planning a surprise for us this weekend.'

'Not another dinner party for your parents?' Claire said. 'I don't think I could bear it, Mark.'

'No, not a dinner party.' He sighed. 'I know Dad's being really difficult about the Gerald business at the moment. He blames me of course.'

'Me too no doubt. I've got no illusions about what your parents think of me.' She looked at him. 'I'd just like to get away for a couple of days. As it happens Danni will be spending the weekend with her mother, so you'll have the place to yourself.'

'Well, that's something I suppose. That girl is so damned rude. I don't know how you put up with her.'

'It goes both ways,' Claire reminded him. 'Perhaps you're not very civil to her.' She looked at him. 'Anyway, what was this surprise you were planning?' she asked.

'You've chosen to do something else so you'll never know now, will you?'

'In other words you made it up to make me feel guilty.'

He had the grace to smile and hold up his hands. 'OK, you win. Who are you going with, anyway? Anyone I know?'

'Is it out of the question that I might like my own company?'

'No, of course not. I suppose I'll just have to rattle around in the house by myself.'

She raised an eyebrow. 'All I ask is that you don't rattle round it with Fay. I draw the line at her occupying my space.'

Mark winced. 'That's not fair. It was over between Fay and me ages ago and you know it.'

'Do I?' She turned away. 'How can I believe that when she rings you here right under my nose.'

'It's complicated,' he said. 'There's Richard.'

'The son who knows you but doesn't realize you're his father.'

'It was what we both decided would be for the best.'

'You mean it was her punishment for your refusing to acknowledge him.'

He shrugged wearily. 'If you like. Seeing him through his education has meant I had to keep in touch with Fay. As for anything else, you can believe me when I say it was dead and buried long ago.'

Claire turned away. 'If you say so. Frankly, Mark it's not really relevant any more, is it?'

'What do you mean?'

'I mean that our marriage was dead and buried long ago too.'

He took a step towards her. 'It needn't be like that.'

Claire shook her head. 'Admit it, Mark. Nothing I ever do is right. Your parents despise me for not giving them the grandchild they wanted. Sometimes I feel that you do too. I believe you've forgotten what started all this.'

'I haven't. I know none of it has been fair on you.'

'First there was the disastrous termination of the baby I wanted. Then I had to watch you have an affair with Fay which produced a child. I let you talk me into the surrogate thing. I was prepared to go along with all the lies it would have entailed. But we were even deprived of that in the end. Ever since I've had to put up with your parents' sniping and not once have you uttered a word of support for me, Mark. Did you feel that that being married to you was enough to make up for it all?'

He frowned. 'Claire! I can't believe that after all these years you're still holding it against me; you're still so bitter. I thought we'd argued all this out years ago.'

'Did you imagine that "arguing it all out" as you put it would make the pain just go away? Anyway we stopped talking to each other years ago.'

For a long moment he stared at her, then he shrugged and turned away. 'Oh, all right then. Go away for the weekend. Have it your way.'

Have it your way. As if she had ever had it her way! She stared at the door as it closed behind him. Part of her had hoped he would beg her not to go. If he'd uttered one word of encouragement – suggested they took a break together – sat down to talk through their problems, she would have given in; cancelled the weekend and gone with him. Deep down there was really only one thing she really wanted if only Mark realized it. Instead he had shown his usual indifference.

When Ruth stepped down from the train Danni could see the strain on her face.

'Mum!' She ran to her and threw her arms around her. 'I've missed you. How are you?'

'I'm fine. A bit tired,' Ruth said. 'More than anything I need a cup of tea.'

Danni laughed. 'You and your cuppa!' She linked her arm through Ruth's. 'Come on, we'll get one in the buffet before we go.'

Ruth looked better for the tea. Some of the colour came back to her cheeks as she drank it. She smiled at Danni across the table. 'Tell me about this job of yours.'

'I think I've told you most of it,' Danni said. 'Claire is a lovely person and I'm learning more every day.'

'And going to art classes too?'

'Yes. Art and design is what I'm doing.'

'Tell me about this young man you've met. Is it serious?'

'You'd like him, Mum. He's nice, really sweet and funny. He wants to be a landscape gardener.'

'That's interesting.'

'His mum doesn't think so. He's been to uni, you see – got a degree and everything. She thinks it's a bit beneath him.'

'That's a shame.'

'Mum . . .' Danni reached across the table to touch her mother's hand. 'What's wrong? There's something, isn't there?'

'I'm afraid so.' Ruth sighed. 'It's Jim's wife.'

'His late wife, you mean? Is he still talking about her non-stop?'

'It's worse than that,' Ruth said. 'As it happens she didn't die at all. She left him but he was too proud to tell me. Now she's back on the scene – wants to come back.'

'Oh, Mum! What does Jim say? He's sent her packing I should hope.'

'That's just it. You know how he always spoke about her, as though she was perfect. Well, it seems he still thinks so, in spite of what she did.'

'You mean he actually *wants* her back?' Ruth nodded and Danni bit her lip as the implications slowly sank in. 'So what are you going to do?'

Ruth looked up at her daughter. 'I'll have to give in my notice at work, of course,' she said. 'I can't keep on working there, not after what's happened between Jim and me.' She glanced up at Danni. 'It means I'll be homeless and out of work. There'll be nothing to keep me in Meadbridge any more so I've been thinking – time for a change; a fresh start. I thought you and I might move somewhere together; somewhere nice; even by the sea perhaps.' Her face brightened. 'We could find new jobs and get a place together. What do you think?'

Danni's heart lurched. 'Oh, Mum.' She bit her lip, unwilling to hurt her mother. 'I really like it here. I've got just the job I wanted and a chance to get a proper qualification. Then there's Rick. We . . .' She broke off as she saw her mother's wounded expression. 'Oh, Mum, I'm sorry if you're disappointed, but I really don't want to leave Haylesmere.'

Ruth looked up. 'What made you come here in the first place, Danni?' she asked. 'I mean, why Haylesmere.'

Danni was taken aback by the sudden direct question. 'I – don't know.' She shrugged. 'I just stuck a pin in the map.'

'Are you sure?' Ruth looked at her intently. 'Are you sure you're not on a mission?'

'Mission?'

'To try and find your father.'

'I tried that once, didn't I?' Danni swallowed hard, willing herself not to blush. 'It was a disaster.'

'I mean your biological father.'

'What here – in Haylesmere?' Danni tried to feign innocence.'Why would I look for him here?'

Ruth hesitated for a moment, then she shook her head. 'No reason. It was just a thought. Forget it. I've got no right to tell you what to do any more, Danni. You must do whatever you want.'

Danni reached across the table to touch her mother's hand. 'Mum, I'm sorry.'

'That's all right. You're a young woman now. You've made yourself a life and a good one by the sound of it. I'm the last person to want to spoil that for you.'

'Are you sure you'll be all right?'

'Of course. I'll have to be. More fool me for trusting another man,' Ruth said bitterly. She smiled and shook her head. 'Take no notice of me, love. I'm sure this young fellow of yours is different. Next time I come and visit I'll have to meet him.'

'Yes, of course.'

Ruth stood up and gathered her belongings together. 'Right, shall we go then? We've got all weekend to talk, haven't we?'

When Fay received Mark's telephone call just after lunch on Sunday she was surprised.

'Mark! How nice. What can I do for you?'

'Are you free this afternoon?'

'For you – of course I am.'

'We need to talk, Fay. All right if I come over?'

'Now?'

'Yes. Will you be alone?'

Fay smiled to herself. 'Richard has gone to watch cricket with some friends from university.' She lowered her voice seductively, 'We'll have the place to ourselves.'

'Right,' he said briskly. 'I'll see you in about twenty minutes.'

Twenty minutes wasn't long. Fay hurried to her bedroom and changed into the new black dress she had brought home from the shop only yesterday. It fitted her like a second skin and the neckline plunged provocatively. She hastily brushed her hair and put on fresh lipstick. What was it that Mark needed to talk about so urgently? Might he have come to his senses at last and decided to divorce his wife?

She regarded her reflection in the mirror. Were the traces of her angry confrontation with Richard earlier still visible? Before he went out the subject she'd been dreading had come up. Richard had announced that he wanted to leave home – find a place of his own. She'd always known she couldn't keep him with her for ever, of course, but she'd visualized him getting a good teaching post somewhere; moving to another town to take it up because he had to. Not choosing to live separately here in the same town so that everyone would know. But that was what he seemed hell bent on doing – finding himself some grotty bed-sit and living a hand-to-mouth existence with this god-awful manual labouring job. And to cap it all he was even proposing to move this Danni girl in with him.

She'd tried to talk him out of it, tried to keep cool, but as usual she'd said too much, letting her tongue run away with her against all her best intentions.

'You can't seriously be thinking of getting yourself hooked up with *her*?' she'd said when she began to feel her argument slipping away from her.

'What do you mean, *hooked up*?' Richard's face took on the obstinate look she knew so well. She knew she was handling the situation badly but she couldn't stop herself.

'Really, Richard, the girl is not our sort. She's nothing more than a common little . . .'

'Stop right there!' Richard held up his hand. 'I don't want to hear any more. I don't want us to fall out, Mum but I want to be with Danni and you're going to have to get used to it,' he said. 'As soon as we can find a place we're going to move in together.' And with that he had turned on his heel and walked out, leaving her shaking with angry frustration.

She only hoped that Mark had something pleasant to tell her when he arrived. She deserved it. So far it had been a hell of a day.

Fifteen minutes later Mark's car pulled on to her driveway. She'd been watching from the window and had the front door open before he had time to get out of the car.

'Darling! Come in.' She held out welcoming hands.

In the living-room she had the drinks tray out ready. Lifting the bottle of gin she raised an eyebrow at him. He shook his head.

'Too early for me. Fay, sit down. There's something I have to say to you.'

'Oh dear, that sounds ominous,' She sat down uncomfortably on the edge of the sofa. 'Fire away. What's wrong?'

'Us,' he said bluntly. 'It's over between us, Fay. It was over long ago, as I'm sure you know. We've been bound together by Richard all these years, but now he's a man. He doesn't need either of us any more.'

His words hit her like a douche of icy water after the altercation with Richard earlier. She laughed uneasily, determined this time to remain calm. 'Really! What brought this on?'

'I'll be frank,' he said. 'I've been doing a lot of thinking lately. I've been blind all these years – thinking that taking over the family practice was everything. Now I know that it isn't. Father's behaviour is impossible to tolerate and I've finally had enough. I'm planning to throw in the towel; make a complete break. Maybe Claire won't want to go along with it. I couldn't blame her. She's had the rough end of things for years. But I mean to do everything I can to try and make it up to her.'

'*She's* had the rough end of things!' Fay got up, her colour rising. 'I don't see why you should consider her. If she hadn't got rid of your child all those years ago you'd have been able to satisfy your father's demands. I'm the one who gave you a son; the one who's been faithful to you even though you refused to acknowledge us.'

'I know that and I'll . . .'

'I do hope you're not going to suggest paying me off!' Fay said. 'because I refuse to allow you to insult me like that.'

'Claire didn't want to get rid of our child,' he admitted with a sigh. 'I made her. Because of that she's had to face a life without the children she wanted so much. All these years I've let her take the blame and lately I've begun to see how selfish I've been. I want to try to make amends.'

'How noble of you!' She sneered. 'Well, don't think that after all the years I've given you – everything I've sacrificed, I'm going to lie down and let you walk out on me just like that! You have a son. You are Richard's father. He may not have been good enough for you to acknowledge but you needn't think you can drop him that easily!'

'But he doesn't know I'm his father. That was your decision.'

'I thought it was kinder to him – at the time. Now I think differently,' she said, her eyes flashing with spite. 'Richard has been desperate for me to tell him who his father is for some time and I think the time has come for him to know.'

'What would that achieve?'

'It would stop him making a mess of his life for a start. He needs a father's firm hand, Mark, someone who'll talk to him man to man,' she went on. 'Did you know he'd taken a job with Rowlands, this local landscaping firm?' Mark shook his head. 'And that he was seeing that girl who works for your wife?'

Mark looked shocked. 'Danielle?'

'Is that her stupid name?' Fay shrugged her shoulders. 'He seems determined to leave me and move into some squalid little bed-sit with the little trollop. She's a bad influence on him. You could put a stop to it.'

'Tell him I'm his father if you want to,' Mark said. 'But I don't see how I could stop him doing anything if he's made up his mind. It's none of my business and none of yours either if it comes to that. Richard is a man now. You might be his mother but you can't dominate his life for ever.'

Fay was rapidly beginning to lose control. Her face was crimson and the veins in her neck knotted as angry tears welled up in her eyes. 'I'm about to lose everyone and everything that means anything in my life and nobody gives a damn,' she said. 'I could have married. I could have had a proper family with a real father for my children.'

He took a step towards her. 'Fay – don't.'

'Don't touch me!' She fumbled for a handkerchief and dabbed at her red-rimmed eyes. 'But you go ahead, Mark.

You make amends and get your life and your marriage back on track – if you can. If you want to know, I think you're making this – this *saintly gesture* of yours too late!'

Mark was silent for a moment, something Claire had said yesterday echoing in his memory. 'What do you mean, too late?' he asked.

'It really hasn't occurred to you, has it, that poor Claire might have stopped loving you? You're so eaten up with your own conceit that you couldn't imagine that she might have turned to someone else.' There was a stunned silence and Fay threw back her head and gave a triumphant yelp of laughter. 'Haven't you guessed that she's having an affair, Mark? Are you still so blindly arrogant that you haven't noticed anything?'

He stared at her. 'Affair? Who could she be having an affair with?'

'Anyone who took her fancy I should imagine! And who could blame her, especially after what you've just told me?' She smiled, jubilant that at last she'd shocked him into silence.

Again he stared at her speechlessly. 'Do you have anything to substantiate your accusation?'

Fay laughed. 'I've spotted her meeting someone – in the car park at the back of the market place.' She waited for this piece of information to sink in, then she asked, 'Where is Claire this afternoon by the way?' She cocked an eyebrow at him. '*Know*, do you?'

Mark's mind was spinning. Could it be possible that Claire had gone away this weekend with another man? Had that been what she meant when she said it was too late? Could what Fay be saying have any truth in it? He gathered himself quickly and put on an impassive face. 'Claire and I have never had secrets from each other. You know that. She knew about our affair. She knows about Richard. And she also knows that it's over between you and me. I'm sure that if there were anyone else she would have been honest with me about it. But it makes no difference, Fay. Whatever happens I shan't be seeing you again after today, so you might as well get used to it.'

'That's what you think. You'll be back,' she goaded. 'You'll come crawling back, just as you always have, when she won't let you into her bed and you need a quick—'

'Shut up, Fay! For God's sake let's at least be dignified about this. You know you'll regret it later if you let your temper run away with you.'

She stood facing him, breathing fast, trying desperately to swallow the anger that rose in her throat like bile, almost choking her. At last she forced her heartbeat to slow and felt her muscles relax. She had one last trump card to play but as her heart stopped pounding a small voice in the back of her mind told her to keep it to herself.

'All right,' she said. 'You can go. You can forget Richard and me – pretend we never existed. And I hope it brings you luck. I hope your conscience will let you sleep at night.'

He shook his head 'My conscience is clear, Fay. I've always tried to do the right thing by you and Richard.'

'If that's what you believe then good luck to you, Mark,' she said with a smile. At that moment the sound of car wheels was heard on the gravel outside the window. 'That's your son. You can tell him now if you like. Shall we do it together or do you want me to leave you to do it alone?'

He flung past her and pulled open the front door. On the drive Richard was getting out of the car. 'Hi, Mark,' he said with a smile.

'Richard.' Mark got into his car and threw the car into gear, spinning the wheels and sending up a shower of gravel as he reversed out of the gateway. Richard stood watching him in bewilderment. Inside the house his mother seemed agitated.

'All right, Mum?'

She shook her head. 'I've got a dreadful headache. I'm

going to lie down for an hour.'

'Mark OK?'

'Oh yes,' she said, trying not to sound bitter. 'Mark is just fine.'

Lying on the bed with the curtains drawn she tried to formulate a plan. George Naylor was entitled to know that he had a grandson. He was entitled to know what kind of man his son was too. She imagined the pompous old man's face deflating and smiled to herself. Perhaps Mark would change his mind about the practice not being the most important thing in his life when he was out on his ear and looking for another job! And once George knew how badly he'd been misled all these years he might even feel the need to alter his will. The tension left her face and her lips curved in a satisfied smile.

'You didn't really think you were going to get everything all your own way, did you, Mark Naylor? It's payback time now!' she whispered into her pillow. 'Time to reap what you've sown.'

CHAPTER TWELVE

Driving back to Haylesmere Claire could not remember when she had felt so tired or downcast.

The weekend had been a disaster. The moment they had arrived at the hotel she had known it was a bad mistake. She felt like a slut, checking in at reception, going upstairs with Adam. The moment the door closed behind them she had turned to him.

'I'm sorry, Adam. I can't do this.'

He had stared at her, aghast. 'What do you mean? Can't do what?'

'I can't stay here with you. I'm sorry – *really* sorry but I've got to go.'

He put his hands on her shoulders. 'Calm down. You're panicking. Just sit down and we'll talk.'

'You're overwrought,' he told her. 'This weekend is just what you need. You've been married to Mark for a long time. It's bound to feel wrong. But we're not children, Claire. We both know what we're doing, what we want.'

'Do we?' She turned huge, anxious eyes on him. '*You* might know, Adam, but I'm further from being sure now than I ever was.' She gave a shuddering sigh. 'I told you ages ago that we should stop seeing each other. Why couldn't you just leave it?'

'You know why.' He reached for her hand. 'Because I love you.'

She shook her head. 'You'll get over it, Adam. You have to. This could wreck your career. You're young. You have your whole life ahead of you.'

'None of it matters without you.'

'Yes, it does!'

'Just tell me one thing.'

'What?' She knew what he was about to ask. And she knew how hurt he would be by the reply she knew she must make. She had to force herself to meet his eyes as he spoke.

'Do you love me? Because if you feel as I do then I know we can overcome anything.'

She drew her hand away from his. 'No, Adam. I love – I *thought* I loved you. But it's not in the way you want. Not as you deserve to be loved.'

'You don't mean that.'

'I do. You must believe me.'

His mouth twisted with bitterness. 'You'll be telling me in a minute that you still love Mark.'

'I've been married to Mark for a long time,' she said slowly. 'Once I loved him more than anything in the world. I've made sacrifices for him; taken the blame for what wasn't my fault. I've put up with his unfaithfulness.'

'So why the hell do you want to stay with him?'

'Because in a funny way those things bind you together as much as happiness,' she told him. 'Oh, I can't expect you to understand. Maybe you will when you've lived a bit longer.'

'Do you have to keep throwing that in my face?'

She reached for his hand again. 'Adam – please believe me. This really is for the best. I promise you. You'll meet some lovely girl of your own age; marry and have a family. You'll be a successful doctor. You can't throw all that away for an infatuation.'

'It's not—'

141

'Yes, it is. And it will pass.'

'Is that all it's been for you?' he asked bitterly. 'A diversion – a bit of a laugh?'

'Far from that, Adam.' She said sadly. 'Far from that.' She shook her head and stood up. 'Will you drive me back to the King's Head?'

'And if I say no?'

She shrugged. 'I'll ask reception to ring for a cab.'

His shoulders drooped. 'OK. You win.'

The drive from Norfolk had seemed interminable. They had hardly exchanged a word. He had dropped her at the tiny village pub where she had left her own car and she watched him drive away with a bitter-sweet ache in her heart.

Luckily there was a vacant room at the King's Head and she stayed for the rest of the weekend. Those two nights felt like the longest and loneliest she had ever spent. She hurt for Adam. He had looked so bereft when he left her. She had her own regrets too. Being loved again had been like a heady narcotic. Being the centre in someone's world had made her feel special. She'd been flattered and deeply aware that it might be her last chance at happiness. But thinking about it in the sleepless, small hours of the morning she had faced the fact that however much Adam thought that what he felt for her was real it would never have lasted. For all the reasons she had given him, and more, it was wrong. She must hope that he would come to realize it and maybe even thank her some day.

The house was quiet when she let herself in. Downstairs in the studio there was a note from Danni on her desk.

Taken Maddie for a walk. Back soon. Hope you had a nice week-end. Danni.

Claire picked up her bag and went upstairs to take off her outdoor things. She closed the bedroom door and looked around her at all the familiar things. She and Mark no longer shared a bedroom. They hadn't for some time. This was her room; her private space; yet in spite of the familiarity of the surroundings it suddenly felt the most alien, the most lonely place in the world. What happens now? she asked herself as she took off her outdoor things and began to unpack her bag. What's left? She had thrown away her last chance of being wanted being happy and loved, for what? To face more years of empty loneliness? It was then that the tears began. All the emotion she had suppressed over the last two days welled up, tearing painfully at her chest and throat. Sinking down on the bed she gave way to the sobs that threatened to choke her, weeping as she hadn't wept since Ruth had walked through the door all those years ago carrying her baby daughter – and Claire's last chance of motherhood.

On her way upstairs to her room on the second floor Danni paused outside her employer's bedroom door. The muffled sounds of Claire's distress made her bite her lip. She hovered uncertainly, her hand reaching for the door handle. Her first instinct was to go in and try to comfort her but something made her hesitate. It was really none of her business. Maybe the cause of Claire's anguish was something private that she wanted to keep to herself. Perhaps she would be embarrassed by Danni's concern. Claire was entitled to her privacy. Better leave her.

On Monday morning Claire was up bright and early. Danni was finishing her breakfast downstairs in the kitchen when her employer breezed in. It was clear at once that she was in an enthusiastic mood.

'Good morning, Danni. We've got a busy day ahead of us. I'm sure you're as eager to get started on the Frobishers' project as I am.'

Danni looked up. 'Of course, but do you really need me to come too?'

Claire looked at her in surprise. 'Of course I do. Most of this is your project.'

'I took Maddie out before breakfast so she's OK, but – what about the housework?'

Claire waved a dismissive hand. 'Oh, that can wait. In fact I'm thinking of getting a woman in to do that. You're far more valuable to me in the business.'

Danni flushed with pride. 'Really?'

Claire smiled. 'Yes, really – if that's all right with you.'

'You bet! What do we do first?'

Claire sat down at the kitchen table and took out her note-book to make notes. 'Well, first I think we'd better go and get the decorators booked,' she said. 'Show them our colour schemes so that they can start mixing the paint. After that I'd like to go to the wholesalers and look at fabrics and carpets. We'll have a tour round the auction houses and pick up some catalogues – see what's coming up in future sales. Finally I'd like to go out to the house and take some final measurements, because although the tradesmen always take them I always like to take my own just to be on the safe side.'

'Right. What shall we do in the afternoon?' Danni asked with a grin.

Claire stared at her for a moment then laughed. 'You're right. It does sound like a tall order for one day but we can try, eh?'

'We certainly can.' Danni was pleased to see that Claire had obviously got over whatever was troubling her the previous evening. 'Did you enjoy your weekend?' she asked.

'The weekend?' Claire's bright smile slipped briefly. 'Oh, yes – it was fine,' she said, gathering up her briefcase and handbag. 'We'll go then, if you're ready.'

The morning passed in a whirlwind of activity. Danni watched as Claire showed the decorator the colours she wanted and he promised to have the special blues, greens and yellows specially mixed to match the cards she had prepared for him. The fabric house was an Aladdin's cave of colour and texture as was the adjoining carpet warehouse. Claire asked for Danni's opinion on every count and seemed to take her views on board, which Danni found flattering.

At the auction house they learned that there were plenty of sales corning up and they retired to a pub to eat lunch and study the catalogues. Claire wasn't sure what the Frobishers' taste was so she made a note to go and show them the catalogues and ask their permission to bid for anything they fancied.

The clock on the car's dashboard was pointing at 4.30 as they drove up the drive of Waterlees Manor, the Frobishers' house. Claire let herself in with the key that had been entrusted to her, then took out her electronic measuring device and went from room to room, measuring floors and windows, Danni following with pen and notebook. As they opened the drawing-room door on the first floor the room was flooded with late afternoon sunlight. Claire drew a deep breath and sat down on one of the wide window ledges.

'Oh, isn't it lovely? I think we'll have to have window seats here.' She looked round the room. 'Can't you just imagine how beautiful it will be in here decorated with all the colours you've chosen?' she asked Danni. 'You have a real eye for colour, you know.' She patted the window ledge beside her. 'Come and sit down for a minute and enjoy the sunshine. You've earned a breather. I've worked you really hard today.'

As Danni sat down beside Claire she noticed the fine lines around her eyes. The make-up, so carefully applied this morning, was fading and she could see the signs of unhappiness and a sleepless night. Reaching out she touched Claire's arm.

'Are you all right?'

'Don't I look all right?' Claire shook her head. 'I'm sorry. I didn't mean to snap. I'm a bit tired actually – didn't sleep all that well.'

'Sometimes I think you try to do too much,' Danni ventured. 'You've got me now, remember. I'm here to take the strain.' To her astonishment Claire's eyes filled with tears.

'Danni! How sweet. I'm quite touched.' Claire hastily dashed away the tears with the back of her hand.

'Did – did something happen at the weekend?' Danni asked, then immediately bit her lip. 'Oh! I'm sorry! Forget I asked that. Sometimes I let my tongue run away with me.'

Claire took her hand and squeezed it. 'You're very perceptive,' she said. 'And you're right. The weekend wasn't fine at all. It was a disaster. Suffice to say that I almost made a horrible mistake.'

'But you didn't. So that's all right.'

Claire sighed. 'Sometimes making the right decision is the hardest thing you can do,' she said. 'The hardest, the most hurtful and the bleakest.'

Danni nodded. 'I know,' she said.

Claire looked at her. 'You said that as though you really do know,' she said. 'Surely at your tender age you haven't been faced with any life-changing decisions?'

'I have, actually.' Danni paused. 'I decided some time ago to find my true father. It all seemed so simple and straight forward at the time.'

'So – did you find him?'

Danni nodded with a sigh. 'Yes. But there it has to end. Coming out into the open about it would cause too much trouble.'

Claire sighed. 'Nothing is ever as simple as it seems,' she said. 'What about this young man you've been seeing? Is everything all right there?'

Danni smiled. 'Rick? Yes, he's lovely. I'm so lucky to have found him.' She looked at Claire. 'As a matter of fact I was going to talk to you about him.'

'OK, fire away. No time like the present.'

'He lives with his mother at the moment,' Danni began. 'But he's got a job – just the job he wanted. And he's hoping to move out and get a place of his own. It won't be much – not to start with, but . . .'

'But he wants you to share it with him?' Claire looked into her eyes. 'And what about you, Danni; what do you want?'

'I'd like to be with him,' Danni said. 'But I like living at Grafton Place too. If it meant that things would be difficult . . .'

'You do what you want,' Claire said. 'What your heart tells you. Your job is safe if that's what's worrying you. If you move out we'll have to rethink your salary and hours and so on. We'd have to do that anyway now that you're working more or less full time with me. But as for decisions, be your own person. Love is a powerful emotion, Danni. Sometimes it makes you do things against your better judgement. Don't allow that to happen. You can't please everyone and sometimes one false move made for the wrong reason can ruin your whole life.' She looked into Danni's eyes for a moment then put on her brightest smile. 'Heavens! Just listen to me. Talk about an agony aunt.' She stood up. 'Look at the time. We'll have to stop off at Marks and Spencer's now to get something quick for dinner!'

The moment was gone, but Danni felt that in those few minutes she and Claire had become closer – far closer than employer and employee. She guessed that Claire's advice had been prompted by the termination she regretted so bitterly. Clearly it had left a painful scar on her memory. She wondered if Ruth had ever known about it.

It was almost a week later when Adam knocked on Mark's door late one afternoon after surgery.

'Come in and have a seat,' Mark invited. 'What can I do for you?'

Adam pushed an envelope across the desk. 'I'm afraid it's my resignation,' he said. 'I applied for a place in an Edinburgh practice a while ago. I went for an interview on my day off and they offered me the job. I start on the first of next month.'

Mark frowned. 'Well, congratulations of course but I do think you might have given me some warning.'

'I know. I'm sorry, but I wasn't sure that I really wanted the job at the time.'

'And how did you manage an interview in Edinburgh in one day?'

'I flew up.'

'So that you wouldn't have to ask for time off?'

'Again, I wasn't sure . . .'

'Hedging your bets?' Mark shook his head. 'The first of the month is only ten days away. I hope you realize how difficult this makes things for me. I'll have to advertise – sift through the applicants and conduct interviews; find a locum to fill the gap. You know how long it all takes.'

'I know. I'm sorry.'

'What with the building work and everything this really is something I can do without at the moment.'

Adam shifted uncomfortably in his seat. 'I – suppose I could turn the job down – either that or ask for a deferment.'

'Oh don't put yourself out,' Mark snapped. 'I daresay we'll muddle along – somehow. We usually do.' He stood up. 'Well, if that's all I'll say good evening, Adam. It's been a long and difficult day and I'd quite like to get home.'

Claire was in the kitchen preparing the evening meal when he walked down the basement stairs. She looked up as he came in. 'Hello. Good day?'

'No, bloody awful as a matter of fact.' He opened the fridge and took out a bottle of wine. 'The builders have come up with yet another snag – something to do with building regulations. Everyone seems to have come down with this gastric flu bug and to cap it all I had Adam in just as I was leaving, tendering his resignation, would you believe? Leaving me *ten whole days* to fill his place!' He poured himself a generous glass of wine and looked at her. 'Do you want one?'

'Yes please.' She continued to stir the sauce she was making. 'So – you're losing Adam?'

He sat down at the table. 'Yes, to some practice in Edinburgh. Seems he can't get far enough away from us!' He took a long draught of his wine. 'Mind you, I can't really say I blame him. What with the building work and Dad's constant interference trying to work at Charlesworth Avenue has been pretty fraught over the past few months. The irony is that we're going to finish up with a state of the art medical centre and no doctors.' He gave a short laugh. 'It'd serve Dad right in a way.' He drained his glass and refilled it, glancing at Claire's back. 'I don't mind telling you, I've thought seriously more than once of backing out and leaving Dad to it myself.'

She turned to look at him. 'You? I thought that Charlesworth Avenue was the be-all and end-all for you.'

'So did I once. That was when I thought that when Dad retired I'd be in charge.' He laughed again. 'Huh! How wrong can you be?'

Hope made Claire's heart quicken. She pushed the pan to the back of the hob and sat down opposite him with her glass of wine. 'If you feel like that what's to stop you moving out anyway?'

He shook his head. 'After all these years?'

'You're still a doctor, Mark; a good doctor. There's nothing to stop you setting up on your own. I'm pretty sure that most of your patients would go with you.'

'I don't think I could do it,' he said quietly. 'It's too late. I've invested too many years in Dad and Charlesworth Avenue.'

Claire was silent for a moment, thinking about the years she had invested too. She waited to see if Mark would show a chink of hope; prompt her to encourage him. He didn't.

'I'd be behind you,' she said, looking at him. 'I'd back you up – a hundred per cent.'

He looked back at her and just for a moment she saw the youthful spark she'd fallen in love with all those years ago come back into his eyes. Then they clouded again and he smiled cynically. 'You'd love to get a pop back at Dad, wouldn't you?' he said.

'I was thinking of you actually,' she said 'Of us.' *If there is still an us*, she added under her breath. She got up and went back to the cooker. 'If you want to grab a shower the meal will be ready in about fifteen minutes,' she said, beginning to stir again.

Rick was waiting when Danni came out of her evening class. She could see at once that he was bubbling over with news.

'Guess what? I think I've found us a place,' he said.

'No kidding!' She slipped her arm through his. 'Where? Can we go and see it? What's the rent?'

He laughed. 'I can show you the outside. If you want to see inside you'll have to wait till tomorrow. It's on the first floor of a house in Market Street.'

'That's right in the middle of the town. Not far from work for me.'

'Exactly. It's a large bed-sit with a tiny kitchen and an *en-suite* shower room.'

'Wow! Luxury,' she said.

'Well, better than I'd hoped.'

'Can we afford it?'

'That's the best bit,' Rick told her. 'The owner is someone I know slightly. She's one of Mum's customers and I've delivered things to her from time to time. She's just bought this house as an investment, to rent out as flats, so it's all newly decorated. Thing is, there's this big garden at the back and I've suggested to her that I can landscape it for her in my spare time. She jumped at the idea and because of that she'll let us have it cheaper.'

'Is your new employer OK with that?' she asked. 'The landscaping bit I mean.'

He nodded. 'He's fine, even offered to let me get the materials from his supplier. It'll be mostly paving and gravel. She's no gardener – wants to keep the horticulture down to a few tubs. It's a doddle really, and for that we'd get the flat at thirty per cent off.'

She pulled his head round and planted a kiss firmly on his lips. 'You're a genius!'

'Have you spoken to Miss Cavendish about giving up your room?' he asked.

'Yes. She's fine – says we'll have to rethink my money and hours but as for moving out, it's not a problem.' She looked at him. 'What about you? Have you told your mum?'

He pulled a face. 'Not yet. I thought it'd be better to wait till we'd found somewhere – got a date fixed for moving. A sort of *fait accompli*.'

She laughed. 'Chicken!'

'You wouldn't come with me to tell her, would you?'

'And let her think it was all my idea? No way! You're on your own with this one, Rick.'

'I thought you'd say that. And you're right of course. I'll do it tonight before I go to bed.'

She pulled the corners of her mouth down. 'I think you'd be better breaking the news first thing tomorrow before you both go off to work,' she said. 'Things always seem worse when you lie awake thinking about them.'

'OK. Let's go and have a drink to celebrate, shall we? Then a walk in the park before I take you home.'

She hugged his arm. 'Oh, Rick. Just think: a place of our very own. I can't wait!'

'What do you mean, you've found a place of your own?' Fay stared at Richard across the breakfast table. 'You've got a perfectly good home here.'

He winced. He'd known she wouldn't take it well. 'We've talked about this, Mum. It's time I stood on my own feet,' he said. 'I'm really grateful for all you've done for me over the years – all the support and everything, but I'm twenty-two and it's high time I started living on my own.'

'Except that you won't be on your own, will you?' Fay said. 'That little – that *girl* will be moving in with you, won't she?'

He nodded. 'I told you – we want to be together.'

Fay laughed. 'You're so naïve. If you think a girl like that will be faithful to you then you're even more stupid than you seem.'

'Why are you so down on her?' he asked.

'Because I know the type; brought up on a council estate with a loose-living mother. No education, no breeding . . .'

'You are a single mother too,' he reminded her. 'Is that how you want other people to see you?'

'It's not the same.' She turned away. 'Your father was an educated man with a good family background, Richard. There's a world of difference between her circumstances and yours.'

'If he's so marvellous why hasn't he married you?' he asked. 'Why has he never been around for me?'

Fay bit her lip hard. Her impulse was to tell him Mark was his father. That he had always been around for him; supporting him financially if nothing else; that it was her fault he'd never known him as a father. 'You don't know what you're talking about, Richard,' she said.

'Anyway, how do you know that Danni's father wasn't educated? And what does it matter anyway? Danni is her own person. She's got guts. She's working really hard to make the best of herself.'

Fay shook her head. 'I'm not going to discuss it with you, Richard. You must do as you please. Go your own way and make your own mistakes just as we all have to. You know your home will be here when you come to your senses.'

He stood up, relieved that she seemed to have calmed down. 'Thanks for that, Mum. I'll have to go now. See you later.'

She nodded. 'Yes. See you later.'

She got up and stood at the window to watch him go. Tall and broad-shouldered. Her son. Hers and Mark's. Yes, he was a man now and she had to face the fact. She'd handled things all wrong, she told herself. If only she'd told Richard when he was a child that Mark was his father maybe things might have worked out differently. She'd been bitter because Mark wouldn't acknowledge his own son – wouldn't leave Claire and marry her. She'd wanted to punish him. But she'd only succeeded in punishing herself. Now she was about to lose the only two people she'd ever cared deeply for. She faced a forlorn future. But if her life was to be bleak and lonely then someone must pay. And pay they would. She'd make sure of it.

CHAPTER THIRTEEN

T HE news item made the front page of the local paper.

WELL LOVED DOCTOR TO PUT UP FOR
LOCAL COUNCIL

Below was the announcement that Doctor George Naylor was to stand as Conservative candidate in the coming council by-election caused by the death of Councillor Tom Crawford. There followed a run-down of George's career and standing in the town as senior partner at the long established Charlesworth Avenue Medical Centre since 1968 when he took over from his late father, Doctor Henry Naylor. The article was extensive and accompanied by a photograph of George with his wife, Mary in their garden. Nowhere in the article was there any mention that he had retired and handed over the reins to his son.

Mark threw down the paper in disgust. 'Typical! He can't even give me the credit for taking over from him at the practice,' he said.

Claire picked up the paper and read the article for herself. 'The one good thing is that he'll probably be too busy to interfere in the running of the practice once he gets in,' she said.

'Want to bet? Anyway, you mean *if* he gets in,' Mark said.

'It'll be just my luck if he doesn't. He'll be worse than ever if that happens!'

Claire got up and began to clear the table. 'When Danni gets back from walking Maddie we're off to an auction sale,' she said. 'So if you're sure you've had enough . . .'

'Yes.' Mark stood up. 'Time I was off anyway.' He paused. 'It's your birthday next week,' he said. 'What would you like to do?'

She turned to look at him in surprise. 'Me?'

He laughed. 'Of course, *you*! What do you think – a meal; the theatre or a film? Is there anything on you want to see?'

Claire was taken aback. For the last two years Mark had been hard put to it to remember her birthday at all. 'Well – I'll have to think about it.'

He crossed the kitchen and put his hands on her shoulders. 'It seems ages since we did anything together.'

'It *is* ages.'

'Then I suggest we put that right.' He bent towards her. 'You know I . . .'

'Phew! We got back just in time. It's starting to rain . . .' Danni bustled into the kitchen with Maddie and stopped short. 'Oh – sorry!'

Mark dropped his hands to his sides. 'High time I was off anyway.' He picked up his case. ' 'Bye then.' He paused for a moment then bent to kiss Claire briefly on the cheek.

'Goodbye.' Claire was visibly shaken by the gesture, colouring pink as Mark ran up the basement stairs.

'Sorry. Did I interrupt something?' Danni asked.

Claire laughed. 'Who knows? I've no idea what Mark was trying to say.' She bent to take off Maddie's lead. 'We'd better get going now, Danni. The sale starts at ten and we have to drive out to Woodbridge.'

As Fay unfolded her copy of the *Courier* the article about Doctor George Naylor sprang off the front page at her. As she read, her heart began to jump with a rush of adrenaline. It couldn't be better. This was just what she needed to put her plan into action. The by-election was to take place in four weeks' time, which meant that canvassing would be well under way by now. The next few weeks would be vital. George Naylor was going to need all the publicity he could get – *favourable* publicity that was. What she found even more advantageous was the invitation at the end of the article: *Anyone willing to help with canvassing or in the committee room please e-mail Doctor Naylor* – there followed his e-mail address. Maybe Doctor Naylor wasn't the only one beginning a campaign, she told herself. And the sooner she began hers, the better!

Armed with Doctor George Naylor's e-mail address she decided to begin by sending him a message. Arriving at *Style and Grace* she told her assistant that she was going to catch up with some paper work; then, in the privacy of the tiny office at the back she switched on her computer and drafted a letter.

Dear Doctor Naylor
You don't know me but I would like to take this opportunity to congratulate you on standing for the council and wish you the best of luck for the coming by-election.
I happen to be in possession of a piece of important informa-tion that I feel you should have. This information concerns your family and is something that I feel will be crucial to your popularity and ultimate success.
It you are interested I shall be in the lounge bar of the Red Lion at six o'clock this evening. Please do not take this letter as in any way hostile. I wish you well and want only to help.
Fay Scott.

She read the e-mail through several times then, satisfied with it, she clicked on 'send' and switched off.

*

The auction sale had been a success for Claire. On behalf of her clients she had bid successfully for several items of antique furniture. When she and Danni got back to Grafton Place it was 4.30.

'I suggest that we have something to eat and then you can take the rest of the day off,' Claire said. 'We've done really well today and I've got two women coming later about the cleaning job so I shan't need you again today.'

'I'll take Maddie out, shall I?' Danni suggested.

'Fine. While you're gone I'll make omelettes. OK with you?'

Dannie walked Maddie round the park, then returned to share her meal with Claire. While they were eating Claire said, 'I've been thinking. How would you like to learn to drive?'

Danni looked up in surprise. 'I'd love to.'

'You'd be even more useful to me as a driver. There'd be so many errands you could do to save me time. I'll pay for lessons. Would you like me to lay it on for you?'

'Oh, yes please,' Danni said excitedly. 'I can't wait!'

Claire laughed. 'Have you been to see this new flat your boyfriend's found yet?'

'No. We're going this evening.'

'And I bet you can't wait for that either.' Claire got up and filled the kettle for coffee. 'I'm going to miss having you around the place,' she said. 'Maddie will miss you too.' She looked down at the little dog who was staring up adoringly at Danni, hoping she'd saved a few tit-bits from her plate.

'I'll miss you too,' Danni said. 'But don't worry. I'll be here bright and early every morning to take Maddie for her walkie.' She reached down to stroke the dog's ears. 'I wouldn't let my little mate down, would I?'

She met Rick at their usual meeting place at six o'clock. He had rushed home to change out of his working clothes and have a quick shower.

'Did you tell your mum where you were going?' she asked him.

He shook his head. 'She wasn't in. She must have stayed on at the shop for some reason. To be honest it was a relief. Things have been a bit fraught between us since I told her I was moving out.'

Market Street branched off the market square and had once been one of the most select parts of Haylesmere. The houses were Victorian, three storeys high and originally built at the height of the industrial revolution for the newly created middle classes.

Number 12 was newly painted and Danni took to it on sight. Already she could see that the first floor had tall windows that would let in plenty of light. The landlady, Mrs Clark took them upstairs and opened the door of Flat 2. Danni looked around it in delight. As she had expected, the two long windows let in a flood of light. The large room which ran the whole width of the house had been partitioned to make a small kitchen and a tiny adjoining shower room. A double bed was concealed in a curtained-off alcove.

'You'd be completely self-contained,' Mrs Clark said. 'And as you can see it's been newly decorated and furnished.' She looked at the two shining faces. 'Well, I'll let you have a few minutes to think about it, shall I?'

As the door closed Danni flung herself into Rick's arms. 'Oh! It's gorgeous!' she enthused. 'You were so clever to find it. I love it and I can't wait for us to move in and be a real couple.'

He held her at arm's length and looked into her eyes. 'You are sure that this is what you want, aren't you, Danni? I mean – really *sure*.'

'Of course I'm sure,' she said, giving him a playful push. 'I want us to be together. You know that.'

'I mean . . .' Rick paused. 'Look, Danni, what I'm trying to say is that to me this is a serious commitment, not just a casual fling. I love you and I'd like to think it was a long term thing – that later on – maybe in a couple of years or so we might even get married and have a family.'

She laughed. 'Wow! We *are* getting heavy, aren't we?'

'I'm not joking,' he said. 'And I think we should talk about it now, before we decide to move in together.' He held her shoulders and made her eyes meet his. 'You've never really said how you feel.'

'Don't be daft. You know how I feel.'

'But I want to hear you say it. I want us to . . .' He swallowed hard. 'OK, it might sound silly to you, but I'd like us to promise each other; make some kind of vow.'

She looked back at him, seeing in his eyes how deeply he felt and realizing that he needed reassurance from her. She took a deep breath.

'It's not easy for me, Rick, this talking about feelings. I've only ever had Mum in my life and we were never big on this in-depth stuff. I've never had any really close friends either, just acquaintances and school-mates; no one I ever really wanted to open up to. But you – you are the very best thing that's ever happened to me and if I don't say so it's because I can't really believe my luck and I'm afraid that if I take it for granted I might lose you. And thinking about that terrifies me . . .' She paused to take a breath. 'We think in the same way as each other. You make me laugh and I want you to be happy and have all the things you've ever dreamed of. Your dreams are my dreams too, Rick.' She lifted her shoulders and laughed a little self-consciously. 'If that's love then – I love you, Rick. And I always will.'

He drew her close and kissed her. 'You don't know how happy that makes me, Danni,' he said with a sigh. 'So – shall we go and tell Mrs Clark we'll take it, on the terms we arranged?'

She grinned and reached up to ruffle his hair. 'You bet,' she said.

*

The lounge bar of the Red Lion was quiet. Fay bought herself a drink and had a word with the barman, telling him whom she was expecting. She took a seat in a secluded corner and settled down to wait.

She had no idea what Mark's father looked like but when she saw a well-dressed, slightly portly man enter the bar and glance around she knew instinctively who he was. The man went to the bar and ordered a drink. He spoke to the barman who pointed Fay out to him and George Naylor picked up his glass and made his way towards her across the room.

'Mrs Scott?'

'*Miss* Scott actually.'

'Good evening, Miss Scott.' He sat down and put his whisky and soda on the table. 'Can I get you anything?' She shook her head, indicating the half-finished gin and tonic in front of her.

'I wouldn't normally meet a woman like this but I'll be frank; I found your e-mail intriguing.' He looked at her. 'I can't spare too much time so I'll come straight to the point. What is this important information you have to tell me?'

Fay took a sip of her drink, her eyes downcast. 'It's just that I think you should know that you have a grandson you're unaware of,' she said.

He stared at her for a moment then shook his head. 'You are mistaken,' he said. 'I have only one son and he has no children.'

'With respect it is you who are mistaken,' she told him. 'Mark does have a son. He is twenty-two and his name is Richard.'

George's colour deepened, but he remained calm. 'I take it you have proof of this?'

Fay smiled. 'I certainly have. I am his mother. I have been Mark's mistress for the past twenty-five years – ever since his wife aborted their child.'

George's eyes blazed. 'Ever since she *what*? What are you saying?'

'Your daughter-in-law found that being pregnant was an untimely inconvenience so she aborted the child she and Mark were expecting. Unfortunately the termination caused complications and she was unable to have another child.'

'And you're telling me that my son and you have had a child behind his wife's back.'

'Not at all. Claire has always known about it, which is probably why she persuaded Mark to try surrogacy a few years later.'

'Surrogacy?' George's eyes were bulging now and his colour had deepened to purple. 'I hope you have irrevocable proof of this slander, madam.'

'It is no slander. I have only Mark's word about the surrogacy,' Fay said. 'Apparently the mother decided to keep the baby after all. As for your grandson . . .' She opened her bag and took out a photograph. 'This is Richard on his graduation day. I think you will agree that he bears a startling resemblance to his father. But there is always DNA testing if you have any real doubts'

George stared at the photograph, momentarily lost for words. 'What is all this about? What do you want?' he asked at last. 'If it's money . . .'

'Please.' Fay held up her hand. 'I haven't come here to blackmail you. Mark has been fair in that respect. He has paid for Richard's education, and made sure that we did not go without.'

'So just what is the purpose of this meeting?'

'I thought it was high time you knew about Richard,' Fay told him. 'My son has no idea who his father is. All his life he has been deprived of a proper family. There have been times when I've longed for a paternal influence for him, but right from the first Mark has refused to publicly acknowledge

Richard as his son. It is something which saddens me deeply.'

'What do you want me to do about it?'

Fay drained her glass. 'I want you to persuade Mark to tell Richard that he is his father,' she said. 'I think my son has the right to know.'

George shook his head. 'Mark is a grown man. I can't tell him what to do.'

Fay smiled wryly. 'According to what I hear you've never stopped telling him what to do. Let's face it, Doctor Naylor, you've never let him have anything his way. You've disapproved of almost everything he's done, which is probably why he's kept you in the dark about Richard all these years!' She picked up her gloves and handbag, pausing a moment to assess the effect she was having. 'The local newspapers would have a field day with this juicy little bit of gossip under the present circumstances, wouldn't they – if anyone were ruthless enough to go to them with it?'

He stared at her. 'You wouldn't.'

'Of course not.' She pulled on her gloves very slowly. 'Not if you do as I ask. After all, it's not much, is it? Only what is due to my son and me.' She looked down at him. 'And you too – as a grandfather, Doctor Naylor – when you think about it.' She began to walk away then turned. 'You can keep the photograph,' she said. 'After all, you've missed your grandson's childhood so you might as well have something.'

'I demand to know the truth about this!'

George Naylor had barged into the house just after nine that evening while Mark and Claire were just finishing their dinner. He threw the photograph down on the table. 'I'm told that *this* is my grandson. *My grandson*, mark you! I demand an explanation!'

Claire glanced at Mark whose face was ashen. 'Sit down, Father,' she said. 'Calm yourself. You should be thinking about your blood pressure.'

'Damn my sodding blood pressure,' George shouted. 'Is it true or isn't it?'

Mark cleared his throat. 'Yes, it's true, but I think there are some things that need clearing up,' He was visibly shaken. 'May I ask where all this has come from?'

George sat down at the table and poured himself a glass of water. 'This Scott woman e-mailed me this morning – must have got the address from the newspaper article. She asked me to meet her – said she had important information. Fay Scott, she says her name is.' He glared at Mark. 'Ring any bells, does it?'

Mark sighed. 'Of course it does. Fay is someone I've known for many years.'

'*Known!*' George gave a bark of laughter. 'The understatement of the century! She says she's been your mistress for the past twenty-five years and that you are the father of her son, Richard.'

'Fay is someone I had an affair with. Claire knows all about her. Fay had a child, a son. But she refused to allow him to know that I was his father. I finished the affair years ago, but as long as I was supporting Richard I couldn't avoid seeing her.'

'That's not the way she tells it.' George countered. 'She says you refused to acknowledge him as yours. Wouldn't have the boy told that you were his father.'

'Not true,' Mark said. 'That was her idea. She was angry because I wouldn't divorce Claire and marry her.'

George ran a hand through his sparse hair and blew out his breath explosively. 'I really can't believe we're having this conversation. It's a bloody nightmare! I can't believe that a son of mine could behave in such an outrageous way.' He directed his attention to Claire. 'Of course you're the one to blame in all this,' he accused.

'*I am?*' Claire looked at Mark.

'I know about your abortion. How *could* you? Because you

didn't want a child Mark had to go and get one from some other woman! I know about this disgusting surrogacy rubbish too. I can't believe that my own son and his wife could have deliberately deceived me; gone against all my principles in this appalling way. I daren't tell Mary. The shame would kill her!'

Mark got up from the table and threw down his napkin. Claire could see his hand shaking. 'Now just you listen to me, Father,' he said. 'You're going to hear my side of this whether you like it or not. How would you have felt if I'd come to you and announced that I had an illegitimate son?' George opened his mouth but Mark went on; 'How would you have reacted to a surrogate child? And before you blame Claire again, it was me who insisted on the abortion. We were at university at the time and we – I felt it was the wrong time. Things went wrong and Claire suffered terribly as a result. She almost lost her life and as a result she had to give up her studies. All hopes of becoming a doctor – or a mother – were smashed for her because of it.' He glanced at Claire. 'But what did I do to make it up to her? I hid her illness from you. I went and had an affair; fathered a child with another woman. All these years Claire has taken the blame for not producing grandchildren for you and I've let her. I'm ashamed of myself. I always have been, which was partly why I agreed to the surrogacy idea. But even that ended in heartbreak for her.' He looked at Claire. 'Why she's still here is a mystery to me. All I know is that we don't deserve her – any of us!'

George stared from one to the other of them, clearly stunned. 'I don't know what to make of any of this,' he said at last. 'I feel I don't know my own son.'

'You never did, Father,' Mark said. 'I don't think you ever wanted to. For as long as I can remember you've always superimposed the image of the son you wanted on to me. You've never even tried to get to know what I was really like. I haven't forgotten the beatings I had as a child whenever I dared to be other than perfect.'

'Discipline!' George blustered. 'I only acted as any good father should.'

'Except that the discipline was never tempered with love or compassion. And nothing changed, did it? No matter what I've done to try to please you it's never been good enough. Even now you can't stop interfering. You still treat me like a student – can't trust me to run the practice. Because of your meddling we've lost all our best doctors. Even Adam Bennett is leaving now. Well, now you can have my resignation too.'

George stared at his son. 'What are you saying? Are you throwing everything your family has worked for all these years away?'

'I think you've done a pretty good job of that yourself,' Mark told him. 'I've wasted too many years trying to please you – trying to do what you wanted – hiding reality from you. Now I know where my true loyalty lies. I'll take my skills where they'll be appreciated.' He held out his hand to Claire. 'And if she can find it in her heart to forgive me I hope Claire will come with me to make a fresh start.'

Claire stood up and went to Mark, her eyes moist. 'Of course I will,' she whispered.

George stood up, shaking his head. 'I can't take all this in,' he muttered. 'Tonight has knocked me for six. I think we'd better talk about this again in the morning.' As Claire moved towards him he held up his hand. 'No, don't bother to see me out.' As he left the room he looked over his shoulder at Mark and Claire saw a new look in his eyes. It occurred to her that if she hadn't known George better she might almost have taken it for respect.

George did not see Danni standing at the foot of the stairs as he came out of the dining-room and headed for the front door. Rick had a seven o'clock start in the morning so they had been to an early film and then he had walked her home. As she passed the dining-room door she heard raised voices and realized that Mark and Claire were not alone. She was passing the door when her attention was taken by the mention of the name Fay Scott.

She paused outside the door and what she heard next made her heart freeze within her. Doctor Naylor senior was shouting. He sounded incandescent with rage:

'Fay Scott says she has been your mistress for the past twenty-five years and that you are the father of her son Richard.' A moment later she heard Mark admit it.

She stood rooted to the spot, her heart frozen. So Mark was the father Rick had never known! Slowly the implications sank in. She and Rick had the same father. She gasped as the reality of the situation hit her. *Rick, the young man she had just promised to love for ever, was her half-brother.*

CHAPTER FOURTEEN

WHEN Danni woke next morning the thought that hit her like an avalanche was that she had no choice but to finish her relationship with Rick. She groaned and turned over, burying her face in the pillow. How was she going to do it? She had lain awake half the night and wept more tears than she could ever remember weeping. She kept imagining the hurt look on his face when she told him and the pain that pierced her heart was almost too much to bear.

She couldn't tell him the truth. Not unless she told Claire and Mark too, and it was too late for that. Telling them who she was now, after she'd inveigled her way into their lives, would make her sound so devious. Either way she couldn't possibly stay here in Haylesmere, working for Claire. She was about to lose not only the man she loved more than anything in the world, but all her dreams of making something of herself at last. All her life she had felt like a nobody – a non-person, but since she had come here to Grafton Place life had really taken off for her. She told herself that she should have known. She was never destined to be an artist – an interior designer. That kind of luck just wasn't for her. Now she would have to go back to where she belonged – working in a supermarket, living on a shoestring in some grotty bed-sit – God only knew where.

She realized suddenly with a pang of guilt that she hadn't

spoken to Ruth lately. That was the trouble with being happy and in love. It made you selfish She reached for her mobile phone and dialled the number. It was early but Ruth was an early riser and she was bound to be up and about. She replied almost at once.

'Danni! I was just getting ready to leave for work.'

'Oh – sorry. Shall I ring you back this evening instead?'

'No, it's OK, I've got plenty of time. It's lovely to hear from you. Are you all right?'

Danni swallowed hard. She had decided not to tell her mother what had happened. It might sound as though she only got in touch when there was a problem. 'I'm OK, Mum. How are you? What's happened? Are you still at Jim's?'

'No, but I've been lucky. I've found a nice little flat and I've landed a good job. It's better paid than the last one and now that I've cleared my debt I'm much better off.' She paused. 'Any chance you could come and stay for a weekend?'

Danni sighed, wondering just how 'little' Mum's flat was and whether there'd be room for her to live there too. 'I – don't know at the moment, Mum,' she said.

'Danni – is something wrong?' Ruth asked. 'You sound a bit stressed.'

'No – no, I'm fine. I'd like to come and visit, Mum, but I don't know when. I'll have to get back to you. I'd better go now.'

'Danni, look, I'll come and see you, shall I? I'd love to see you and I could tell you all about the new job. Listen, love, you've never actually given me your address. I've got a pencil – just give it to me now.'

'Sorry, Mum, you're breaking up,' Danni said quickly. 'I think my phone needs charging. I'll get back to you. 'Bye.' She switched off quickly. She couldn't have Mum coming here to Grafton Place. The cat would be well and truly out of the bag if she ran into Mark or Claire. She'd have to think of something. She looked at her watch. It was almost time to get up and face Claire. Somehow she would have to tell her she was leaving but what excuse could she possibly make? What a mess! If only she hadn't decided to come and look for her biological father none of this would have happened.

Meanwhile Claire was singing in the shower. She and Mark had spent the night together. They had made love for the first time in months. Lying awake afterwards far into the small hours he'd opened his heart as never before and told her things about his childhood that shocked her – things he'd never disclosed to her: How afraid he had been of his tyrannical father almost from babyhood; how traumatic it had been when he was bundled off to a harsh boarding school at barely seven. He described the holidays at home that were something he came to dread, with his father constantly bullying him, forcing him to do the kind of sports he hated and was no good at.

'He knocked all the decent humanity out of me,' he confessed. 'Even when I fell in love with you I knew that he had to approve or it wouldn't work, which was why I panicked when you became pregnant. I realize now that I've lived my whole life in a constant state of anxiety. It becomes a habit when you grow up knowing nothing else.' He sighed. 'I regret the affair with Fay more than I can say. It's one of the worst things I've ever done. But after the termination – after we married you seemed to turn away from me, turn in on yourself. Deep down I knew it was all my fault, but I was in denial. I tried to blame Dad but I knew inside that I had no one to blame but myself. It was all due to my weakness.' He looked at her. 'I didn't like myself much at that point, Claire. I refused to face it. Then Fay told me she was pregnant and you know the rest. When Richard was born I knew I had to tell you or I'd be trapped for ever.'

'It took courage, telling me,' Claire said softly.

'But it took you more courage to you to stay with me.' He

sighed. 'Then tonight, hearing him yelling at us like that – in our own home, something suddenly snapped inside my head. It was just as though I were waking up for the first time in my life. You have no idea how liberated I feel. It's as though a great burden has been lifted from my shoulders,' he said. 'Now I can start living the life I want to live at long last.' He looked at her. 'I'm just so full of regret and shame for all I've put you through.'

'It hasn't been easy,' she admitted. 'But it's over now.' She kissed him. 'I can't tell you how proud of you I was tonight. It was wonderful to hear you standing up to him at last. And standing up for me too.'

He drew her close. 'From now on it's us, you and me. No one else matters. The affair with Fay – it was never meant to hurt you.'

'I know'

He was silent for a moment then he said. 'Adam leaving. It's because of you, isn't it? He's in love with you.' He raised his head to look at her. 'I almost lost you, didn't I? It would have been no more than I deserved, but I go hot and cold just thinking about how close I came to losing everything that matters to me.'

'How did you know?'

'Instinct. I saw the way he looked at you when ever you came to the surgery and I felt that you were attracted to him too. When you know someone really well you can sense these things. I just didn't know what to do about it. After all, I cheated on you so I could hardly complain.'

'I couldn't have left you,' she said. 'What you're saying is true and I'm sorry. I've been so lonely, Mark. I admit that it felt good to have someone wanting me again, but I know I could never have done it. Poor Adam,' she added. 'I hope he'll find happiness with someone else.'

He paused. 'So many people have been affected by all this. Not least Richard.'

'Are you going to tell him?' She looked at him. 'Do you want to bring him here to the house? I'd like to meet him, Mark.'

'Would you? He's a very nice young man. I think you'd get on.' He sighed. 'As for Fay . . .'

'What was her motive for telling your father, do you think?'

'Revenge – spite, who knows? All I do know is that I'm grateful to her. I'm glad it all came to a head, even if it has shown up my shortcomings.'

'The way I see it is that it proves that in spite of what your father did to you you've remained the man I saw when I fell in love with you.' She smiled. 'It's nice to know I was right.'

He kissed her. 'What did I ever do to deserve you?' he whispered.

'What do you mean, you can't move to the flat with me?' Rick stared at Danni incredulously.

'I just can't, Rick. I can't explain so don't ask me to. It wouldn't work.'

'Why do you say that?' He was shaking his head as though the thought just wouldn't sink in. 'And – why has it taken you this long to come to that conclusion?'

'You don't get it. It's not just the flat, Rick,' she said. 'I can't see you any more either.'

He laughed. 'Oh come *on*. You're winding me up.'

'No, I'm not. It – it's over, Rick – you and me. We're finished.'

His face assumed the hurt look she had been dreading. 'You can't just say you can't explain so I'm not to ask you. I deserve better than that, don't I?' When she failed to answer he probed again. 'Have you met someone else?' When she still did not reply he shook his head angrily. 'It's Mum, isn't it? Somehow or other she's got to you. Well, I can tell you now that I'm moving out whatever happens. I think she's going round the twist. Do you want to hear the latest? She suddenly

171

told me a couple of days ago that Mark Naylor is my father. Yes, *Doctor Mark Naylor,* your boss's husband. I've known him for ever but I only ever knew him as Mark. I never even knew he was a doctor or where he lived. Now she calmly tells me that he's my dad.'

She looked at him. 'Don't you believe her?'

'I don't think I'll ever believe a word she says again. Why couldn't she tell me when I was a kid? Why couldn't *he*? OK, I know he's married to someone else, but in that case why did he hang around and why suddenly come out with it now – if it's true, that is? If you ask me I think they're both barking! Look, Danni, I'm not living at home any more whatever happens so if it's Mum holding you back you needn't worry.' He grasped her shoulders and turned her to face him. 'Danni – tell me you're not serious – that it's just cold feet or something. I love you and you say you love me, so what can possibly be wrong with moving in together?'

Looking into his eyes she felt that she had never loved him as much as she did at that moment. A crazy thought struck her. If no one knew what would it matter? Neither of them had a father's name on their birth certificate. Why throw it all away for the sake of a few shared genes? Then reason kicked in. It would be wrong – incestuous. She would never dare to have children with Rick. He would have to know eventually and when he did he wouldn't thank her for keeping it from him. She couldn't bear to tell him – to see the horror on his face. Better to make a clean break now.

'I've thought about it, Rick,' she said. 'Thought about it very carefully and I've decided that I – I don't love you enough. You said you hoped we'd get married. I realize now that I don't want that. I don't want to marry you.'

His eyes were brimming with tears as he grasped her shoulders and made her look at him. 'Say that again,' he said, his voice rough with emotion. 'Say it while you're looking at me.'

The lump in her throat was almost choking her but she

made herself look into his pain-filled eyes as she forced out the words. 'I don't love you, Rick. I'm sorry.' She swallowed hard. 'Better to find out now than – than when it's too late.'

Claire was alone in the house a couple of evenings later. Mark was at an area health authority meeting and she was taking the opportunity to tackle a stack of neglected paperwork downstairs in the studio. As she worked her thoughts were with Danni. She was worried about the girl. She wasn't herself. She had been preoccupied for days now. She didn't look well either, tired and hollow-eyed as though she wasn't sleeping. Claire guessed that it had something to do with the boyfriend but Danni clearly didn't want to talk about it so she hadn't pressed her.

Suddenly there was an unexpected ring at the front door bell. Assuming it was someone collecting for charity she sighed, put down her calculator and went upstairs to answer it. Opening the door she was surprised to see her mother-in-law, Mary Naylor, standing outside. She braced herself, expecting an admonishment over the scene with George, so when Mary smiled amicably she was taken off guard.

'May I come in, my dear?' Mary asked.

Taken aback at the 'my dear' Claire held the door open. 'Mary! This is a surprise. Yes, of course. I'm afraid Mark is out,' she said, leading the way through to the drawing-room.

'Oh, I knew that,' Mary said. 'That's why I'm here. I wanted to speak to you alone.'

Claire looked at her mother-in-law. 'Can I get you anything – coffee?'

'Thank you, no.' Mary sat down. 'I'll come straight to the point. I've come to apologize,' she said. 'Though the word sounds woefully inadequate for the disservice George and I have done you over all the years.'

Claire hardly knew what to say. 'Apologize?'

Mary nodded. 'First for the scene George made here the

other night. He had no right to burst in on you like that.'

'He told you?'

'Everything. I'm so sorry my dear. And now I want to tell you our side of it all. I'm not going to make excuses for myself or for George, but I want you to know that there are things in the past that even Mark doesn't know about. It might go some way to helping you to understand.'

Claire felt deeply uncomfortable. 'Please – there's no need . . .'

'Oh, but there is.' The older woman leaned back in her chair and took a deep breath. 'For you to understand I have to go back a long way.' she began. 'We had a child before Mark was born. A little boy, born a year after we were married. George had just qualified. He idolized him. He was everything he'd ever wanted in a son: strong, good-looking, happy and good-natured.'

'What happened?' Claire whispered.

'He died at six; meningitis. We were both devastated of course, but George was almost crazy with grief. He couldn't get over the fact that as a doctor he hadn't been able to save his own son.'

'I'm so sorry,' Claire said. 'But then you had Mark.'

Mary sighed. 'Only after three miscarriages,' she said. 'George was desperate for another child but for me it was hell, the dashed hopes, the sense of failure again and again, the disappointment on George's face. But then, as you say, at last we had Mark. I was so relieved when the baby was safely born and he was a boy. But I soon saw that George regarded him as a replacement and not a new child in his own right. He even insisted we give him the same name as the child we lost, Mark. He destroyed all the photographs and wouldn't have him spoken about again. The new Mark was to be the embodiment of the first one.'

Claire was slowly beginning to understand. 'But he wasn't,' she said.

Mary shook her head sadly. 'He didn't even look like him or have the same characteristics. George went from disbelief to disappointment – finally to anger. He bullied the child unmercifully. It was as though he was punishing him for not being a clone of his dead brother. Much against my wishes he sent him off to boarding school at a tender age.' She looked at Claire. 'Can you imagine what it was like for me, seeing my little boy so miserable? I felt powerless to protect my own child.'

'But surely later, when Mark decided to study medicine. . . ?' Claire put in.

'Yes, he had to concede then that Mark was doing something right. As you know, the practice has been in George's family for generations and it was a foregone conclusion that Mark would take over when George retired.'

'But when we failed to produce a grandson – a new heir, George discovered another stick with which to beat Mark?'

Mary nodded. 'And I'm afraid I was spiteful to you too,' she said. 'I remembered what I went through trying to give George the child he wanted. I thought you chose not to have children out of selfishness. I never knew about your termination and the disastrous aftermath. I never guessed that Mark had been unfaithful. I simply blamed you for causing him to suffer his father's disapproval all over again.' She looked at Claire and shook her head. 'And then there was the failed surrogacy. How it must have hurt you to lose that baby too. And how you must have hated me,' she said sadly.

'Not hated,' Claire said. 'Resented, perhaps. But I resented Mark more for standing back and letting me take all the blame.'

'Rightly so! And there was no excuse, but now perhaps you can partly understand why he did it. George turned him into a nervous wreck as a child. Later, as a man, George became his weakness, his Achilles Heel.'

'I think that particular spectre has been laid to rest,' Claire said. 'Mark and I have had a long talk. Having stood up to his father at last he feels free, ready to make a new start.'

'I'm so glad.'

Claire looked at her mother-in-law. 'What are you and George going to do about Richard, Mark's son?' she asked.

Mary shrugged. 'It appears that the young man has been kept in the dark as much as we have,' she said. 'I think we should respect his wishes as to whether he wants to meet us or not. We owe him that much at least.'

'Thank you for telling me all this, Mary,' Claire said. 'Coming here tonight must have taken a lot of courage.'

'No more than you were owed,' Mary told her. 'I hope I can make up for it in the future. I admire you more than I can say for sticking to Mark all these years in spite of everything. And, I have a sneaking suspicion that George does too. I think the relationship between the four of us is going to be much better in future. That is if you're prepared to give us another chance.'

'Of course we will,' Claire said. 'I love Mark. I confess that it hasn't always been easy.'

'It can't have been.' Mary stood up. 'But I'm grateful to you for it. I hope the two of you can make a fresh start.' At the door she paused and turned to Claire with the hint of a twinkle in her eyes. 'By the way, it was my idea that George should stand for the council,' she said. 'And we've just heard that the only other candidate has decided to stand down so he'll get in unopposed at the by-election. You can be sure he'll be too busy to interfere in the practice once he takes up his council duties.'

Claire smiled. 'Thank you.' She took the older woman's hand and pressed it warmly. 'For everything.'

Mark had just seen the last patient of the day when his door opened. He did not look up from writing his notes at once, expecting it to be a receptionist or one of the practice nurses coming in with a query. When he did glance up he was aston-ished to see Richard standing there.

'Richard. What can I do for you?'

Richard's face was dark with anger. When he spoke his voice shook. 'You sit there and calmly ask what you can do!' He approached Mark's desk and stood looking down at him. 'You can answer me one question is what you can do.'

Feeling at a disadvantage, Mark stood up. 'Of course. Anything.'

'Are you or are you not my father?'

Mark drew a deep breath. 'Yes, Richard. I am.'

'Then why has it taken you and my mother twenty-two years to decide to tell me?'

'It was her choice; not mine.'

'Why?'

'It's complicated, Richard. Perhaps you should ask her.'

'Do you think I haven't?' Richard stared at him and Mark saw for the first time how much his son resembled him. It was almost like looking at a youthful photograph of himself. 'I feel right now that I don't know my mother,' Richard went on. 'How can I believe anything she tells me when she's been lying to me all my life about something as fundamental as who my father is.'

'Believe me, Richard, I wanted you to know,' Mark said. 'I wanted to have a father-son relationship with you, but the only way I was going to get that was to leave my wife and marry Fay – your mother.'

Richard shook his head. 'I *hate* all this,' he said passionately. 'The cheating, the dishonesty of it all. I hate being a part of it – the *major* part of it! I'm ashamed of my mother and I want you to know that I'm more than ashamed to be your son!'

Mark flinched. He hadn't expected such bitter vehemence. 'Perhaps you don't know the full truth of it all,' he said.

'I know enough. I know that you're a cheat and a liar,' Richard said. 'I know that you betrayed your wife and that my mother encouraged you to. I know that you lied to me – pretended to be someone else when all the time—'

'I also made sure you never went without,' Mark interrupted. 'I supported you through your education and I kept a roof over your head.'

Richard threw back his head and laughed. '*Great*! That was all it took, was it – a few pieces of silver – conscience money? Well good for you!' He drew a folded paper from his pocket and threw it on to the desk. 'You also made sure I went through life with that – a birth certificate with *father unknown* on it.' He watched as Mark picked up the document and looked at it. 'Fathers are supposed to be role models,' Richard went on. 'But I can tell you here and now that you are the worst role model any son could be unlucky enough to have.' He snatched the certificate from Mark's hand. 'I just wanted you to know how I feel,' he said. 'Because I hope this is the last time we ever speak to each other. I never want to see you again as long as I live.' He strode to the door and turned, his hand on the handle. 'Goodbye – *Doctor*.'

After he had gone Mark sat for several minutes, his head in his hands. The encounter had shaken him. He had expected – he didn't know what; to be accepted with open arms, welcomed as Richard's father? He had visualized introducing his son to Claire and his parents – seen them all as a family at last. Now he saw how naïve he'd been. And where did Fay fit into it all? She was, after all Richard's mother. Even if she had started it all by sending his father that e-mail she was owed some consideration. Now it looked as though her actions had backfired on her too. He sighed, suddenly remembering the little rhyme his mother was fond of quoting to him as a child. '*Oh what a tangled web we weave when first we practise to deceive.*'

CHAPTER FIFTEEN

IT was late on Friday afternoon when Ruth arrived at Church Street. She knocked twice on the door of number 28 and was about to give up when she heard a movement on the other side of the door. A moment later it opened to reveal a breathless Mrs Bell.

'Sorry to keep you, love,' she wheezed. 'Only I was upstairs and my arthritis don't let me move as fast as I used to.' The old lady peered closer. 'Oh, it's young Danni's mum, isn't it? Mrs – er . . .'

'Blake,' Ruth supplied. 'Yes. I'm here on the off-chance. Do you happen to have a room vacant?'

Mrs Bell nodded. 'You're in luck, love. One of my regulars has gone off on holiday. A single do you?'

'Fine,' Ruth said with relief. 'It's only for a couple of nights.'

'Come on in then.' Mrs Bell opened the door wide. 'I'll take you up. It's on the first floor. Then I expect you could do with a cuppa.'

'That would be nice.' Ruth followed as Mrs Bell led the way upstairs. The room looked out over the street and was one of Mrs B's best. The old lady stood in the doorway, puffing gently, one hand to her side. 'There you are then. Make yourself at home, dear. Come down when you've unpacked and have your tea in the kitchen with me,' she invited.

'If you're sure it's no trouble.'

'Bless you no. It'll be nice to have company. Do you know, sometimes I hardly see a soul from breakfast till teatime.'

Ruth unpacked her overnight bag and went downstairs to the kitchen where Mrs Bell was waiting with her big brown teapot and two mugs.

'Ah, there you are then,' she said as Ruth came in. 'Sit you down and help yourself to a biscuit.' She passed a tin with a picture of the Prince and Princess of Wales on the lid. 'Now, how is young Danni? Here to see her are you?'

'Yes, though she doesn't know I'm coming,' Ruth said. 'I'm a bit concerned about her. I keep ringing her but her mobile phone seems to be permanently switched off.'

Mrs Bell shook her head as she passed a steaming mug of dark-brown tea across the table. 'If you ask me them mobile things are a curse,' she said. 'People walk about with the bloomin' things glued to their ears, jabberin' away into thin air. It'll all end in tears if you ask me. It's a wonder more of 'em don't walk under buses!'

'The thing is, because we've always kept in touch by phone I don't know her address,' Ruth said. 'And I was wondering if you'd got it.'

'There! See what I mean?' Mrs Bell said. 'Relying on a mobile phone just lets you down in the end.' She dipped her biscuit in her tea and sucked on it thoughtfully.'

'So – do you happen to know it?' Ruth asked.

'Know what, love? Oh, Danni's address. Well, no, not really.' Mrs Bell raised her eyes to the ceiling. 'I do remember her asking me how to get there when she first went for the interview and I know I said to her that it'd be tuppence to speak to her soon, living in a posh area like that.'

Ruth tried hard to contain her impatience. 'So where is it?'

'Very posh – now, let me think. Something or other designs – interior or some such. Gresham Park, was it? No! Grafton Place. That's it! I remember it now. Posh houses in a square with a sort of park thing in the middle. I went to visit a friend there years ago. She was a housemaid to—'

'Grafton Place – what number?'

The old lady pursed her lips. 'Mmm – sorry – don't think she ever said what number it was. Would it be any good looking it up in the phone book?'

'Not unless you can remember the name of the designer she's working for.'

'No. See what you mean.' Mrs Bell was thoughtful for a moment then she said. 'Perhaps if you was to go there there'd be a sign up outside. But in any case you could always ask,' she said. 'I can certainly tell you how to get there.'

Ruth brightened. Light at the end of the tunnel at last. She drank the last of her tea and stood up. 'No time like the present,' she said. 'I'll go now if you can give me directions.'

'Now?' Mrs Bell looked doubtful. 'Time's getting on. Don't you want to have something to eat first?'

'No,' Ruth said. 'I've only got the weekend and I've been worried about her.'

Ruth got off the bus and walked the short distance to Grafton Place. It was, as Mrs Bell had said, a very smart area. She walked all the way along one side of the square and eventually decided to knock on one of the doors. Choosing number 54, she walked up the steps and rang the bell. A moment later a girl opened the door carrying a small child on her hip.

'Yes? Can I be helping you?'

The girl had a foreign accent and Ruth guessed that she was an au pair. 'I'm sorry to trouble you but I'm looking for an interior design place somewhere around here,' she said.

The girl shrugged. 'Please to wait – I ask.' She disappeared and a few minutes later an older woman appeared. 'Can I help you?' she asked.

'I'm looking for a design firm – interior design. I only know that it's Grafton Place.'

'Of course. It's just a few doors along. It's at number 64. Cavendish Interior Design. It's in the basement. You'll see the sign.'

'Thank you.'

Ruth walked on, counting the numbers as she went. As she reached number 58 a car passed her and drew up a little further along. A man got out and stood for a moment, locking the car. Ruth stopped in her tracks, the breath catching in her throat. It had been almost twenty years and she couldn't be absolutely sure, but something about the dark hair, now turning grey – the build; the set of his head – evoked strong memories. Mark Naylor! It could not be a coincidence that he lived in the street where Danni was working. Now she understood why Danni hadn't wanted to reveal her address. Wondering what to do next Ruth suddenly realized that the man, who now stood at the top of the steps, was looking curiously at her. As she turned in a panic-stricken attempt to escape he called out, 'Hello there! Can I help you?'

Reluctantly she stopped and turned. He had retraced his steps and now he stood facing her just a few feet away. Any doubt she'd had dissolved. It *was* Mark Naylor.

'Are you looking for someone?' he asked. There was no sign of recognition in his eyes until she began to stammer a reply then his eyes suddenly widened with disbelief.

'My God! It's Ruth Emerson. It is, isn't it?' he said.

She nodded, her mouth too dry for words.

'What do you want? Why have you come here?' His eyes narrowed. 'If it's money . . .'

'How *dare* you!' she said, flushing crimson. 'I've paid you back every penny I owed; never missed a single month.'

He looked shamefaced. 'I know you have. I'm sorry. I didn't mean . . . It was such a shock, seeing you. So why are you here?'

'I'm looking for my daughter.'

'Your daughter? You mean the child that you – that we. . . ?'

'Yes.'

He shook his head. 'What makes you think you'll find her here?'

'You might not realize it but she's a young woman now and I have reason to believe she's working for your wife.'

'You mean – Danielle?'

'That's her name.'

'But she never said. What the hell has she been playing at?'

'I think she's been trying to make a living whilst getting the education I could never afford to give her,' Ruth told him.'

He coloured. 'Does she know you're coming? Were you planning some kind of confrontation?'

'Of course not. She has no idea I'm coming. I didn't even know she was working here. I had to find out from a previous landlady. I've come because I've been worried about her. She's seemed so unhappy lately.' She looked at him squarely. 'You might find it hard to believe, but we ordinary people do have lives of our own.'

'I suppose you'd better come in,' he said, leading the way down the basement steps. 'This is my wife's studio,' he said as he opened the door. 'It's where Danni works most of the time.' He opened the door and walked in. Claire looked up from her drawing board.

'Hi! What time is it? Don't say I'm late with . . .' She broke off as she saw that Mark was not alone. 'Oh! Sorry, I didn't know we had—'

'Don't you recognize her?' Mark interrupted.

'Hello, Claire.' Ruth stepped forward. 'I've come to see Danni,' she said. 'My daughter.'

The colour drained from Claire's face. '*Ruth*!' she whispered. 'Danni is your – I had no idea.'

'I didn't know she was working for you,' Ruth told her. 'We've kept in touch by phone. All I knew was that she had this marvellous job and a place to live. She was so thrilled, but lately I sensed that something had gone wrong. She's sounded so unhappy lately, then she just switched her phone off. I had to come.' She looked at them both. 'To think that if I hadn't I might never have known.' She looked around the studio. 'Is she here?'

'She's taken the dog for a walk,' Claire said. 'She'll be back shortly.' She looked at Mark. 'I think we need to talk.'

He shrugged. 'What is there to talk about?'

'Who knows?' She looked at Ruth. 'Do you think Danni knew who we were when she answered my advertisement?'

'I've no idea. I only put her in the picture about the circumstances of her birth a few months ago,' Ruth said. 'She was asking so many questions, but I made her promise not to try and dig up the past. She has such a talent for art. It hurt me that I couldn't afford to support her through art school. Finding this job has been a life-saver for her.'

Claire shot Mark a look. 'I'm glad I was able to help,' she said. 'She's such a lovely girl. She and I have built a strong bond in the time she's been with me.'

'So why is she so unhappy now?' Ruth asked.

'I don't know. I wish I did,' Claire said. 'I agree that she hasn't been herself for days now. I'm glad you're here, Ruth. Perhaps she'll tell you what's wrong.'

Mark cleared his throat. 'Look, I can't stay. I only came back for something I left in my study. I've got surgery at six.'

'Of course. You go,' Claire said. 'Ruth and I will talk this through.'

Mark was in the kitchen when Danni came down the basement stairs with Maddie. She unhooked the lead and watched as the little dog ran through to the studio.

'Look at her. You'd never think she'd just had a long walk, would you?' She turned and noticed that Mark was looking at her oddly. 'What?' she said. 'Have I done something wrong again?'

'No. There's a visitor for you in there.' He nodded his head towards the studio. 'You might be surprised.'

184

Danni pushed the studio door open and stood staring.
'*Mum!*'

Ruth looked at her daughter. 'Oh, Danni. How could you?'
she said. 'You promised me you wouldn't.'

'I know.' Danni glanced at Claire. 'I'm sorry. To begin with
I found Mark because I caught flu and needed a doctor. When
this job came up I had no idea that this was his home and you
were his wife. It felt almost like fate.' She looked from one to
the other. 'I was never going to say anything,' she assured
them. 'I'd made up my mind not to. I soon saw that it would
cause too much trouble.'

'Your mother has been worried about you,' Claire put in. 'I
have too. You've been so preoccupied – not at all your usual
happy self.'

'I know,' Danni averted her eyes. 'It's nothing to worry
about.' She looked at her mother. 'There was no need for you
to come all the way over here.'

'You wouldn't answer your phone,' Ruth said. 'I've left you
countless messages but you haven't replied to any of them.
What was I supposed to think?'

'Is it something to do with your boyfriend?' Claire asked
gently.

Danni looked up sharply. 'Yes.' She swallowed hard at the
lump in her throat, willing them not to be kind to her – struggling against the knot of tears that threatened to erupt and
betray her.

Claire stood up. 'Look, I've got to go out and buy something for supper.' She smiled at Danni. 'You know what I am
– the world's worst housekeeper. Mark won't be back until
after surgery. Why don't you make your mother a coffee and
have a talk while I'm gone?'

Ruth looked at her gratefully. 'Thank you.'

Claire took her jacket from the hook behind the door,
picked up her handbag and left, closing the door behind her.
There was silence as they heard her footsteps going up the

basement stairs, then Ruth said:

'Want to tell me about it?'

Danni covered her face with her hands. 'In a minute.'

'Danni – you're not pregnant are you?'

She looked up sharply. '*No!* I almost wish I was. It's worse than that.'

'How?' Ruth's patience was wearing thin. 'Danni – are you going to tell me or aren't you?'

'I told you about Rick,' Danni said. 'He's the best thing that ever happened to me. We were going to move in together. We'd found a flat and everything was perfect. I really love him, Mum. And he loves me.'

'So where's the problem?'

'I found out the other night that he – that Mark is his father. It seems he had an affair years ago and Rick is his son. That makes him my half-brother.'

Ruth bit her lip. 'Oh, Danni. Have you told Claire? Does she know about this boy?'

'Yes, she knows. I haven't said anything. I couldn't. Until today she didn't know who I was. Anyway there was some kind of row and I overheard it by accident. I didn't want it to sound as if I listen at doors.' She paused, closing her eyes against the painful memory. 'I've finished with Rick.' She looked up, tears beginning to trickle down her cheeks. 'It hurt so much, Mum. I couldn't tell him why and I had to say I didn't love him any more. I can't get the look on his face out of my head.' She swallowed hard. 'I was wondering whether I could come home to you.'

Ruth got up and came to put her arms round Danni. 'Of course you can, love. You don't need to ask.'

'I was so happy here,' Danni said against Ruth's shoulder. 'I love working with Claire. It was perfect. We get on together so well and she's taught me so much. She was even going to pay for driving lessons for me. My life was really going some-where, Mum. Now – now it's all ruined.'

'You could still stay on,' Ruth told her. 'This Rick – he's your first real boyfriend. There'll be others. You'll get over it and so will he. You're young and—'

'*No!*' Danni pushed her roughly away. 'You don't understand. It isn't some silly schoolgirl crush. It's real – for both of us. I'll never want anyone else. And the thought of Rick and another girl just – just destroys me, which is why I can't stay here where I might run into him.'

Ruth held her daughter and let her cry silently against her shoulder. This is all down to Mark Naylor, she told herself angrily. How many more lives was he going to mess up with his mindless self-indulgence? A thought occurred to her.

'Claire will soon realize,' she said. 'Now that she knows who you are.'

Danni shook her head. 'She won't have connected my Rick with Mark's son,' she explained. 'His name is really Richard. Rick is just what he likes his friends to call him.'

'Then you're going to have to tell her.'

'I know.' Danni sighed. 'Oh, Mum, what a mess.'

Mark had seen his last patient and was preparing to go home when a call came through from reception.

'Can you see a temporary patient, Doctor? I know surgery is over but she says it's urgent.'

He sighed. 'What's her name?'

'Mrs Marks.'

'All right, send her in.' He sat down again at his desk, glancing at his watch as he waited. He wondered how Claire had got on with Ruth and Danielle, hoping that whatever the problem was would be cleared up by the time he got home. He'd had enough for one day. The door opened and he looked up at the patient.

'What can I . . .' His heart sank. '*Fay!* What the hell. . . ? What's all this Mrs Marks rubbish?'

She sat down and smiled. 'Rather appropriate, don't you

think? Just missing the apostrophe. Have you had a visit from your esteemed father?'

'I have, and you needn't think anyone was intimidated by your attempt at troublemaking,' he told her. 'What you attempted to do was tantamount to blackmail. We have only to go to the police.'

'But you won't.' Her eyes glittered. 'because as you know there were no witnesses to our conversation and never once did I even hint at financial demands. I merely told him the undisputable truth.'

'With what motive?'

'I thought it was time you learned a lesson,' she told him.

'So consider yourself avenged.' He looked at her. 'You might be interested to know that I also had a visit from your son.'

'*Our* son,' she corrected.

'Not according to him. He told me in no uncertain terms what he thought of me. He also said that he never wants to see or speak to me again.'

Her triumphant expression faded. 'And you might be interested to know that he said more or less the same to me.' She opened her handbag and fumbled for a handkerchief. 'My own son.' Her voice trembled. 'The child I gave birth to and sacrificed everything for.'

'Except that he's not a child any more. You have only yourself to blame, Fay,' he told her. 'This is all your doing. If you'd told him years ago that I was his father none of this would have happened. You've been keeping it up your sleeve as a kind of insurance, haven't you; to use as a last resort – a weapon? Well I'm afraid it's backfired on you.'

She dabbed at her eyes. 'Did you know that he's planning to move into some poky bed-sit with this Danni creature?'

He frowned. 'Danni?'

'You must know the wretched girl,' she snapped. 'She works for your wife. I wouldn't put it past you to have engineered the whole thing!'

Mark stared at her, momentarily speechless with shock. 'Are you saying that Richard and Danni are. . . ?'

'An *item* is the term you're looking for,' she said.

'And they're planning to live together?' A cold feeling gripped his stomach.

'Oh very good,' she sneered. 'Pretend you don't know, why don't you?'

He stood up. 'I'd like you to leave now, Fay.'

She glared at him. 'Don't think you can dismiss me like one of your minions,' she said. 'I could still go to the press. I could still make things hot for you. How would your father like to see his practice in ruins? I don't suppose many people would want their medical needs catered for by an amoral philanderer.'

'Do what the hell you like, Fay!' he said wearily. 'I don't give a damn any more. Go to the papers. Go to the police. Go to the bloody Prime Minister for all I care. I've had enough. Just get out and don't come back. You've done your worst and much good may it do you.'

She got to her feet looking a little less confident. 'Don't think you'll come out of this unscathed,' she said. 'I know a lot of people and I'll make sure they all know what you are.'

'Perhaps you'd like to start with my receptionists,' he said. 'Then there are the nurses and the other doctors, not to mention the pharmacist. Oh, and don't forget the cleaners will you!' He walked to the door and opened it wide. She shot him a look of pure venom as she walked through it. He closed the door on her retreating back and sat down at his desk again, his head in his hands.

'Oh my God,' he groaned. 'What have I done?'

CHAPTER SIXTEEN

$\mathbf{A}$s Danni and her mother sat side by side on the train back to Meadbridge they were silent, each occupied with her own thoughts. Danni was remembering the incredible scene with Mark the previous afternoon. He had knocked on her door as she was packing to leave.

'May I come in, Danni?'

She'd been surprised to hear his voice. After a pause she'd opened the door to find him standing outside looking grave.

'May I come in? I want to talk to you.'

She turned without a word and he followed her into the room. 'Mum and I are leaving in the morning,' she said.

'I know.' He sighed. 'Can we sit down? I've got something I want to say to you.'

She indicated the one easy-chair and sat down herself on the edge of the bed.

'Danni, Claire has told me everything. How you applied for the job not knowing that she was my wife. How you met Richard and the unfortunate outcome.'

She shrugged. 'You make it sound so simple.'

'I don't mean to trivialize your feelings,' he said. 'You are the innocent victim in all of this and I realize how hurt you must be. I can't tell you how sorry I am, Danni. I know I'm the cause of it all and I want to try to make amends to you.'

'There's nothing you can do,' she said. 'Not for me anyway.

190

I have to leave – go home to Meadbridge and try to start again.'

'That's what I can help with – if you'll let me,' he said. 'When Ruth decided not to fulfil her part of our bargain all those years ago I was angry. Having a child meant so much to Claire; to me too. For me it meant a chance for us both to start again – repair what I'd already almost ruined. That was why when your mother decided to renege on our arrangement I told her she'd have to repay the money we'd paid her. Claire tried her hardest to make me relent. To be honest it began as a bluff. I thought it might force Ruth's hand – make her change her mind. But it didn't. She loved you too much to part with you. And who can blame her?'

Danni looked at him. 'I never knew any of this until recently. Because of you we lived close to poverty for years,' she told him. 'I wish you could see some of the places where we had to live. Mum couldn't afford to let me stay on at school and I had to work in dead-end jobs that I hated.'

He shook his head. 'I know. I know all that now and I'm sorry. Back then you were just a tiny baby,' he said. 'Not a real person. Not to me anyway. After you and your mother left I tried to forget the whole episode. It's only since you came here – since I saw you as a young woman – saw how well you and Claire got along together that I realized that you would have been a daughter to be proud of.'

She stared at him in amazement. 'I thought you didn't like me.'

He smiled. 'To be honest I couldn't help being a bit jealous of the bond you and Claire had,' he said. 'That was before I knew who you really were.' She opened her mouth to speak but he held up his hand.

'Don't say anything for a minute. Just listen. Hearing about you and Richard really brought it all home to me. Through me you've been the unwitting casualty of all the mistakes I've made and I want to try and make up for it.' He looked at her.

'I'd like to pay for you to go to art college. I'll support you right through the course; make you a monthly allowance. No need to work part time to make ends meet. I think it's the least I owe you. What do you say?'

'No!' She shook her head, her chin thrust forward stubbornly. 'It's too late.'

'It needn't be. Think about it, Danni. You have your whole life ahead of you. Claire says you have a genuine talent. She's all for my suggestion. She even suggests that if you like you could come and work with her again when you've qualified. You and she could extend the business – be equal partners.'

'*No!*' She stood up. 'If I get my art and design qualification it'll be through my own efforts,' she told him. 'Not paid for by you because you want to ease your conscience and feel better about yourself. Mum says that now she's out of your debt she'll be able to help me. I'll go to college part time and stack supermarket shelves to pay my way. I *won't* be beholden to you for anything.'

Sitting on the train Danni relived the scene in her mind as she had a dozen times since yesterday afternoon and told herself she had done the right thing – the only thing she could have done if she was to hang on to the tattered shreds of her self-esteem.

Ruth, on the other hand, was remembering how annoyed she'd been when Danni had told her she'd turned down Mark's suggestion. Unable to forget it she turned to Danni now.

'Why did you have to be so hasty yesterday?' she asked. 'Why couldn't you let Mark pay for you to go to college? He'd never miss the money.'

Danni shook her head. 'We've managed without his help all these years,' she said. 'I want him to live with his conscience. It's Claire he needs to make it up to, not me. We'll be fine, Mum. We don't need Mark Naylor.'

Ruth looked at her daughter and realized suddenly how

much she had grown up over the past months. 'And what about Rick?' she asked tentatively.

Danni flinched. 'I've got no choice, have I?' she said. 'By now he probably knows why I left. It helps a bit to think that. There's nothing either of us can do about it.'

Ruth took her hand and squeezed it. 'You'll be OK, Danni,' she said. 'You're strong; much stronger than I've ever been. I was cross when you turned down Mark's offer but I'm proud of you too. You'll meet another nice young guy and be happy again. You'll see.'

Danni shook her head. 'There'll never be another Rick.'

'Yes, there will. By the time I was your age I'd had lots of boyfriends. Come to think of it, I was already married.'

'And look what a disaster that was.' Danni turned to look at her mother. 'If it hadn't been for that waste of space, Tom Emerson and his gambling, you'd never have got into a mess with the Naylors.'

'And you wouldn't even have been born,' Ruth reminded her gently. 'So some good came out of it, wouldn't you say?'

'Sometimes I wonder. All I'm grateful for is that Tom wasn't my father,' Danni said vehemently. 'In fact, come to think of it I never really had a father at all, did I?'

'I suppose that's true.' Ruth looked thoughtfully at her daughter's face and felt angry again. It wasn't right that a girl of her age should be so bitter and unhappy. She pressed her hand again. 'We'll be all right, you and me, Danni,' she said. 'We've still got each other and after all that's all that really matters.'

But that night as she lay in the darkness, listening to the muffled sounds of her daughter's misery through the thin wall of her bedroom Ruth knew that it wasn't really all that mattered. There was something preying heavily on her mind; something she had hoped might never have to come out. Now she had to face the fact that it almost certainly would have to. She shrank from the thought, knowing that once the secret was out the loving relationship that she and her daughter had always shared would be destroyed.

Claire was working in the studio a week later when there was a ring at the bell. She put down her brushes and dusted her hands then went to answer it. A young man stood outside. She smiled at him.

'Hello. Can I help you?'

'Is Danni here?' he asked.

Instinctively Claire guessed who he was. 'It's Richard, isn't it?'

'Rick,' he corrected, his chin lifting proudly in a way that stopped the breath in her throat. It was a gesture of Mark's that she knew so well. She held the door open.

'Please come in,' she invited. 'I'm afraid that Danni isn't here. She left with her mother last week. She won't be back.'

'Do you have any idea why?'

Claire bit her lip. 'Perhaps it's your mother you should be talking to, Rick.'

'I've moved out,' he said. 'I'm not going back. She's cheated and lied to me all my life. I don't want to see her again.'

Claire sighed. To the young things were so straightforward – so black and white. Realizing that she was going to have to deal with this herself she said, 'Sit down. You'd better tell me what you know and perhaps I can fill in some of the blanks for you.'

He sat uneasily on the edge of the chair she drew up for him. 'I know that my father is . . .' He looked at her apologetically 'Your husband.'

'It's all right.' She smiled. 'I've known about you for a very long time. I just wish we could have met in happier circumstances.'

'Me too. At least he was honest with you, which is more than my mother was with me.' He shook his head. 'What I can't understand is why Danni suddenly said she didn't want

194

to be with me any more. I didn't believe her then and I still can't get my head round it.'

'I can see that I'll have to explain,' Claire said. 'It isn't easy, Rick, and even when you know you're not going to like it. But you're owed a proper explanation.' She took a deep breath. 'I have always been unable to have children. Almost twenty years ago Mark and I paid a woman to have a baby for us – with Mark as the father. That baby was Danni.'

He stared at her, momentarily dumbstruck. 'Oh God! I – don't know what to say.' He paused, letting the information sink in, then he looked at her. 'So – if that's the case, why wasn't she brought up by you?'

'Because when she was born her mother couldn't bring herself to give her up.'

He frowned. 'I see. So – did she come here to find her father?'

'I think she did – initially.'

His face cleared. 'I remember now. She told me once that she knew who her father was but she could never tell anyone because it would upset too many lives.'

Claire nodded. 'She found out that you were Mark's son by accident and couldn't bring herself to tell you that you and she were . . .'

He flinched 'Half-brother and sister?'

'I'm afraid so,' Claire said. 'I know it broke her heart to part with you.'

He looked desolate. 'So – that's it then. It's final, isn't it? I'll never see her again.'

She reached out to touch his hand. 'I'm so sorry, Rick. I know she loved you very much. It's all such a terrible tragedy but I do believe that what Danni has done is for the best. It must have cost her a great deal.'

He stood up. 'Thank you for telling me,' he said. 'Don't get up, Mrs Naylor. I'll see myself out.'

She watched from the studio window as he walked up the

area steps. 'Poor boy,' she said to herself. Could anything be more cruel? Suddenly she saw why Mark's father was so averse to modern infertility procedures.

As Mark walked through the town one Saturday afternoon three weeks later he hummed a tune under his breath. He was on a mission – looking for a present for Claire. In two weeks' time it would be their wedding anniversary and this year he had made up his mind to do something special. Things were looking up. They had never been so happy. It was almost like falling in love afresh. The work at the surgery was finished. The new extension was furnished and equipped. Only yester-day he had appointed a new junior doctor to replace Adam Bennett, and two more nurses. Best of all, his father had been elected on to the town council two weeks ago.

George was in his element and had told his son regretfully on the evening of his election that he would have to take a back seat as far as the practice was concerned from now on. In future his priority would be his council duties. Mark could barely conceal a gleeful smile. *God help the council*, he'd muttered under his breath.

But George wasn't quite done with interfering in family matters. One of the first things he had done was to unearth a long-forgotten deed on the houses in Grafton Place. When they were first built there was a ban on their use as business premises.

Apparently it had never been repealed.

'Of course I shan't point out to anyone that Claire's virtu-ally breaking the law,' he'd said with a jovial chuckle. 'But it might be policy to take that sign of hers down. You know ...' He gave Mark a conspiratorial wink. 'Just in case.'

Trust Dad! 'Typical of him to find out the one thing that would make life difficult,' Mark had said to Claire as he helped her take down the *Cavendish Interior Designs* board from the basement wall.

He was walking past the town's largest estate agency when something in the window attracted his attention.

Lease of shop premises for sale with storage rooms above, suitable for conversion to living accommodation.

Mark leaned closer to look at the photograph and was surprised to see that the shop in question was *Style and Grace*. What was Fay up to now? On impulse he went inside.

'The shop was a ladies' boutique,' the girl behind the desk explained. 'But the previous owner is not selling it as a going concern. She's moving on – taking the business name and all her stock with her to start again in Yorkshire.'

Mark heaved a sigh of relief. So Fay was going. She had finally let go. On impulse he asked, 'Would it be possible for me to have a look at the place now?'

'Certainly sir.' The girl went into an office at the back and came back with a labelled key. 'One of our negotiators will take you round there now.'

Standing in the empty shop twenty minutes later Mark looked round and felt a little *frisson* of excitement. He was pretty sure it was exactly right for what he had in mind. Back at the office he put in an offer.

Ruth was worried about Danni. She was working in a newsagent's shop and hating every minute. When Ruth had reminded her that enrolment for the next term's art and design classes was to be held that week Danni had dropped a bombshell.

'I'm not going.'

'Why not?' Ruth stared at her daughter. 'I told you I'd pay. I can easily afford it now.'

'I've given it up.'

'What do you mean, you've given it up?' Ruth was shocked. 'Danni! You can't. You're talented. It's all you've ever wanted to do.'

'Well, I don't want it any more.'

Ruth stared at her incredulously. 'Don't want it any more?'

'Mum! You sound like a parrot,' Danni snapped. 'Look, it's going to take me years to qualify at this rate. I'm better off training for something else. I'll see if I can get on to one of those re-employment schemes and earn while I'm training.' She shrugged. 'You never know, perhaps I'll marry some rich old guy or a footballer or something and end my days in luxury!'

'Don't be flippant, Danni. Why didn't you let Mark pay for you to go to college? You might as well have accepted seeing that he wanted to do it.'

'Why should he pay for me? I'm nothing to him and he couldn't have foreseen that I'd meet Rick. I'd have felt obliged to pay him back and I don't want to live for years in debt to him like you did.' Seeing Ruth flinch she said quickly. 'Sorry, Mum. I didn't mean it to come out like that, but I think we both have to put the Naylors behind us now.'

'But you were so fond of Claire,' Ruth said. 'You loved working with her. You could always go back. I know she'd have you like a shot.'

'You know why I can't go back there.' Danni tossed her head. 'I've made up my mind to forget any of it ever happened. Cavendish Design; Mark and Claire – Rick too. I'm going to wipe them all out of my memory. It'll be like this year never happened – like none of them ever existed. It's got to be a completely new start or nothing.'

Ruth looked at her in dismay. 'So – what are you going to do, then?'

'I don't know. I'll see what's on offer.'

But Ruth wasn't taken in by Danni's bravado. She was pale and she'd lost weight. The vitality had gone from her eyes. Ruth still heard her crying into her pillow late at night too, long after she should have been asleep. Ruth knew that in spite of her protestations Danni was desperately unhappy and longed to be back at Haylesmere. She knew also that it would be a very long time before she got over Rick.

Mark passed the envelope across the breakfast table. Claire looked at it, then up at him.

'What is it?'

He laughed. 'Only one way to find out.'

'It's too thick for a card,' she said, turning it over in her hands.

'It's your anniversary present,' he told her. 'Go on, Claire – open it.'

She slid a knife under the flap and drew out the contents. She looked at it and then at him. 'An estate agent's brochure – for a shop?' she looked again at the leaflet, frowning. 'Isn't this Fay's place?'

He nodded. 'She's gone, Claire. Fay has left at last. We've seen the last of her.'

She shook her head. 'But I don't understand. What's this for?'

'It's yours,' he told her. 'I was passing the agent's and I saw it was for sale – the lease, that is. It's in a marvellous position, Claire, and with the ban on running the business from here . . .'

'Are you telling me you've actually *bought* it?'

'Yes! It's your anniversary present. Just wait till you see it. It's got so much potential. There are rooms upstairs too. You could turn them into a self-contained flat and let it to help with your expenses. There's even separate access at the back. It's perfect.' His eyes were shining with excitement. 'I can't wait for you to see it.'

'Well – you've certainly got it all mapped out.' Claire couldn't help smiling in spite of herself. To begin with she'd been quite shocked by Mark's insensitivity – presenting her with his ex-mistress's shop as an anniversary present. On the other hand it was a nice touch of irony. She knew the shop too, and she had to agree that it would make a wonderful base for her business. 'Danni would have loved it,' she said wistfully.

He nodded. 'You miss her, don't you?'

'To think she should have been our daughter, Mark,' Claire said. 'It would have been such a success. She and I really got along together.'

'And if it hadn't been for me she'd still be here.'

Claire sighed. 'What a tragedy. Who would have thought she and Richard would meet?' She looked at him. 'It makes sense of what your father is always saying, doesn't it?'

'I suppose he does have a point,' he acceded. 'You can't stop progress though, whatever anyone says. Anyway . . .' He stood up. 'It's my day off, so shall we go and look at the shop first? After that I've booked a special lunch for us and then this evening I've got tickets for that show you've been longing to see.'

Claire looked round the empty shop. Once the changing-cubicles had been ripped out there would be ample space for everything. She would still use her studio at home for much of the creative work, but here she could make a stylish venue where prospective clients could discuss their needs in comfort. She half-closed her eyes, visualizing a smart desk and comfortable chairs – soft, muted colours; a deep-pile carpet, or maybe a polished wood floor. She imagined designing the place to create a restful yet sophisticated atmosphere. She could display some large blown-up photographs of some of her finest room settings taken from the album where she kept all of her work. There would be ample space to hang generous fabric and carpet samples and at the back she would have an office where the business side of her work would be done, out of sight of the public. She would have flowers and . . .

'So? I take it you approve.' Mark had been watching her.

She turned to him with shining eyes. 'Oh, Mark, it's lovely. I could do so much with it.'

'That's what I thought.' He put his hands on her shoulders and looked into her eyes. 'You don't mind, do you, that it was Fay's? I didn't buy it for her you know.'

'I know – and I don't mind at all.'

'Promise?'

'Promise.'

'I can't tell you how wonderful it is to see you looking happy again,' he said. 'I know I haven't made you happy and I really don't deserve you but I'm going to try so hard to make up for all the neglect and the hurt I've caused you over the years.' He cupped her chin with his hand. 'I can't think why you've put up with me this long but I'm so grateful that you have.' He brushed her cheek with his lips. 'I do love you, you know. I always have. It was just . . .' She put a finger against his lips.

'No recriminations,' she said softly. 'I love you too or I'd have left long ago, so let's say no more about it.' She looked around her. 'It was so good of you to think of this. I'm going to have such a ball doing it all up.'

Danni stood behind the counter at Readmore's. It was 8 a.m. and she'd been at work since five, taking delivery of the papers, sorting and marking them and packing the paper-boys' bags. The last of the boys had now departed and she looked at her watch, wondering if she could risk leaving her post for a few minutes to make herself a cup of tea.

She popped through to the grubby little kitchen at the back, filled the kettle and dropped a teabag into a mug. She did the early shift on alternate weeks with the proprietor. When she started work at five she was finished at lunch-time, but by the time she'd walked back to the flat she was too tired to think of doing anything else with her day. Standing waiting for the kettle to boil she wondered how much longer she could stick this job or indeed Meadbridge. Although she had grown up in the town she felt she didn't belong here any more.

Everyone she'd known at school seemed to have either moved on or got married. She had nothing in common with any of them any more. Not that she ever really had had.

Her heart ached for Haylesmere, for Claire and the job she had left behind. As for Rick, she tried hard to push all thoughts of him from her mind. Sometimes she almost succeeded, except late at night in the quiet darkness of the small hours when images of him invaded her mind, refusing to give her any peace. She knew she must soon do something about training for a job that would be more rewarding but she had no idea what. She was permanently exhausted and could summon neither enthusiasm nor interest for anything. A deadly lethargy seemed to have turned her body to lead and her brain to mush. There was no future, she told herself; so why bother to plan for one?

She made her tea and carried it through to the shop where she found an elderly man in a flat cap standing at the counter bristling with impatience

'Ah! So *that's* where you were – tea drinking!' he accused. He slapped a newspaper on the counter. 'This is the second time this week that kid has delivered the *Guardian* to me!' he complained. 'I don't read this rubbish. I have the *Daily Mirror*; always have. You can keep this and you know where you can stick it!'

Danni took a deep breath and counted to ten under her breath. Unfolding the paper she pointed to the pencilled address on the top. 'Is this your address?'

'No! It flamin' well ain't!' he said. 'I've just said, ain't I? It's next door.'

'There's a new paper boy on your route,' she told him. 'He's obviously a bit muddled with the numbers. He's put the papers through the wrong doors, that's all.'

'I know that! I'm not stupid! *Twice* in one week he's done it and it ain't bloody good enough!'

'I'll try to see that it doesn't happen again,' Danni said. 'But there was no need to come to the shop; you could just have swapped with your neighbour.'

'*Him*? I don't speak to him or his toffee-nosed bitch of a missis. It's your job to make sure the papers gets to the right address. If you can't you shouldn't be doing the job, you silly mare!'

Danni felt her cheeks flame. 'Don't you speak to me like that,' she said, trying hard to keep her temper. 'I've explained: it's not my fault.'

'It *is* your fault and I'll speak to you any way I see fit,' the man insisted, his face puce. 'Maybe someone should speak to your boss about the way you're messin' folks about – out the back drinkin' tea all day instead of seein' that folks gets their right paper.'

Danni's control snapped. 'Oh, get lost you bad-tempered old git.' She took a *Daily Mirror* from the pile on the counter and pushed it under his nose. 'Here – take this and you know what you can do with it.' He began to back away from the counter. 'And from today I'm taking you off the delivery list,' she shouted. 'I'm not paid to stand here listening to old mingers like you swearing and shouting at me. If you can walk to the shop you can collect your own sodding paper!'

His face was purple as he stared at her, temporarily shocked into silence. He shook the paper at her. 'You ain't 'eard the last of this!' he shouted. 'I'll get you sacked for this!'

'No you won't!' Danni pulled off the overall she wore. 'You won't because I'm leaving – *right now*!' She walked round the counter and the old man beat a hasty retreat as she bore down on him. She slammed the door and turned over the 'closed' sign, then she found a piece of paper and scribbled a hasty resignation note for the shop's owner. She took her coat from the hook on the back door and let herself out.

When she arrived back at the flat Ruth was preparing to leave for work. 'Danni! What are you doing home? Are you all right?'

'No, I'm not all right!' She threw herself into a chair and broke into a torrent of tears. 'Nothing's all right, Mum. Nothing will ever be all right again. I've walked out on that job. I'm not putting up with being sworn at. I hate it! I hate everything.'

Ruth's heart sank. She'd been prepared for Danni to be upset and depressed when they'd left Haylesmere but she'd told herself that she was young – she'd soon bounce back. All she needed was a change of scene and some time. But it had been weeks now since she'd come home and if anything she was getting worse, not better. Now she'd made herself unemployed again. The old pattern was re-establishing itself. She went to Danni and put her arms round her.

'Don't cry, love. Look, I'll ring in sick and we'll spend the day together.'

Danni shook her head. 'No! There's no need for that. Just leave me. I'll be all right.'

'No,' Ruth said firmly. 'I'm going to make you a proper cooked breakfast and you're going to tell me exactly what happened. We're going to have a talk, you and I. There are things you need to know and this seems as good a time as any.'

Claire was in her element, supervising the refurbishment of the shop. There had been a lavish article with colour photographs in the local papers, announcing the opening of the new premises, and she had put advertisements in several of the county magazines too. The sign outside had been repainted. Already, *Cavendish Interior Design* was emblazoned above the shop in tasteful flowing script. The new woodblock floor had been laid and tomorrow her furniture and all the samples were being delivered. She would be open for business on Monday and she couldn't wait.

She had decided that the window would contain only a flower arrangement and a sign, briefly outlining the services she could provide. In the small office at the back her new computer sat on the desk she had brought from home and she sat down to send her daily batch of e-mails. Clicking on 'receive' she was surprised to see that there was one from Richard Scott.

Congratulations on your new venture, Mrs Naylor. Best wishes from Richard. She read it thoughtfully. When she had heard that Fay had left for Yorkshire she had assumed that Richard had gone too. She had only half believed him when he had said he didn't want to speak to his mother again. Clearly they'd parted on bad terms, but she had assumed that by now he would have forgiven her; clearly it wasn't so. If he had seen her article in the local paper he must still be in Haylesmere. On impulse she clicked on 'reply'.

Dear Richard. Thank you so much for your good wishes. Are you still in the neighbourhood? If so do feel free to drop in and see me. Best wishes, Claire.

After Ruth's fry-up of bacon, eggs and tomatoes with fried bread Danni felt stronger. Ruth came to the table with a pot of freshly made tea and sat down opposite her.

'That was lovely, Mum,' Danni said as she pushed her plate away. 'But are you sure it's OK for you to take the day off?'

'It's fine,' Ruth assured her. 'I've taken a day's holiday so you needn't worry. Now, tell me what happened to upset you at the shop.'

Danni recounted the dispute with the man in the cap. But in telling it she suddenly saw the funny side and soon she and Ruth were laughing. Encouraged by Ruth's amusement she imitated the man's accent and mannerisms, making her mother laugh even more till at last Ruth said:

'Why don't you go back? If you make your boss laugh as much as you have me I'm sure he'll understand.' But Danni shook her head.

'I can't go back,' she said, suddenly serious again. 'At the moment I feel I can't work anywhere. I had my dream job and that's all over. I know I'll have to find another way to earn a living and I will. But I can't face it yet, not just at the moment.' She looked at her mother. 'You said you had something to tell me. What was it?'

'Yes.' Ruth's heart gave a lurch and she moistened her lips, pouring two cups of tea to give herself time to think. 'I confess I don't know where to begin, Danni,' she said, looking up. 'You're going to be so shocked.'

'Mum!' Danni laughed nervously. 'Stop it. You're scaring me now. What can you possibly have done that's so awful?'

'I told a lie,' Ruth began. 'A really big one. I've gone on lying too – to you – even to myself in the end. It's something I regret more than I can tell you. Like all lies this one has grown and grown so that I've had to tell more lies to cover it up.'

'OK, so you told a few porkies. Who hasn't?'

'This was a bit more than a porkie, as you call it. It happened a long time ago; before you were born.'

Danni looked puzzled. 'So – why does it concern me?'

'Because you are at the heart of it. It can't go on, Danni. It has to end here and now.' Ruth reached out to touch her daughter's hand. 'Please don't hate me for this.' She swallowed hard. 'The surrogacy – it was a fake. Mark Naylor isn't – never was, your father.'

For a moment Danni was speechless with shock. Wide-eyed, she asked, 'So – you're saying that my father was. . . ?'

'Yes. Tom. My husband. The one man you never wanted for your father.'

Danni stared at her mother. 'But – how can you be sure?'

'I'm sure all right. I always have been. I agreed to be a surrogate for the Naylors in good faith, but even before things could be put into motion I found out that I was pregnant with Tom's child.' Ruth wrapped her hands round her teacup. 'I hoped and prayed that I was wrong but I did a test and it was positive. It was a shock – a potential disaster. I thought about it long and hard and in the end I decided to bluff it out – go along with it. We desperately needed the money to pay off Tom's debts. We were getting all kind of threats. God only knows what would have happened if I hadn't agreed.'

'But you told me he left you because he hated the thought of you carrying another man's child.'

'He did. I never told him the truth. I daren't. He'd have been sure to let it slip some night in the pub when he'd had a few and if word had reached the Naylors everything would have been ruined.'

Danni was shaking her head. 'But Mark – he's a doctor. He's no fool. He knew you were married so there was always a chance. Wasn't there some way he could check that the child was his?'

Ruth shrugged. 'Perhaps. Who knows? He trusted me. Sometimes I think he closed his eyes to the possibility because they wanted a baby so much. And God knows we desperately needed the money.'

'So you went ahead with it – paid Tom's debts and ended up losing everything – your husband, your home – your job.' Danni looked at her mother. 'And finished up with a child to bring up alone and a massive debt.'

Ruth nodded. 'Over the years I even managed to convince myself that it wasn't a lie – that you *were* Mark's child; that I hadn't deceived anyone. But deep down the truth was always there, niggling away at my guilt like a raw wound.' She looked at Danni. 'You've got a fool for a mother, Danni. A liar and a stupid, gullible idiot. I even messed up your life through my selfishness and my cheating, keeping you when all the time you could have had a good life with well-off parents; an education and everything you could ever have wanted.' Her eyes filled with tears. 'I wouldn't blame you if you despised me.'

Danni paused, looking long and hard at her mother. 'Despise you?' she said. 'For keeping me? Everything you went through was for that waste of space Tom Emerson. OK, I'm not over the moon to find that he's my father, but it doesn't matter because he's never going to know.' She looked at her mother. 'Did you know that Claire had a termination when she was at university?'

'No!'

'It was Mark's baby but it happened at the wrong time. Things went wrong which was why she couldn't have any more children.'

'Oh my God!' Ruth's eyes filled with tears. 'And I took you from her.'

'You did what you felt you had to do, Mum,' Danni said. 'And I just hope that I turn out to be like you and not like Tom because I've got the best Mum in the world.' She stood up and went to her mother. 'Don't ever think I blamed you after all you've done for me?'

'I always hoped I'd never have to tell you,' Ruth said. 'When you came home I was determined to make it up to you in any way I could. I hoped you'd settle down again, go to college and make a new start. But it hasn't happened. I didn't realize how much you cared for that young man but I've had to watch your unhappiness. I've seen you pining for Rick and in my heart I knew that the only way I could make it right was to do the decent thing – come out in the open and tell you the truth, what ever it cost.' She hugged her daughter. 'I couldn't let you go on being so miserable.' She looked at Danni. 'I lied to Claire and Mark. It was a terrible – a wicked, unforgivable lie.'

'But you paid back every penny they gave you. You spent years of hardship to do it. I think you've more than paid for your mistake.'

Ruth paused. 'They'll have to know now, of course.'

'Why should they?'

'I think you'll have to tell them – when you go back to Haylesmere.'

'But I'm not going back.'

Ruth held Danni at arm's length. 'I don't think it's quite sunk in yet, has its love? Don't you see? You and Rick are not related in any way. There's nothing in the world to stop you being together!'

Danni caught her breath. '*Oh!*' Her heart gave a joyful leap as the realization hit her. 'But if I were to go back it would all have to come out. I'd feel I was letting you down, Mum – betraying you.'

'Not if it's what I want and I ask you to do it.' Ruth shook her head. 'I betrayed Claire and Mark all those years ago. I betrayed you too, and I've been paying the price for it ever since. You've had to pay the price too and nothing can hurt me any worse than that. I've been carrying this burden for so long, I can't tell you what a relief it'll be to be able to put it down at last.' She hugged Danni. 'Why don't you look up the trains and go today? No time like the present.'

CHAPTER SEVENTEEN

In Grafton Place a thick carpet of leaves lined the pavements. The trees in the park had turned from green to russet and gold since Danni left. Only a few weeks had elapsed since the series of events that had shattered her happiness, yet it felt more like years.

As she drew closer to number 64 her heart began to beat faster. She looked forward to seeing Claire again though she wondered what kind of reception she would get once she said what she had to say. As for Rick, she refused to allow herself to think about him. Suppose he had met someone else in her absence? He might possibly have discovered the truth about their blood tie. It would have shaken him as much as it had her. But in any case he must feel badly let down by her. Either way he would surely be trying hard to forget her and make a new start. She longed to find him and put things right, but she couldn't be sure that it would ever be the same between them. By not confiding in him she might have damaged their relationship beyond repair.

On reaching number 64 she paused by the area steps. Something was missing. Claire's sign for Cavendish Design had gone. A feeling of panic clutched at her heart. Could they have moved? If they had how would she find them? She walked up the steps and rang the bell. An unfamiliar woman answered the door. She wore a print overall and a sour expression. She looked Danni up and down suspiciously.

'Yes?'

'Does Mrs Naylor still live here?'

'Who wants to know?'

'I'm Danni Blake. I used to work for Mrs Naylor. Is she in?'

'At this time of day? No. She's at the shop.'

Danni frowned. 'Shop. What shop?'

The woman raised an eyebrow. 'Surely you'd know if you used to work for her?'

Danni swallowed the sharp retort she longed to make. 'If you could just tell me where the shop is I needn't trouble you any further.'

'If you'd like to leave your name and a telephone number I'll tell her when she gets home,' the woman said. 'It don't do to give out personal details to all and sundry.' At that moment there was a shrill bark and a small brown furry bundle hurled itself at Danni.

'*Maddie*!' Danni picked up the little dog and submitted to having her face licked all over. 'Maddie, I've missed you so much,' Danni said burying her face in the dog's fur.

Convinced at last that the girl on the doorstep wasn't a criminal the woman relented. 'Mrs Naylor's shop is in the High Street; just off the market square,' she said. Then, snatching a reluctant Maddie from Danni's arms she closed the door firmly before she could be asked any more questions.

Danni turned, walked down the front steps and back in the direction of the town.

She saw as soon as she turned into the street that the shop that had been run by Rick's mother and once known as *Style and Grace* was now no longer a fashion boutique. Even from where she stood on the corner she could see that the sign had changed. Now, to her surprise she saw the words *Cavendish Interior Design* in elegant flowing script, royal blue on white, painted on the fascia above the bow window.

211

Surprised, Danni walked along the street for a closer look. A large flower arrangement and a photograph on an easel stood in the window. It was a large coloured photograph of an elegant house which Danni instantly recognized as the exterior of the Frobishers' house, which she and Claire had worked on together. There was another photograph of the drawing-room and Danni felt a little glow of pride remembering that she had had a hand in its design. A discreet sign in the front of the window laid out the services that Cavendish Design could provide and an addition at the bottom of the sign read: Garden landscaping: an additional service provided by *Rowlands Landscaping*. Phil Rowlands. Taking her courage in both hands she pushed open the door and walked in.

'Good afternoon. What can I . . .' Claire looked up from her desk in the corner of the office and gave a gasp. She pulled off her glasses and stared open-mouthed. '*Danni!* Is it really you?'

Danni laughed. 'It was last time I looked,' she said.

Claire stood up and came across to hug her warmly. 'It's so good to see you. What brings you to Haylesmere? Where are you staying?'

'I wanted to see you,' Danni told her. 'I went to the house but I was told you were at the shop. At least I was once Maddie had vouched for my credentials.'

Claire laughed. 'You've met Mrs Haynes then, our tame dragon!'

'Not so tame, I'd say.' Danni looked around her. 'This is lovely – really posh. It was quite a surprise to hear you had a shop.'

'It's a long story. I've been here a few weeks now. It used to belong to Fay Scott.' Claire looked at her. 'You know, Richard's mother.'

'Yes. I remember.'

'She's moved. Gone up north – Yorkshire.' There was a pause during which Danni wondered whether Rick had gone with his mother, then Claire asked, 'Where did you say you were staying?'

'I didn't. I haven't sorted that out yet. I need to talk to you, Claire. You and Mark as a matter of fact.'

'Then you must stay at Grafton Place. Your old room is still there and vacant. I'm sure Maddie will be delighted.'

'What about Mrs. . . ?'

'Haynes? She doesn't live in. She's really quite nice when you get to know her; just fiercely protective.' Claire looked at her watch. 'Look, I might as well shut up shop for the day. We'll drop in at the supermarket for something nice for dinner and a bottle of champagne as this is a celebration.' She went into the room at the back and returned with her coat and bag while Danni waited, feeling distinctly uncomfortable.

'Look, Claire,' she said, 'I don't want you to go to any trouble. In fact when you hear what I have to say you might not feel like celebrating after all. In fact you might change your mind about asking me to stay.'

Claire stopped in the act of taking her keys from a drawer to look at her former employee. 'What is it, Danni? You're beginning to scare me.'

'I'd rather wait until Mark is home.'

'No way!' Claire went across and locked the shop door, then she took off her coat. 'After what you've just said I'm not being kept on pins for the rest of the afternoon. Come through to the back. I'll put the kettle on. I want to hear this right now.'

The little room at the back of the shop was set out as an office with a desk and two chairs. Leading off it was a tiny kitchen where Claire went to fill the kettle.

'Sit down,' she called through to Danni.

Danni took a seat and presently Claire came back with two mugs of tea and a tin of biscuits. She sat down opposite Danni and looked expectantly at her. 'OK, I'm ready. Whatever it is you'd better hit me with it.'

Danni took a deep breath. 'The surrogacy,' she began.

'Yes?'

Danni decided to come straight to the point. 'It was a fake,' she said. 'It wasn't intentional but after Mum agreed to go through with it – and before Mark could go ahead with – with the – procedure she did a test and found that she was pregnant already – by Tom, her husband.'

Claire let out her breath on a sigh of relief. 'Is that all? I thought it was something terrible.'

Danni stared at her. 'But it *is*! Mum lied to you. She took your money under false pretences because she was desperate to pay Tom's debts, but she's lived with the guilt of it for years. She even lied to me about it. She only told me because she could see how unhappy I was about splitting up with Rick.'

'Poor Ruth,' Claire shook her head. 'You know, I always had a feeling she might have already been pregnant,' she said. 'Just a woman's instinct – something about that certain look a woman gets in the early stages. I couldn't be sure of course and I certainly wasn't going to express my doubts to Mark. I told myself that the baby might just as easily have been his. And if the truth is known maybe it didn't matter to me all that much whose child it was as long as I would be getting it in the end.' She looked up. 'So how's that for selfish?'

'You're not angry then?'

Claire reached out to touch her hand. 'Why should I be angry with you? You are the innocent party in all this. Poor Ruth has paid a terrible price for what happened, in every way possible. The one thing she was lucky in was having you for a daughter.'

'We do have to tell Mark though, don't we?' Danni asked.

'Only if you really want to? You could say it's all water under the bridge now.'

'But I *need* to, Claire. I want to make things right with Rick, you see.'

'Yes of course you do. I wasn't thinking. He came to see me

– wanted to know if I knew why you'd dropped him so abruptly. I had to tell him that you'd just found out that you were half-siblings.'

'So – has he gone to Yorkshire with his mother?'

Claire shook her head. 'No. He couldn't forgive her for lying to him all his life, holding back his father's identity. He was deeply hurt by it.'

'Is he still working for Phil Rowlands?'

Claire smiled. 'Yes, he certainly is. It was through him that Phil and I teamed up. We're not in partnership or anything; at least not yet, but we recommend each other and so far we've teamed up on a couple of projects and it seems to work really well.'

'I saw the notice in the window,' Danni said. She sighed. 'I really miss working with you.'

'Have you started a new course at college?' Claire asked.

Danni shook her head. 'I decided not to – couldn't see the point any more.'

'That's a shame; and a terrible waste. You really do have talent, Danni.' Claire reached across to touch her hand. 'Was it because you were depressed – about Richard.'

'Partly, I suppose – among other things. Everything just seemed to go pear-shaped and I just gave up.'

'So – what are you going to do – about Richard, I mean?'

Danni felt herself blush. 'To be honest I haven't a clue; don't know where to start.'

Claire peered at her. 'Would you like me to fix something? I could invite him to dinner.'

Danni shook her head. 'No. Thanks, Claire but I'd rather talk to Mark first and then try to see Rick on my own.'

'Well, it's up to you.' Claire stood up. 'Come on. First things first. Let's go and organize some food.'

Mark was as surprised to see Danni as Claire had been. Claire insisted that they eat first before Danni dropped her bombshell, but Mark sensed that there was something brewing and dinner was a strained affair; each of the three of them attempting to make small talk but failing. As Claire brought the coffee tray to the table she said:

'OK, I was wrong. We should have got this out of the way first. Danni has something to tell you, Mark.' She looked at Danni. 'Do you want to tell him or shall I?'

'I will,' Danni said. Straightening her shoulders she took a deep breath. 'I'm not your daughter, Mark,' she said. 'I never was. Ruth was already pregnant when she agreed to be a surrogate mother for you.'

There was a moment's silence as Mark leaned back in his chair, looking first at his wife and then at Danni.

'Is this supposed to make some kind of difference to me?' he asked.

Taken aback, Danni looked at Claire. 'Mum lied to you,' she said. 'She took your money under false pretences. She only did it because she was desperate to help Tom and she's suffered for it ever since because . . .' Mark held up his hand.

'She was the one who suffered,' he said. 'I can see now that she lost everything because of it. And to my shame I made everything worse for her. Because of my vindictiveness I made sure that she – and you lived in poverty. I think you could say that she's paid back the debt in more than full measure.' He patted Danni's shoulder. 'None of this is your fault,' he assured her. 'You're a person in your own right; a young woman whom Claire and I have come to like and respect. Ruth did a good job bringing you up in spite of all the difficulties. No.' He reached out and took Claire's hand. 'Right at the root of all this – before we even knew Ruth – was a selfish man who had no thought for anyone but himself. And that was me. So if there's any blame to be apportioned you know where to look.'

There was a moment's silence then Claire said, 'Danni split with Richard because she thought there was a blood-tie between them. Now that she knows there isn't . . .'

'Of course!' Mark hit his forehead with the heel of his hand. 'We must do something about it.' He looked at Claire. 'Why didn't you invite him over?'

'I didn't want that,' Danni put in. 'I should have been honest with him but I chickened out. It's up to me to put things right.' She looked at Claire. 'If you could just find out where he's working.'

'I will. I'll ring Phil this evening.' Seeing the look on Danni's face she held up her hand. 'Don't worry. I shan't give anything away.'

Later that evening Claire came to Danni's room. 'I've had a word with Phil,' she said. 'I had to tell him a bit about what was going on but I've sworn him to secrecy. If you want to see Rick you can go to where he'll be working tomorrow lunchtime. Phil will stay well out of the way so that you can have some privacy.'

Danni's heart quickened. 'Thanks, Claire.'

'You might be surprised when I tell you where it is.' Claire sat down on the bed. 'Remember that neglected garden that Richard was so fond of?'

'The one he was trying to restore?'

'Yes. It seems that someone has bought it. They plan to demolish the house and rebuild. Phil's hoping we might get the commission if we play our cards right but that's a long way off yet.'

'I hope they won't demolish the garden,' Danni said. 'That would break Rick's heart.'

'No. It seems that the new owner wants Richard to continue with his work in the garden. He's been beavering away non-stop in his spare time, Phil says, which is why he'll be there tomorrow in his lunch-hour. So now it's up to you.'

'Thanks. I'm really grateful.'

Claire stood up and went to the door. 'Better get some sleep then.' She paused a moment then looked back. 'Danni, if all goes well tomorrow you're more than welcome to your old job back. You do know that, don't you?'

'Oh, Claire!' Danni felt tears prick her eyelids. 'Thank you.'

'Don't thank me. I really need someone and I'd like it to be you.' She smiled. 'There are some rooms upstairs at the shop. I'm having them converted into a little flat. Maybe you and ...'

'*Don't!*' Danni held up her hand. 'It's like tempting providence, as Mum always says. Let's just wait and see. Who knows, this time tomorrow I might be back in Meadbridge.'

'Well, I'm not buying that,' Claire said. 'Anyway, get to bed now. Don't rush in the morning. You've had a traumatic day. If I don't see you in the morning, good luck!'

'You already knew, didn't you?'

Claire and Mark were alone in their room later that night getting ready for bed. She looked at him through the dressing-table mirror as she took off her make-up. His expression confirmed her suspicion. 'All these years and you've never said a thing.'

Mark sat down on the bed. 'It was our last chance,' he said. 'After my affair with Fay and then Richard's birth I felt pretty rotten. I wanted you to have the child you longed for; the child I felt I owed you. Yes, OK I guessed just as you did about Ruth, but I chose to turn a blind eye.' He sighed. 'I should have known she'd change her mind the minute she held the baby.'

Claire stared at her reflection in the mirror, her eyes reminiscent. 'It was so awful, Mark. Ruth saying she couldn't part with the baby – you shouting at her, saying she'd have to pay you back. It was like some kind of nightmare.'

'And it drove us even further apart,' Mark finished for her. 'I've always known that. I just didn't know what I could ever do to make it up to you. The look on your face when you held that baby in your arms haunted me. I was so bloody angry with Ruth.'

'And deep down you resented me for making you feel guilty.' Claire turned to look at him, her eyes wide with remembered pain. He stood up and crossed the room to her.

'Darling.' He raised her to her feet and held her close, stroking her hair. 'Forgive me,' he said, his lips against her cheek. 'I don't deserve you. I couldn't have blamed you if you'd left me. But I promise you that from now on you're my first and only priority – all that matters is your happiness.'

They clung to each other for a long moment then Claire looked up at him and said, 'It's odd, isn't it, that we've got Danni back again. She may not have ever been our daughter but I have a feeling that this way is probably even better.'

'Danni is her own person,' he said. 'She belongs to no one – except maybe Richard – in time.' He held her a little away from him, his eyes glinting. 'There's something else,' he said. 'Something no one knows yet.'

'What? Tell me.'

'I bought that derelict old house and garden that Richard loves so much,' he told her. 'I'm the mystery buyer. It's my way of making up to him for all the years he was deprived of a father. When the garden is finished I shall tell him it's his to do as he likes with.'

She stared at him, wide-eyed. 'But – how did you know about it?'

'I was talking to your colleague, Phil Rowlands,' he said. 'He gave me the idea.'

'What about the ruined house – what are you going to do with that?'

He shrugged. 'Haven't a clue. But between you and Phil Rowlands, Danni and Richard I don't foresee too many problems, do you?'

Laughing, she hugged him. 'Doctor Mark Naylor, you're a devious, scheming . . .' He put his fingers over her lips.

'Now then. Can't have you calling me names, can I?'

'I was going to say a devious, scheming angel,' she told

him. 'Though on reflection I don't think angel suits you.'

He laughed. 'I don't think it does either!'

Danni hardly slept that night and when she woke in the morning she thought at first that she had dreamed the whole thing. She looked at the bedside clock and was surprised to see that it was already half past eight. She got up quickly, showered and dressed and went down to the kitchen where she found Mrs Haynes washing up the breakfast dishes. This morning the housekeeper seemed more amenable.

'Good morning,' she said with what passed for a smile. 'You wouldn't believe the trouble I've had, keeping this dog from coming upstairs to get you. Funny how they seem to know when there's a visitor in the house.'

Danni bent to pick Maddie up. 'I expect she remembers that I always took her for a walk first thing,' she said. 'I'll take her now if you like, then perhaps she'll settle down.'

'Not till you've eaten you won't! There's bacon and eggs already drying out in the oven,' Mrs Haynes said. 'So put that hound down and eat your breakfast, girl.' She looked Danni over scathingly. 'You're far too skinny if you ask me.'

Although she had no appetite Danni obediently ate her breakfast, then took Maddie for a walk. When she came back she asked if she could help with the housework but Mrs Haynes looked scandalized. 'I should just think not!' she said. 'I don't know what Mrs Naylor would think if she heard I'd let you loose with the vacuum cleaner.'

Danni laughed. 'I used to do it when I lived here,' she said. 'Surely there's something I can do?'

The housekeeper looked thoughtful. 'Well, there are one or two things we need from the shops. Maybe that'd keep you occupied for a while.'

Danni took the list gratefully and set off. It was still two hours before she could go to meet Rick. Two hours that stretched before her like two centuries.

*

The old house was off the beaten track – quite a long walk from the nearest bus stop. Danni wore the only clothes she'd brought with her, jeans and a jacket and sensible trainers. Hardly glamorous but she had no choice. All she'd stuffed into her backpack was a change of underwear. It was warm for late autumn; one of those mellow blue and golden days to cherish before the winter sets in. But the walk was further than she had realized and by the time she reached the lane she was hot and weary.

A van with *Rowlands Landscaping* painted on the side was parked outside, confirming that Rick was there. The battered wrought-iron gate stood open and at once she saw a huge difference. The trees and shrubs had been carefully pruned, the borders weeded and the driveway newly gravelled. She could hear someone working at the back. The regular metallic sound of spade on earth told her that someone was digging hard and above the shrubs a thin thread of pungent smoke rose, suggesting that there was a bonfire smouldering somewhere.

She put her hand on the gate and found it gave easily. She saw him as soon as she turned the corner – his back bent over his spade as he toiled over a dead tree-root.

'Looks like hard work,' she said.

Rick straightened up and turned. His face, tanned from a summer working in the open, was a mixture of emotions. Disbelief, surprise – shock.

'*Danni!*' He stuck his spade into the ground and straightened up, narrowing his eyes against the sunlight. 'Hi. It's good to see you.'

'Good to see you too.'

'What brings you here? How did you know where to find me?'

'I could say I guessed,' she said. 'Or I could say that some

221

mystic sixth sense drew me here, but as it happens Claire found out from Phil.'

'Well – whatever, it's a nice surprise.' He rubbed his hands down the sides of his jeans. 'Look at me. I'm filthy.'

She took a step towards him. 'You look pretty good to me,' she said softly. 'Here, in this place you love – working. It's how I've been remembering you.' She reached out to touch his arm. 'When I heard about your mum leaving and Claire taking the shop over I thought maybe you'd gone too.'

'Not a chance!' he said vehemently. 'Mum's gone up to Yorkshire to make a new start. We had a row. I couldn't forgive her for keeping me ignorant about who my father was all those years, especially when it was a man I already knew.'

'So you decided to stay on?'

'This is where I belong,' he said. 'She always hated me doing this job but it's what I want – all I ever wanted. I don't think she ever really knew me. I decided the time had come for me to live my life as I want to live it.' He shrugged. 'Maybe one of these days she and I will be friends again. But for now . . .'

'At first I thought I was too late. And that would have been awful because I've got something to tell you – something fantastic. It's why I'm here. I've found out that we – you and I – we're not related; not in any way at all.'

He stared at her. 'We're *not*? Are you sure?'

'Positive. My mum told me. It's something she'd been hiding for years.'

'Oh my God – *Danni*,' he breathed.

'It was so awful when I found out that Mark was your father. I couldn't tell you the truth about me then. I thought you might not want to know. It was all so . . .' She swallowed hard at the threatening tears. 'I've missed you so much, Rick. So much I thought sometimes it would kill me!'

'Oh, Danni – *Danni*.' He reached out to pull her close, kissing her hard. 'I thought I'd never see you again. I can't tell you how horrible everything has been without you. Phil's been marvellous and when this place was sold and the new owner let me continue restoring the garden it just about saved my sanity.' He looked at her. 'How did you find out the truth though? What happened? I want to hear all about it.' He pointed to the old summer house, which now had a newly thatched roof. 'I was going to knock off for something to eat.' He took her hand. 'Come on. You can tell me about it while we eat.'

In the summer house, sitting on the floor with the aroma of creosote in their nostrils they shared the sandwiches Rick had brought with him and Danni told him about Ruth's confession. She went on to describe the awful job in the newsagent's shop, making him laugh with her imitation of the difficult customer who had finally made up her mind to walk out. As he laughed she looked at him, suddenly serious.

'I don't know what you see in me, Rick Scott,' she said. 'You with your university education and me with my big bolshie mouth. Speak first and think later – that's me! Always getting myself into bother. I'm not elegant and stylish like your mum and I put my foot in it right up to my eyebrows and I'm always messing things up.'

He slipped an arm round her shoulders and drew her close, laughing softly. 'Those are all the things I love about you, silly,' he said. 'You don't suffer fools gladly. You know what you want from life and where you're going.'

'I used to think I did. Lately I haven't been so sure.'

'Well, whatever and wherever it is, I hope we'll be sharing it. You're the best thing that ever happened to me, Danni. I thought I'd lost you for ever but now we know it's all right I'm not letting you out of my sight again.' He looked at his watch and sighed. 'Except that now I have to get back to work. Phil and I are working in the park at the moment.' He looked at her. 'You don't have to get back to Meadbridge today, do you? Will you still be here later?'

She grinned. 'Try and stop me! Claire has offered me my job back.'

'Great!' He got to his feet and brushed the crumbs from his jeans. 'Before we go come and see the Italian garden. I've managed to get the fountain working.'

Hand in hand they stood beside the pool as the little fountain sparkled in the sunlight. The stone statue of the girl with her water ewer smiled her serene smile at them. Danni stood on tiptoe to kiss him.

'It's lovely, Rick,' she whispered. 'You've put so much love into this place. Who knows, one of these days we might even be lucky enough to come and live here together.'

He smiled down at her. 'Now that *would* be a dream come true,' he said. 'But you never know. You came back, didn't you? That proves that dreams do come true sometimes.'